A DEREK STILLWATER NOVEL

THE

# SERPENT'S KISS

# MARK TERRY

MIDNIGHT INK
WOODBURY, MINNESOTA

FIRST EDITION
First Printing, 2007

Book design by Donna Burch
Cover design by Kevin R. Brown
Cover Detroit skyline photo © Photographer's Choice by Getty Images

Midnight Ink, an imprint of Llewellyn Publications

**Library of Congress Cataloging-in-Publication Data**
The Cataloging-in-Publication Data for *The Serpent's Kiss: A Derek Stillwater Novel* is on file at the Library of Congress.
ISBN: 978-0-7387-0882-9

Midnight Ink
Llewellyn Publications
2143 Wooddale Drive, Dept. 978-0-7387-0882-9
Woodbury, MN 55125-2989, U.S.A.
www.midnightinkbooks.com

Printed in the United States of America

For my sister Beth.
The extended Terry family's rock.
Love ya, sis.

# 1

*7:47 a.m.*

THE SERPENT WAS COILED to strike. That was how he thought of it, how he thought of himself.

He stood on West Grand Boulevard in Detroit, leaning against the bus-stop shelter in front of Henry Ford Hospital. Behind him, the hospital towered seventeen floors of red brick, *Henry Ford Hospital* written in giant white script across the top of the building. It was a complex, actually, with at least half a dozen buildings and a couple of parking garages, right there on the corner of the John Lodge and the Boulevard, dominating an entire city block plus more if you counted the parking lots. It was a brisk autumn day, a hint of fall in the air, gray clouds scudding across the lid of the sky as if they had someplace important to go.

The Serpent wondered about the wind. He wondered if the wind would cause problems. It was a technical problem, and he was pleased with technical problems. The whole idea had started out as a technical problem. The wind, though, was a part of the technical problem that he hadn't given much thought to.

He wondered if he should study on it some more, but then he decided it was too late. There came a time in every experiment—every project—in which you just had to jump in and … strike!

He liked that. Liked the melodrama of it. It didn't bother him that it sounded like something out of a bad movie. He thought it sounded cool. The Serpent.

He fingered the cell phone in his hand. It was a Nokia flip phone with the usual kitchen sink of additional nonsense built in—calendar, video games, calculator, voice recorder, digital camera. The Serpent glanced at the tiny screen of the phone and typed in the number. All he would have to do now was push the green call button. Coiled to strike.

It was time to remind the world of the power of Aleph. It was time for Aleph to rise again.

The Boulevard was busy. Just down from the hospital was the Fisher Building, a gorgeous Kahn architectural jewel, forty-some stories of tan marble and sandstone with a green verdigrised copper peak, the very tip of which was gold. He heard the roar of cars on the Lodge, a highway sunk into a massive concrete canyon with forty-foot vertical concrete walls that split the city in two. In the Motor City, everybody drove. On the Lodge, seventy miles per hour was just getting started. Above on the surface roads was a different story. Cars jammed the Boulevard, going nowhere fast. Somewhere close, a car had broken down. People were impatient. He could see it in their faces, the way they craned their necks. He heard the honk of horns.

A street person walked by and eyed him, heading for the corner in tattered black pants and an army jacket. He looked old, thin, with a scruffy white beard. Under one arm was a cardboard sign that said HUNGRY AND HOMELESS. The Serpent thought the guy was going to his day job, there on the corner, spend eight, nine hours holding the sign as hundreds of cars went by, every twelfth car giving him a buck or a five maybe. How much did the guy take in each day? Fifty bucks? A hundred? More?

The Serpent shrugged his shoulders against a strong blast of cold wind and looked across the street at the Boulevard Café. They were all there, he thought.

The Serpent—he smiled at the thought—prepared to strike, his finger on the green call button.

# 2

*7:53 a.m.*

JOHN SIMMONS ORDERED HIS last meal. If he had known it was going to be his last meal, it's unlikely he would have ordered a farmer's omelet, hash browns, and wheat toast with a large orange juice and coffee. But that's what he always ordered at the café across the street from Henry Ford Hospital. In fact, if he had known it was his last meal, the Boulevard Café would not have been on his list of restaurants at all.

Once a week, ten friends, all faculty at Wayne State University or Henry Ford Hospital, got together for a casual breakfast. For reasons known to no one, they met at the hole-in-the-wall Boulevard Café, a restaurant none of them liked that much, and some of them loathed. It had become a peculiar tradition, and Simmons, if he bothered to think about it, suspected that the low-class aspect of the place was part of the charm. A better reason was probably that the tradition had started with the hospital people, who could just walk across the street. He glanced out the plate-glass window at the early-morning traffic clogging up the Boulevard. The hospital valet entrance sported huge, almost disproportionate triangular-shaped eaves over it. It reminded him of the brim of a baseball hat built out of red brick and concrete.

Melanie Tolliver, a researcher at the hospital, asked, "Where's Rebecca?" Tolliver's green eyes sparkled with barely concealed nosiness.

Simmons shrugged, taking a sip of his coffee. "Called and told me she'd be late. Didn't say why."

Melanie brushed frosted brown hair off her forehead and cocked an eyebrow. "Everything okay? I mean—"

"Yeah. Fine." Simmons shrugged again and looked around the restaurant, which was crowded. There were nine of them, one short of their usual ten. The Boulevard Café's nonsmoking section was about the size of a phone booth, so they ended up in smoking, which was blue with cigarette smoke. None of them smoked. "Christ, can't we—"

"Don't start," Brad Beales said from across the Formica table, which wobbled whenever anybody leaned on it. Brad was a linguist and stood six-six in his stocking feet. He looked like a Q-tip. Tall and skinny with a shock of fluffy white hair haloing his long, thin head. In a falsetto voice, Beales said, "*We like Margie.*"

Simmons and Beales laughed, but Melanie shot them a disapproving frown. "It's convenient."

"It's a dive," complained Simmons.

Beales shrugged, a half-grin on his face. "Food's cheap."

"Well, we've avoided food poisoning so far, anyway," Simmons said. He was going to go on, but he bit back his complaint. He glanced at his watch, wondering where Rebecca was. She'd sounded a little stressed when she had called this morning. She'd called to tell him

5

she'd be late. When he asked why, she just said, "I'll be late. That's all," and hung up. It wasn't like her. Of course, three or four times a week she spent the night at his place or he spent the night at hers. He knew Melanie was wondering if they'd had a fight. He wondered too. But no. Everything had been okay. Everything *was* okay.

A popping sound from somewhere nearby caught his attention. Not a large pop, like gunfire. More like the pop of a champagne cork. Like that.

It registered for just a moment. Simmons looked up, a quizzical look on his face, then dived back into his coffee. Margie, their regular waitress, arrived with a couple of plates. She could have been on the Russian weightlifting team in the sixties. She was round-faced and round-bodied but looked like she could heft a bus. She wore her steel-gray hair pulled back in a blood-restricting bun and generally looked as if she were driving in second gear in a third-gear world. She delivered Simmons's omelet and hash browns, no toast. The woman was incapable of delivering a whole order. It had to arrive in sections, like a seven-course meal. Toast, apparently, was the second course.

Beales had chocolate-chip pancakes covered with chocolate syrup and whipped cream. Melanie said, "Are you ever going to grow up?" Her bowl of steaming oatmeal was placed in front of her. Her toast was also missing in action.

"As the great Mr. Buffett said, '*Mah umer draz ho raha hoon, laykin dunia dar nahien.*'"

Melanie sighed. "I give up. Turkish?"

"Urdu. Pakistan, you know?" Beales spoke nine languages, seven of them fluently. "'*I'm growing old, not up.*'"

Jorge Gomez, an administrator at the hospital, said, "Warren Buffett said that?"

"*Jimmy* Buffett," Beales said.

"But chocolate-chip pancakes? I mean, really ..." Melanie trailed off, looking at John Simmons. "John, are you okay?"

John's hand went to his throat. His face contorted in a grimace, and his skin began turning red. "Can't—" he gasped out, and tried to scramble from the booth, but fell sideways off the end of the table onto the black-and-white tiled floor.

Somebody screamed and Melanie started after him, but she suddenly gasped and placed her hand against her chest as if struggling to expand her lungs. Around her, others in the restaurant were doing the same thing. Screams choked into silence. And one by one, they died.

# 3

*8:13 a.m.*

JILL CHURCH STOOD JUST outside the bathroom door, hands on hips. "Michael! You're going to be late."

The water in the shower ran and ran and ran. She couldn't understand why her sixteen-year-old son took such long showers. She had timed him once at thirty minutes.

No answer. She banged on the door, glancing at her watch. "Michael!"

The water shut off. "Okay, okay."

"Hurry—"

Her cell phone rang somewhere in the house. "Damn," she muttered, and turned, trying to arrow in on the loud chiming of Bach's *Toccata and Fugue*, which she had chosen for her cellular's ring. She checked her purse first. No go. She paused for a moment, looking across the island into the living room. Where had she left it?

Jill, pulse quickening, chased the sound down into her bedroom. The phone perched on her rolltop desk, the one in the corner where she paid bills and sometimes read files she brought home from her office in the Federal Building in downtown Detroit.

She snatched up the phone and flipped it open. "Church here."

"Jesus Christ, Jill! We've got a situation here." It was Matt Gray, the special agent in charge of the FBI's Detroit Field Office. "What took you so long?"

"What's up?" she said, ignoring the question.

"Probable terror attack in the New Center Area. West Grand Boulevard just across from Ford Hospital. All hands."

Jill's stomach clenched. Her worst nightmare: a terror attack on her turf. Out of the corner of her eye, she saw Michael saunter out of the bathroom in only his underpants. He was almost six feet tall, his shoulders broad, his hips narrow. For a moment, she felt like she'd been caught off-guard. Her son, her baby boy, was a man. He glanced over his shoulder at her, eyes narrowing, then disappeared into his bedroom, the door slamming behind him. She refocused on what Gray was saying.

"…the Bureau's HMRU will be called in. Right now the DFD and DPD are first responders, but we expect to lead as soon as things are under way."

She listened to a few more details before clicking off. She rushed out of her bedroom and pushed open Michael's bedroom door without knocking. He was pulling on a black T-shirt with the rapper J Slim on the front, Slim's sneering white face framed by two hands flipping the bird.

"You're not wearing that shirt to school," she said.

"Mom, I'm going to the concert tonight." Even though his voice had deepened into that of a man's, it still had a child's petulance to it.

Her jaw set. "We went over that. Not on a school night. You've got school tomorrow."

"Mom, it's the only show, and Ray's got tickets."

"I don't have time to argue with you right now. We've got a crisis—"

"Everything's a fucking crisis," he muttered, and turned away. Michael grabbed his black nylon backpack and brushed past her.

"Michael—"

He spun, face twisted in an ugly grimace. Jill's heart nearly broke. The resemblance to his father was so strong. The high cheekbones, dark hair, snapping blue eyes the color of cobalt. But mostly it was the set of his mouth. How she hated to see that angry, hurt look on her son's face. *Just the teen years*, she thought, but knew it wasn't quite right. Michael was falling out of her protective orbit, and that was natural. That was good, normally, but he was being pulled into the orbit of a world that she knew wasn't good for him. It was dangerous, and she was a little scared when she thought about it.

She stepped forward and gave him a quick hug, feeling a tug on her heart again as he flinched from her touch. She kissed him on the cheek. "Have a good day. I'll see you tonight."

Their eyes met. There was something there, something she couldn't read. Had she surprised him by not rebuking him about the profanity? Was it the kiss? What was going on inside his head?

"Bye," he said, and loped past her and out the door. She heard the roar of his eight-year-old Honda Civic, and then he was gone.

Grabbing her purse, she made sure her Glock 9 mm was in the clip on her belt, snagged her briefcase and cell phone, and hurried after him, heading for her crisis. It was only when she was firing up the engine of her Honda Accord that she realized he was still wearing the offensive J Slim T-shirt.

# 4

DEREK STILLWATER LIMPED ACROSS the salon of his cabin cruiser, the *Salacious Sally*, and inspected the contents of his two partially packed Go Packs. *My passport*, he thought, and did a slow turn around the salon, looking to see where he had left it. There it was, on the end table next to the brown leather couch. He walked over, favoring his left leg, which was causing him a lot more problems then he wished it were. It had been five weeks since the surgery, but he wasn't recuperating as fast as he wanted to. The surgeon was thinking they might have to go in and do more work.

Derek was afraid it wouldn't heal all the way. That was his Inner Pessimist talking, he thought. *Tell that gloomy prick to butt out,* he told himself, and picked up the passport and crossed back to the backpack and duffel bag he called his Go Packs—short for Get-Up-and-Go Packs. He kept them ready 24/7/365, just waiting to be called in for some national emergency or threat of Armageddon.

But no, not this time. Not anymore. He had something else to do. Unfinished business.

The special phone wailed. He stared at where it rested next to the backpack. Derek ignored it and checked his Colt.

The phone continued to wail, a loud siren sound, intermittent. Persistent.

It stopped ringing.

He shoved the Colt into the pack alongside the passport. He had made arrangements so he could take it with him to Mexico. It had been a hassle, but he had pulled strings, insisting.

On the table were a few more items. Bottled water. Money in several different currencies—pesos, euros, dollars, pounds. A pair of binoculars. A bottle of water-purification tablets. Spare batteries. A box of granola bars. An atropine injector, an antidote for a variety of biological and chemical warfare agents.

The phone rang again. This time he picked it up and clicked on the receive button. General James Johnston said, "Derek, we've got —"

"No," Derek said, and clicked off. He dropped the phone back on the table and carefully packed the last of his equipment into his Go Packs. He thought he could hear the thrum-thrum of an approaching helicopter. The *Salacious Sally* was berthed at Bayman's Marina on the Chesapeake Bay, just outside Baltimore. Helicopters weren't that unusual.

The phone rang yet again, the high-pitched wail impossible to ignore. Derek picked it up. "You forget," he said into the phone. "I quit. I don't work for you anymore."

13

General James Johnston, now the secretary of the Department of Homeland Security, said, "We've got a situation in Detroit that we need you for. HMRU's on their way to pick you up now."

"Tell them the detour's not necessary. I'm not going. I'm going to Mexico. My flight leaves in four hours. I plan to be on it."

"We've got people working on Fallen," Johnston said. "Everybody in the world's looking for him. You don't need to chase him down yourself. Especially alone."

"He'll contact me down there. It's a game to him."

"We need you in Detroit."

"Did you miss the part where I resigned, Jim? Five weeks ago. Letter of resignation. I quit. You remember? Not on the motherfucking payroll! I'm going to Mexico—"

"Sarin gas," Johnston said. "Somebody let loose sarin gas in a restaurant in Detroit less than an hour ago. Looks like about sixty people dead."

The sound of the rotors of the battered Huey the FBI's Hazardous Materials Response Unit used was roaring toward him. Derek clutched the phone, cursing to himself. Why couldn't he let go of this tiger's tail?

"When this is done..."

"Mexico," Johnston agreed, his deep, rough voice not showing any smugness or satisfaction. "With full backing of DHS."

"Damn you, Jim. Damn you to hell."

"Godspeed, Derek. Take care of yourself. Keep me informed."

# 5

MATT GRAY, THE SPECIAL agent in charge, glared at Jill Church as she walked over to where he stood. Gray was tall and thin with salt-and-pepper hair and had the pinched, angry face of a toddler whose mother had told him no for the first time. Jill knew they were in big trouble because Gray was wearing combat boots with his suit. It was something she'd seen only in Baghdad, when politicos like Donald Rumsfeld or Paul Bremer were out and about, wearing their suits with army boots, like, *I'm really a military tough guy, but the suit says I'm better than you.*

"About time," he growled.

Jill didn't comment or try to explain that she lived in Troy, one of the northern suburbs. Gray knew it and he didn't care. Gray, despite his position as SAC, didn't handle tense situations diplomatically. He was also heading the FLA for this situation—the federal lead agency in the CONPLAN, the United States Government Interagency Domestic Terrorism Concept of Operations Plan. That meant he coordinated all efforts in dealing with a domestic terrorism attack, working with the local police, emergency medical personnel, and whoever else was involved until FEMA could be brought in, if necessary.

"Where are we?" she asked. Her gaze roved the scene. The Boulevard Café was peculiar. It appeared to be a two-story red brick building, except the main floor jutted out by itself and was painted a shade of off-white that resembled custard. There was an awning across the front done in bright green. Massive white pillars—Doric or Ionic, she didn't know—rose up as if someone had wanted to make the place look like the White House. It didn't. It just looked weird, not that it was all that strange in Detroit. This was a city whose major sculptural artwork was a big fist.

On either side of the Boulevard Café were parking lots jammed with cars. She suspected they were used by Henry Ford Hospital employees.

The Detroit Fire Department's hazmat team had set up a red and white inflatable tent that resembled one of those blow-up jumping playgrounds for little kids. The scene was otherwise mobbed with ambulances, two fire engines, and assorted cop cars. There was also the media. The satellite vans for Channels 2, 4, 7, 50, and 62 were all present and accounted for. Above them, helicopters jockeyed for space.

Gray said, "Fifty-two."

Jill turned her attention away from the scene and focused on her boss. "What?"

"Fifty-two dead," he said. "Everybody in the damned restaurant. No survivors. Kitchen staff, wait staff, customers."

Jill felt something slide down her spine and curl into her stomach. Something that felt suspiciously like an electric eel. *Fifty-two.*

Swallowing back bile, she said, "Okay. What do you—"

"The HMRU are on their way, ETA fifteen minutes. They're going to land at the pad behind the hospital." He waved behind him. "They'll be handling the scene processing. Nobody's going anywhere until they go in and do their forensic thing as best they can."

Gray craned his neck, his blue eyes popping in anger. His navy blue suit fit him poorly, baggy at the shoulders, the pants too long. His face flushed an unpleasant shade of red. "The Department of Homeland Security's sending one of their troubleshooters over. Guy's name is Derek Stillwater. Heard of him?"

"His name sounds familiar."

"He was involved in that mess a while back." Gray paused. "He's still under investigation for that mess."

"I thought he—"

"Secretary Johnston has reinstated him and we're stuck with him. I don't trust him. You're assigned to him. Tell him you're the FBI liaison to DHS. But your job is to keep an eye on him and make sure he stays out of our way."

"I'm a babysitter," Jill said, the bitterness there in her voice.

Gray scowled at her. "Yes, Church. You're the babysitter. Get over it. I don't trust Stillwater. Bullshit him. Keep him in the dark. Keep him out of the way. That's your job. Do it."

# 6

*8:59 a.m.*

Jill leaned against a metal railing alongside a red brick stairway at the northeast corner of Henry Ford Hospital. It was a plaza of sorts, a parklike area between the six-story Education and Research Building and a fifteen-story high-rise that looked like apartment buildings—probably for residents—and two parking garages. There were tennis courts, not in use, and next to those was a helicopter landing pad painted red, with blinking red lights at each corner. Henry Ford Hospital security had cordoned off the area. A marrow-quivering roar echoed between the buildings as a big old military Huey hovered overhead, approaching for landing.

Jill scowled. She had read the file on Derek Stillwater she'd downloaded from the HQ databases, and she wasn't wild about what she'd read. There had been a lot of incidents of heroics, and a lot of incidents of insubordination. The man was a cowboy.

The Huey thundered to a halt, and she walked over as the rotors came to rest. The door opened and a number of FBI agents in navy

18

blue windbreakers clambered out, hauling gear. She stood waiting. Finally, when the last agent climbed out, she said, "Derek Stillwater?"

The agent, a grim-faced black man built like a refrigerator, jerked a thumb over his shoulder, back into the Huey.

Jill stepped over. She saw a man leaning against the far interior wall of the chopper, his face pale. A backpack and a duffel bag were at his feet. Sweat beaded on his forehead, and his hands were clenched into fists.

"Derek Stillwater?" she asked, wondering what the hell was going on.

He nodded and seemed to come to life. He grabbed the bags and jumped out of the chopper. He tossed the bags at her feet, leaned with one arm against the helicopter, and vomited all over the landing pad. Dragging in air, he wiped his forehead with his sleeve and turned to her.

"Sorry."

"Problems with flying?"

He shook his head and picked up his bags. "No. Problems with scenes of biological and chemical warfare."

She cocked an eyebrow. "You're Derek Stillwater, right?"

"That's me. Who are you? My FBI babysitter?"

She blinked. "Agent Jill Church. I'm your liaison."

"Uh-huh. Agent Church, I don't work for the FBI. Got that?" Color returned to his face, and she was startled to see his entire demeanor change. There was authority in his voice. He was tall and good-looking, an intensity about him.

"I didn't say you did. I'm here to help you communicate with the Bureau."

He looked at her. His blue eyes blazed like a gas jet. He stepped into her personal space. She held her ground, puzzled because suddenly she felt like he was familiar. She didn't know why. Had they met?

More puzzling was the wave of emotion that swept over her. Negative emotions, like a sudden case of the blues or depression. She shook her head.

Stillwater said, "The Bureau is investigating me, and you damn well know it. But I don't work for you. I work for DHS, and my job is to—"

"—coordinate, evaluate, and investigate. Yes, I know. And you're some sort of expert on biological and chemical warfare."

"Where are we going?"

They locked gazes. Jill again had that peculiar sense of déjà vu. She tore her eyes away. "Follow me," she said.

# 7

DEREK TOOK IN THE scene before him. The Detroit Fire Department had set up a red inflatable tent as its transition area for the hazard site. The Detroit PD had shut down the street. The FBI HMRU guys trailed ahead of him into the tent. Walter Zoelig, the head of the HMRU, was conferring with somebody in a blue suit wearing army boots. Derek pointed to Zoelig. "Who's he talking to?"

Jill said, "Matthew Gray, the SAC."

Derek nodded. "I'm going in."

"The tent?"

He turned to face her. "I'm going into the tent and then into the scene. Unless you're coming in too, find me after I come out." He hesitated, then handed her his backpack. "I don't want this in the tent. You keep an eye on it for me, okay?"

She opened her mouth to protest, but he had already turned away and headed for the tent. Derek met a Detroit fireman at the sealed entrance. He was a black man with massively wide shoulders, a narrow waist, and a gold tooth. "This is for authorized personnel only," he growled.

Derek held out his DHS ID. "I'm authorized," he growled right back.

The fireman looked at it, nodded, and peeled open the doorway. Derek ducked inside with his duffel bag and took in the agents from the HMRU in one corner stripping down and climbing into their hazardous-materials suits. Derek joined them, tossing his bag down next to a lanky agent named Andrew Calloway. Calloway looked at him and said, "Not a false alarm this time."

The HMRU spent most of its time chasing down false alarms for biological and chemical terrorist attacks. Typically, Derek or some other DHS troubleshooter tagged along.

"I don't know whether to be happy or sad about that," Derek said, stripping off his clothes and hauling his own hazardous-materials suit from the bag. It crinkled. It was a baby blue Chemturion protective suit manufactured by ILC Dover in Delaware, the same company that made space suits for NASA. He spread it out on the ground, unzipped it, and slithered awkwardly into it.

"You're happy some fifty people got killed with sarin gas?" Calloway asked.

Sitting up, Derek said, "You know what I mean. I'm happy we're not wasting our time. I'm not at all happy this happened."

"You should get out of this business."

Derek struggled to his feet and zipped the suit up to his neck. "We should all get out of this business. Got the tape?"

Calloway handed him a roll of duct tape.

"You first," Derek said.

Calloway pulled his square plasticized facemask over his head. Derek sealed the zipper, then tore off pieces of duct tape and sealed Calloway's ankles, wrists, and neck. He helped put a single air tank on Calloway's back and hooked it to the intake port. He turned the knob on the regulator and tapped Calloway's shoulder. Calloway turned around. Through the mask, Derek saw the agent's face was already covered with sweat. He shouted, "I'll check for leaks."

He examined the suit. Everything seemed okay. He gave him a thumbs-up. Calloway helped Derek seal his suit and checked for leaks, and then the two men headed out of the tent toward the crime scene.

It was a short, cordoned-off walk to the restaurant. Inside the suits it was noisy and hot and claustrophobic. Derek followed Calloway through the door and felt the sense of claustrophobia get even worse. Like so many inner-city businesses, the windows were covered with metal bars, as if they were all for prison cells. Just inside the entryway was the cash register, on one corner of a long diner counter. Off to the right were four booths all crammed in front of the main window. Derek quickly counted eleven dead bodies.

Straight ahead, parallel to the counter, was what should have been a clear walkway, though it wasn't very wide. Along the wall on the left were two-person booths. The problem was that there had been seven people eating breakfast at the counter, perched on stools. When they died, they fell to the floor into the aisle. At the back of the aisle was the kitchen. Before you hit the kitchen, the restaurant angled to the left. There were bathrooms and the main dining area. But getting there would require negotiating over or around the dead, tangled on the black-and-white linoleum in pools of vomit and excrement.

"This is such a glamorous job," Derek muttered.

Calloway turned awkwardly back to him. Through the clear helmet, Derek could see how chalky white the agent's face had become. "*What?*" he shouted.

"I said, '*I love my job*.'" Derek had to shout to be heard over the fan in the suit.

"Fuckin' A," Calloway shouted. "Five years till retirement." He turned around and began to stumble over the corpses. Waiting for a little space, Derek followed.

The main room was worse. There must have been thirty people in this part, and they were all dead. He stood next to the chalkboard listing the day's specials—farmer's omelet, Texas bacon cheeseburger, chicken gyro, and each one came with a bowl of soup for $5.99—and took it all in. Cheap vinyl seats or black metal and plastic chairs. Plastic flowers and vines. A mirror on one wall.

The damned place was crowded with Detroit firefighters in hazardous-materials suits. The addition of five FBI agents and one DHS troubleshooter didn't help. They were practically tripping over each other, trying to get organized. At least they were photographing and videotaping the scene, he thought.

But Derek wasn't seeing what he was looking for. He shuffled over to one of the FBI agents, Leon LaPointe, point man for the HMRU. He put his faceplate close to LaPointe's. "What's the source of the sarin?"

"Beats the fuck out of me." LaPointe had curly black hair and an angular, hatchetlike face. Sweat dripped into his eyes, causing him to blink repeatedly as he shouted.

A firefighter stomped over. "Who're you?" Through his mask, Derek saw an older man, his dark brown skin pocked and scarred.

LaPointe made introductions. "Who're you?"

"Thomas Fitzgerald," the firefighter shouted. "That's Captain to you guys. I'm the head of this unit. Come over here."

They followed him to the center of the room. There was some sort of quasi-divider there, with a row of padded bench seats on both sides. It looked like it might have been some sort of internal support for the building, but it was hard to tell. There were poles that went up into the roof, but otherwise the divider seemed to hide plastic plants and be a space for large plastic-covered menus. Fitzgerald pulled back a panel to reveal several small red metal cylinders about the size of propane canisters for camp cookstoves. Each of them was aligned to a single nozzle and regulator, which had been hooked to a radio receiver.

"Shit." LaPointe turned to make eye contact with Derek. "That's not exactly lunch boxes and umbrellas, is it?"

"No," Derek said, expression grim. Aum Shinrikyo, the Japanese cult that had unleashed sarin gas on a Tokyo subway in 1995, had filled lunch boxes with sarin, worn masks onto the subway, punched holes in the boxes with umbrellas, and left. It had been a primitive, largely unsuccessful way of distributing the gas—that nonetheless killed a dozen and injured over five thousand. This device in front of them was something entirely different. If this device had been used in Tokyo, the numbers would have rivaled the attack on the World Trade towers.

Derek looked around, heart racing, focusing on the people who had been closest to the device. The group facing the front of the restaurant appeared to be three separate parties at three separate tables, two people each. The group on the side facing the back of the restaurant appeared to be nine people together, sitting at tables pushed side by side.

"Captain," he said, "once you get the pictures and video, you need to get the names of everybody before you move the bodies."

LaPointe had managed to cross his arms over his chest in the bulky suit. He watched Fitzgerald closely. Fitzgerald looked outraged. "You nuts? How we going to do that? Let's get these poor people off to the morgue."

"No," Derek shouted. "ID them in place. I want a drawing of every single body with a name attached to it."

Fitzgerald thumped Derek on the chest with one heavily gloved hand. "You some kind of ghoul? *You* do it. That's way outside what I'm going to do today. *You do it.*"

Derek stared at him. He said, "I need a clipboard, paper, and a pen. And I need somebody who can write, because I'm going to be the volunteer who gets to go through the bodies looking for driver's licenses. Or are you going to assign someone? *Captain.*"

Fitzgerald said, "I'll get you a clipboard, paper, and pen. I'm not assigning any of my men to work for you."

"Fine."

LaPointe said, "I'll do the writing."

Derek turned to him. "Thanks."

"I hope you're wrong, Stillwater."

Fitzgerald, who had been striding away, turned back and leaned toward them. "What? What did you say? Wrong about what?"

Derek didn't answer. LaPointe said, "Dr. Stillwater's got a theory, don't you?"

Derek shrugged. It was a largely wasted gesture in the Chemturion.

"What? I didn't hear him offer no theory. This is the work of some crazy dudes. Terrorists."

"Maybe," Derek said.

"Maybe? What else could it be?"

"A murder," Derek said. "That's just one option. But if it's targeted, it was targeted at someone—or something—specific. So we need to know who's here and where they were so we might be able to narrow things down. That's why I want the names."

Fitzgerald scowled. "What you're sayin' is you think some wacko killed fifty-two people using sarin gas because he wanted to murder one person?"

"It's one theory to work with," Derek said.

"Why?"

"Why what?"

"Why do you think that?"

Derek hesitated. Then, "Because the Boulevard Café is a weird-ass target for a bunch of terrorists, don't you think? Some greasy-spoon café during the breakfast rush in Detroit?"

"So? That cult hit a subway."

"I know."

"So you could be wrong."

"Always a possibility."

Fitzgerald stared.

"I need that clipboard and stuff, Captain," Derek said.

"Yeah. I'll get right on it." Fitzgerald stumbled off.

LaPointe tapped Derek on the shoulder. When Derek turned, LaPointe said, "This *is* a weird target. Why not the hospital across the street?"

"Why not anyplace else? Terrorists hit discos and subways and restaurants and businesses. This could just be another random target," Derek said.

"But it doesn't feel high-profile enough. Does it?"

Derek shook his head. It didn't. It felt wrong and it felt worse— it felt expectant. Like the other shoe was waiting to drop. Whoever had done this had done it for some reason. Derek built a career on that, on studying the hows and whys of biological and chemical terrorism and warfare. Terrorists had an internal logic to what they targeted. It wasn't always obvious to the observer until later, but there was always some sort of warped, bent logic to their decisions.

To Derek, something about this attack felt strange. It was just intuition, but he had relied on that intuition over the years to keep his ass intact in some extremely hairy situations. He didn't ignore his intuition, especially when it came to biological and chemical weapons.

His intuition told him the Boulevard Café was chosen for a reason.

And his intuition told him that the attacker wasn't done yet.

# 8

MATT GRAY WAVED JILL Church over to the FBI command center, an RV with an unusual number of antennas sprouting from its surface. Gray's face was turning purple, which was never a good sign. She walked over and he snarled, "So what's with Stillwater?"

Jill shrugged, which she knew infuriated Gray. "He's inside."

"Yeah? What for?"

"Matt, I think it's his job."

He glared at her. "We're supposed to isolate him. You know that, right? I want him isolated. I told you that."

"What did you want me to do, handcuff him?"

"You'd like that?" He smirked at her.

"You want to go on the record with that statement?" she said, voice low, keeping her temper in check—but not rolling over and playing dead, either. "Want another swing at a sexual harassment lawsuit? We had so much fun the first time."

29

Gray flushed even more, but his gaze drifted away from her. "Sorry," he said. "Out of line. It's the pressure. Now, why's he inside?"

"He's an expert on this stuff, Matt. Chemical weapons."

"He's something. You're aware—" He broke off, staring over her shoulder. "What the fuck?"

A Detroit fireman walked toward them, a sheet of paper in his hand. He looked hot and sweaty, a young guy with red hair cut short, his blue eyes dulled by stress and fatigue. His pale, freckled complexion had a grayish green tinge to it, like the underside of a mushroom. His gaze jerked back and forth between the two of them. "Is one of you Agent Church?"

"Me," Jill said, raising a hand.

The fireman said, "Um, can I talk to you for a minute, uh, alone? I've got a message for you."

"For me?"

"Um, yeah."

Jill thought this fireman looked about twenty. Not much older than her son. He'd clearly been inside the restaurant. What was this all about?

"Who's it from?" Gray demanded.

The fireman eyed him. "I'm … I'm just supposed to give this to Agent Church."

Gray reached out to take it, but Jill held up her hand and took the paper. On it were scribbled fifteen names and addresses. "Who's this from?"

The fireman nervously said, "Um …"

With a disgusted sigh, Jill walked away from Matt Gray, the fireman following close behind her. "That better?" she asked, once they were out of earshot of her boss.

"Yeah. Sorry. I mean, this hardass from Homeland was real specific he wanted this given to you and nobody else."

"The hardass...?"

"Yeah. Dr. Stillwater. He told me to give it to you and nobody else but you." He swallowed hard, Adam's apple bobbing.

She wondered if Stillwater had threatened the kid. The kid acted a little afraid. Of course, what the kid had seen today...

"What is it? Is there a message?"

"Uh, yeah. Dr. Stillwater says he wants you to start running background checks on these fifteen people. They're, uh, he says those fifteen are top priority."

"Are they—where'd he get these names?"

"Um..." The firefighter licked his lips. "Some of the people inside. You know, the victims? He's gettin' names and IDs and he won't let anybody move the bodies until he's got sketches of where everybody is."

"Holy hell," she muttered. "And these are..."

"He said to tell you they were at ground zero in there."

She stared at him, mind racing. She glanced back down at the list, running through the names: Jonathan Simmons, Melanie Tolliver, Brad Beales...

"Well," she said, almost to herself, "at least it's something to do."

"Yeah."

"Is that it?"

The firefighter looked even more nervous than before. He wiped sweat off his forehead. "Well, uh, Dr. Stillwater, uh, he said that you should do it yourself and not delegate it. He especially said I shouldn't give it to Matt Gray. You were to do it."

"Is that it?"

"Yeah. Just . . ."

"What?"

"I think he meant it. That guy's got brass balls or something. I mean, the captain wanted to bring the bodies out and this guy stood him down, man. Took right over. One of the FBI's HMRU guys said go along with him, he knows what he's doing."

She glanced back at the list, then over to Matt Gray. "Okay," she said. "Thank you. Well done."

When the firefighter walked back to the tent, she returned to Gray, who remained standing by the control center, watching her.

"What the fuck was that all about?" he demanded, hands on hips.

She told him.

Gray snatched the list out of her hand, quickly scanned it, then crumpled it up and threw it in the dirt. "Who the hell does he think he is? We don't work for him. Go do your job, Church. Keep your head down and keep Stillwater boxed in. Understand?"

"Yes, sir."

Gray spun on his heel and strutted over toward a group of TV reporters. When she was sure he wasn't watching, she picked up the crumpled list of names and headed for her car.

# 9

DEREK WALKED OUT OF the staging tent, his hazardous-materials suit cleaned, dried, and carefully folded back into his duffel bag. The cool October air felt awesome after an hour in the suit, stepping over and around dead bodies. The only saving grace was that the suit prevented him from smelling the stench of body fluids and death. He took in a deep chestful of air. Cool and sweet. He looked around for Jill Church but didn't immediately see her. His temper flared, wondering what she'd done with the list of names he sent out for her.

Going through the personal belongings of dead people was hot, uncomfortable, unsettling work. Pulling wallets from pockets, opening purses, looking at ID badges. So many dead. Most of the dead were employees at Henry Ford Hospital, across the street. Some worked for the HMO next door, Health Alliance Plan. A few came from Wayne State University, and a few were from the neighborhood, people just stopping off for coffee or breakfast before going to their jobs or coming home from their night-shift work.

LaPointe sketched the restaurant and labeled the names of every single person on the chart as Derek read off the information. A tedious but vital process.

Derek tucked the final names and his copy of the map into his back pocket. LaPointe was taking a break before overseeing the removal of the bodies from the restaurant to a makeshift morgue being set up in the basement of the hospital.

"Stillwater!"

Derek turned. Jill Church strode toward him, jaw tight, eyes blazing. She stopped in front of him.

"Did you start on those lists?" he asked.

She looked around. Nervously, Derek thought. "Yes," she said, voice low. "I did. We've got a problem."

"*We* do?"

"Yes," she said. "*We* do. I went through my chain of command and gave that original list to my SAC."

"God damn it! I told you—"

"And he threw it away. My job isn't to investigate. My job is to put little walls up around you and keep you out of this business."

"Give me the goddamned list." He held his hand out, snapping his fingers at her.

"I've got a question for you," she said, not turning over the list.

"God damn it. I have a job to do, Church. You have my permission to go stick your head in the sand. But I'm not going to do that. Give me the list."

"Can I trust you?"

He stopped. "That's up to you."

Jill caught his shirt sleeve. "I read some of your file."

"The FBI's file is a little biased."

"I can't decide if you're a bad guy or a hero. But I'll tell you something. I'm a very overpaid babysitter, and I *did* run those names you gave me. So my question is this: Do you know what you're doing?"

He met her gaze and was struck by a sense of familiarity, of déjà vu. Had they met before?

"Yes, Agent Church," he said. "I know what I'm doing."

She nodded, as if to herself. "Then let's go. Those first fifteen names? Some of those are really, really interesting."

# 10

*10:30 a.m.*

MARY LINZEY STALKED BACK and forth behind the Channel 7 Action News van, glaring at anyone who came near her. They were sitting on top of the biggest news story in years, and it was growing stale. The FBI SAC, Matthew Gray, had just come over and done a stand-up, saying practically nothing useful. It would make a decent sound bite, but it didn't contain anything of substance.

She tried to think who they could talk to, who they could interview. There was the SAC, and there were the HMRU guys in their space suits, but so far they hadn't made themselves even remotely available. She had noticed one of the guys from DHS driving off with one of the FBI agents. It might be a scoop to talk to him, but she didn't know where he'd gone. Nobody seemed to know. When she suggested that Steve Shay, their reporter, ask Gray about the Department of Homeland Security, Gray had merely said that the DHS was present in an advisory capacity.

A shout from over by the restaurant caught everybody's attention. Someone said, "They're bringing them out!"

*Thank God*, she thought. *Finally, something to put on tape.* Her cameraman, Ed Wachoviak, was a pro, perfectly capable of framing Shay so they could still see these corpses brought out by the anonymous FBI agents in their creepy space suits. She knew damn well the network would be using this. She should get over there and make sure everything ran smoothly. Make sure Steve didn't trip over his own tongue and say something really stupid.

Her cell buzzed. Not hiding her irritation, she punched receive. "Mary Linzey here, WXYZ."

"You're a producer at channel 7, right?"

"Yes." She tapped her foot impatiently. Who was this? Some guy, his voice sounding kind of strange. Distorted. "Yes, I'm a producer with channel 7. What can I do for you?"

"I have a statement to make."

She sighed. Mary was thirty-seven years old, had a master's in communications, and had been twice divorced. Her life revolved around her job. She had no children. She was a pro, through and through, and had spent years dealing with nuts. She figured this guy for a nut.

"A statement about what?" She ran her hand over her short hair, worn cropped to her skull.

"I am the Serpent."

Definitely a nut. "The Serpent? What's that supposed to mean?"

"Are you at the Boulevard Café?"

"Everybody's here. So what?"

"I made it happen," the voice said.

She stood up straighter, suddenly on high alert. "Made what happen?"

"I planted the sarin gas in the restaurant. And I'm going to do it again."

*"What? Say that again?"* Mary's heart was racing now, adrenaline pouring into her veins.

"You heard me. I have a statement."

"No, no, no," she said desperately, looking around for Steve and Ed. "Why should I … why should I just take your word for it?"

Silence. She thought she'd lost him. Maybe he was a crank after all. Then the voice said, "The gas canisters were red. There were six of them, all connected with a regulator. They were placed in a cabinet in the main room of the restaurant that was part of a booth seat and divider. They were set off via cell phone."

*I can verify that*, she thought.

"I have a statement to make."

"I … I can record this." She could, too. "Just give me—"

"I am the Serpent," he said.

"Why the Serpent?"

The voice was silent again. Only now she didn't think he would click off. He was going to wait her out. This guy was for real. Probably. Finally the Serpent came back with, "Are you taping this?"

Mary fumbled through the back of the news van, looking for the digital voice recorder. She snatched it up, thrilled to see the jacks were still there. "Just a second. I'm getting the recorder. Hold on."

"Better hurry," the voice said. "I'll give you thirty seconds or I'll go to someone at Fox."

"Don't do that! Don't do that! I've got it. Here. Just a second." She slammed the microphone jack into the cell phone and hit record, deeply satisfied that the batteries were charged. "Go ahead," she said.

The Serpent was silent for a long moment.

*Don't shut up on me now*, she pleaded, cell phone pressed against her ear. Then the Serpent spoke, and Mary didn't know whether to be thrilled to be on top of this story or sick to her stomach.

# 11

*10:35 a.m.*

JILL DROVE AND TALKED, filling Derek in. "Those first fifteen names," she said. "There were two of them that got flagged big-time."

"Flagged how?" Derek drummed his fingers on the armrest, a bundle of nervous energy, impatience oozing from every pore.

Jill felt the same way, but she hid it better. They were stuck. Closing traffic for a block around the hospital was creating an incredible kind of gridlock. The New Center Area, one of the healthier areas in the city, was a nexus for several major roadways—the Lodge, West Grand Boulevard, Pallister, I-94, Woodward Avenue. She had gotten away from the initial crime scene but was now sitting bumper to bumper on West Grand Boulevard in front of the Fisher Building. They just needed to make it to either Second or Woodward, but they weren't going anywhere.

"I ran all the names through our database."

"FBI?"

"Yes," she snapped. "That's who I am, right? FBI. Anyway, I ran those fifteen names, not expecting anything. But two names got flagged."

"Which ones?" He held the lists in his hands, flipping through them to find the first one with fifteen names.

"John Simmons and Bradley Beales."

"Okay," he said, finding their names. He compared their names to the sketch of where the bodies lay. "They were sitting together, a group of nine. Right at ground zero. In fact, it looks like they were sitting opposite each other. What's so special about these guys?"

"Beales first," she said, pointing to her laptop. "He got flagged by the CIA."

Derek snapped open the laptop, trying to ignore the fact that they might as well have stayed where they were, with the progress they were making. People were getting impatient, honking their horns and yelling. Nobody was moving.

"Why?"

"Well," Jill said, scowling out the windshield, "first, he took a trip to Pakistan this summer."

"Okay. So he's got bad judgment. Pakistan sucks. It's not my idea of Vacation Land, but some people like hostile hellholes. Why's the CIA in an uproar?"

"You see, Beales is a linguist at Wayne State University. He was taking the trip to Pakistan, apparently, to practice his new language, which is Urdu."

"Urdu."

"Right. Primary language of Pakistan. The other thing is, you see, Beales spoke a whole bunch of languages—Urdu, Hindi, Farsi,

Arabic, whatever the Turks speak. Turkish, I suppose. He worked for the CIA, translating documents."

"But not at Langley."

"I asked. Apparently not. But he has a very high clearance and he's definitely on the payroll. His being killed in a terrorist attack rings a few bells in Washington."

"I bet." Derek thought about it. Not only had Beales been on the payroll of the CIA, but he was an expert in the languages of an awful lot of foreign terrorists—the Muslim extremists, anyway. It was a nexus of some sort, and it made his spider-sense tingle.

"Who's the other guy? John Simmons."

"Simmons is at the Wayne State University Department of Public Health. He's also associate director of the Wayne State University Center for Biological and Chemical Terrorism Research, the CBCTR."

Derek focused his entire attention on her now. "Which is what?"

Since they weren't going anywhere anyway, she took her eyes off the road and turned to him. "Sort of a think tank. You know, since 9/11 there's been so much money thrown around that a lot of universities got in on the act and set up these terrorism centers. They're generally run by people who know a lot about different aspects of terrorism—public health, emergency medicine, sociology, epidemiology. So they work cooperatively with various universities and keep tabs on what's going on with the government and try to stay on top of things. It's what academics do, right?"

"I suppose. Is Beales involved with the—"

"CBCTR? Maybe. It's not clear. But Simmons definitely is."

"It makes you wonder, doesn't it?" He sank lower into his seat, knee jiggling the laptop. He hadn't bothered to turn it on yet.

Jill nodded. "And I think we need to get over to Wayne and track down the office of the CBCTR, if there is such a place, and find out a lot more about John Simmons and Brad Beales. But we're stuck in traffic."

"You got a bubble?"

"Yes, but I don't think—"

Derek angled his way out of the door. He stuck his head back in the car. "Put it on."

"What are you going to do?"

"Get traffic moving."

He took his Colt out of its holster and held it with his right hand, palming his ID from the Department of Homeland Security in his left. He strode up to the car ahead of them and tapped the gun on the window, holding the badge up. The driver of the GMC Jimmy's eyes grew as big and round as jawbreakers, and he cracked his window. "What?"

"You need to move over. We need to get past you."

The driver, sweating in a white dress shirt and dark tie, said, "Where the hell am I supposed to go?"

"Up on the damned sidewalk," Derek said. "I don't really care. But you move the fuck over, got me?"

The driver stared, then began to nudge his Jimmy over a bit more, as close as he could safely get to the car parked at the curb. Behind him, Jill had put the siren and bubble on her car and kicked them on.

There wasn't room.

Derek frowned, and then gestured for the driver to get out.

"What?"

"Get out, please."

43

Slowly the driver complied.

Derek took his place, backed up the Jimmy as far as it would go, and then shifted into gear and floored it. With a huge crunch, the Jimmy slammed into the Buick Regal parked at the curb. Downshifting, Derek kept going until there was space to slip through. He forced the Jimmy up onto the sidewalk and backed it up. He waved Jill to move her car up onto the sidewalk. The driver of the Jimmy stood frozen, eyes wide, jaw agape. He didn't protest, probably because Derek still had his gun out.

When Jill pulled the car up on the sidewalk, Derek slipped in beside her. "Let's go," he said.

"I can't believe you did that," she said.

"Hurry up. You think some of these people won't start driving down the sidewalk now that we've given them the idea? Go!"

Thinking that when Matt Gray heard about this she could kiss her government pension and benefits goodbye, Jill began driving west down the sidewalk of West Grand Boulevard. In her rearview mirror, she saw three cars follow her lead. *Damn*, she thought. *He was right.*

# 12

ONCE THEY GOT OFF West Grand Boulevard, traffic thinned enough so Jill could get off the sidewalk and back onto the street. She wound around traffic, driving from Second to Palmer to Cass, really picking up speed, and then cut over on Warren past the Wayne State Bookstore and Welcome Center, hooking a right on Woodward to Alexandrine to the Detroit Medical Center. The Medical Center was a complex of about fifteen buildings, running about eight blocks long and two or three blocks wide. It made up the VA Medical Center, Hutzel Women's Hospital, the Kresge Eye Institute, Harper University Hospital, and the Karmanos Cancer Institute, as well as Detroit Receiving, the major trauma center for the city.

"Where the hell are we going?" Derek said, clutching the chicken-stick handle on the door. Jill roared into a parking garage.

"I know where we're going. Just follow me."

They ditched the car in the parking garage, and Jill led him down a flight of steps, into a walkway, and then into the University

Health Center. She moved confidently. "You've been here before?" Derek asked, racing to keep up.

"From time to time, yes. One of the weaknesses of the FBI is we don't always know the cities we work in as well as the local cops. I've tried to get to know the area well. I'm not originally from Michigan."

"Where are you from?"

"Around," she said vaguely, concentrating on their route. Derek wasn't sure he could have found his way back to the garage, they had taken so many turns since leaving her Honda behind.

"Nice driving back there," Derek said when they stopped to catch their breath.

"If this is a wild goose chase," Jill said, "maybe I can take up NAS-CAR, because I sure as hell won't be with the Bureau." There were plenty of professional medical people in white lab coats or scrubs, as well as probable patients standing around waiting. Nobody paid Derek and Jill much attention except for a burly security guard who was keeping an eye on them but giving them distance. "There," Jill said, pointing to a name on a placard. "Let's go."

"Lead on. I'm on your turf." Derek fell into step beside her.

The Wayne State Center for Biological and Chemical Terrorism Research resided in the Department of Public Health but really didn't exist as a physical entity. What Jill was looking for was somebody—preferably a secretary—who worked for John Simmons. John Simmons, she knew, worked in the Department of Public Health, which she found listed on the placard. When they arrived at the DPH, the secretary was an older black woman with graying hair pulled into a bun and gray plastic-framed bifocals perched on a long, thin nose. She wore a very professional-looking navy blue suit and skirt and a striped blouse with a fluttery collar at her throat. A diamond and ruby brooch decorated her lapel. When Jill started to speak, the woman held up her hand and pointed to a radio on her desk.

"They're saying something about that terrorist attack. Just a second." She leaned over and turned up the volume.

"The attacker has apparently made contact with the media," a deep male voice said. "The terrorist, identifying himself as the Serpent, contacted Mary Linzey, a producer with WXYZ, the local ABC affiliate, channel 7. He provided details about the device used in the attack for proof of his legitimacy, and made an official statement. We're waiting for a tape of his statement to be ... yes, here, it's being played on TV. Here ..."

There was a lot of fumbling, and then a computer modified voice said: "I am the Serpent. I am responsible for the sarin gas attack at the Boulevard Café at eight o'clock this morning. If I don't receive three million dollars from Wayne State University by 11:45 a.m. today, transferred into account number 84-532-68873-23 at the Bank of Bermuda Limited, I will set off another sarin gas attack at noon and more people will die. This is not an empty threat. I repeat: The money must be in account 84-532-68873-23 by 11:45 a.m. or many more will die."

The deep voice on the radio station came on to repeat what the Serpent had said, but added nothing new. The secretary, hand trembling, turned the radio down. She distractedly focused her attention on Jill and Derek. "Isn't that awful? I'm so sorry. What a tragedy. Some people! May I help you?"

Jill offered her FBI identification and introduced herself. "We're here to speak to somebody about John Simmons."

"Dr. Simmons isn't—" She broke off. "Oh dear Lord. The Boulevard Café! That's ... oh dear God! Is he okay? Was he there? That's where they usually go on Wednesday morning, I think."

"How many of them?" Derek asked. "How many usually go?"

"How many? I'm not ... ten, I think. That's been going on for a while."

"Anybody else from this department?" Jill asked. "Do you know the names of the people he went with?"

"What's this about? I'm sorry, do you need a warrant?"

"This is about the sarin gas attack, ma'am," Derek said. "And trying to stop the next one."

"Oh. Oh Lord!" Her hand flew to her mouth. "I'm so ... let me think. He and Dr. Beales. Dr. Beales isn't from this department, not exactly. Dr. Beales and Dr. Simmons work together a bit with the CBCTR. That's the Center for Biological and Chemical Terrorism Research—"

"Yes, we know," Derek said. "Okay. All right. Dr. Beales and Dr. Simmons. Anybody else you know?"

"Well, Dr. Harrington, but ... well, William Harrington, but he hasn't gone in quite some time."

"May we speak with him?"

She seemed startled. "Dr. Harrington called in this morning. He said he was feeling ill. He's ... "

Derek took a look at the fifteen names. A woman walked by, saying, "Cassandra, have you heard? Oh! Sorry!"

Derek and Jill studied the woman. She stood slightly over six feet, a big-boned, solid woman who nonetheless looked feminine in a gray wool pantsuit and black pumps. Her hair, expertly frosted, curled back to shoulder length, and her makeup was subtle. Somewhere between fifty and sixty, Derek estimated.

"What's going on?" she asked.

"Oh, Dr. Taplin-Smithson," Cassandra said. "Perhaps you can help them. This is Agent Jill Church with the FBI, and this is..." She faltered, her hand gesturing at Derek.

"Dr. Derek Stillwater, Department of Homeland Security," he said.

"Oh," Cassandra said. "Yes. I'm sorry. I guess I didn't catch your name. Anyway, this is Dr. Taplin-Smithson. She works with Dr. John Simmons on several research projects. Perhaps she can help you."

Taplin-Smithson frowned. "What's this about?"

"May we go to your office?" Jill asked.

When Taplin-Smithson hesitated, glancing at her watch, Derek said, "It's a matter of national security, Doctor. Please. It's urgent."

Taplin-Smithson nodded. "Follow me." She spun on her heel and strode down the hallway.

# 13

*11:09 a.m.*

LAUREN TAPLIN-SMITHSON'S OFFICE LOOKED like a bomb had hit it. It was a square room with a window looking east, the blinds drawn. The sole lighting came from an old lamp that looked like it had been picked up at a flea market. The office was dominated by a large, shabby wooden desk that appeared to have been painted a few dozen times over the years. Although the major surface color was maroon, its sharp corners and edges were worn in patches to reveal bits of baby blue and, beneath the blue, banana yellow. The desk itself, probably chosen because of its size, supported a large widescreen laptop attached to an even larger flat-screen monitor that was currently displaying what looked to be a graphical representation of a fireworks starburst.

A boom box sitting on the windowsill played the local NPR station, WDET, which was covering the terrorist events in the New Center Area. All the wall space was taken up by bookshelves—cheap ones, made out of cinder blocks and one-by-twelves painted green. The books and manuals on the shelves were stacked every which way, some upright, some piled on their sides, some leaning at angles. Papers and printouts in manila folders were piled on every horizontal surface. Post-it notes were everywhere.

"May I see your ID?" Taplin-Smithson asked, pointing to the two chairs in front of her desk. They were old overstuffed armchairs, with faded afghans thrown over them to hide what appeared to be rips billowing wayward stuffing.

Jill and Derek provided identification. Taplin-Smithson focused on Derek. "It says PhD. What's your degree in?"

"Microbiology and biochemistry."

"Dual?"

"Biological and chemical warfare were the actual topics I researched," Derek said.

"That would explain your presence. How can I help you?"

"John Simmons," Jill said. "What can you tell us about him?"

Taplin-Smithson shrugged. "Smart. Good guy. He's a physician with an interest in public health and government and public responses to large-scale health emergencies—pandemics, epidemics, natural disasters. He's involved with the terrorism research center."

"Are you?" Derek asked.

"No. I'm a biostatistician and an epidemiologist. That's where I've worked with John. Is...was John at that..." She waved her hand at the radio.

"Yes," Derek said. "I'm sorry."

Taplin-Smithson sighed and wiped the back of her hand across her eyes. "Damn. Who else?"

"Fifty-one other people," Derek said.

"I know, I know. But—"

"John Simmons usually had breakfast there with a regular group of people?" Jill asked.

"Oh sure. The Breakfast Club. Kind of a joke. Like that eighties movie about the kids who got detention? Anyway, they've been going for a few years. Are they …" She stopped, swallowed. "Are they all dead?"

"We're trying to determine exactly who was in the usual group," Jill said.

"Well, there were typically ten of them. Were there ten? Do you have the names?"

Jill didn't answer. Instead, she asked, "Can you give us the names of some of the people he usually went with?"

The professor leaned back in her chair, a battered cloth rocker that looked very comfortable. She tapped her fingers. "Well, Brad Beales, for sure. He's a linguist here at Wayne and is associated with the terrorism center. Melanie Tolliver. She's over at Ford Hospital. So is Jorge Gomez. Hmm, well, Bill Harrington used to go, but that's over now. He doesn't go. I bet Rebecca still does, though. Well, I'm pretty sure of it. I guess I don't know the others, though if you give me some names, I'm sure I could confirm them."

Jill scanned the list of names. "Sally LeVidic?"

"Yeah. She's at Ford. Hypertension research."

"Wei Ling-Wei."

"Sure. Same lab."

"Ron Yaught."

"Hmm. Don't know him. Just a second." She tapped at her computer keyboard, the graphic disappearing. The Wayne State University online directory came up, and she typed in Ronald Yaught. A listing of him in the languages department popped up. "Huh.

Somebody Brad must have brought in. Don't know him, though. Anybody else?"

"Stefan Carabaccio."

"Biostatistics. At Ford," she said, tone leaden. "I know him. God, he died too? Dammit." Her voice broke with emotion.

"Who's Rebecca?" Jill asked.

"Rebecca Harrington." Taplin-Smithson's face turned even glummer. "Did she die there too?"

"No," Derek said. "She didn't." Jill shot him an annoyed look, but he ignored her.

"Huh," Taplin-Smithson said. "John was there but Rebecca wasn't. That's a little strange." She seemed almost to be talking to herself.

"Why is that?" Jill asked.

Taplin-Smithson sighed and leaned back in her creaking chair again. "Well, that's why Bill Harrington wasn't there. He used to go. It was a pretty tight group. Then John Simmons and Rebecca Harrington had an affair. Bill and Rebecca got a divorce about a year ago. John and Rebecca have been together ever since."

Jill and Derek thought that over for a moment. Jill broke the silence. "What did Rebecca do?"

"She's an administrator here, over at Karmanos."

"Did she and Simmons live together?"

"Noooo, I don't think so. Not that I heard, anyway."

"How did Bill Harrington and John Simmons get along?" Derek asked. "Especially with Simmons working under him?"

"Oh, Bill's only over him in the terrorism center. Bill Harrington's lab's in the biochemistry department, but his office is here. The terrorism center is one of those ... well, you know how institutions and think tanks and universities sometimes work. There's no physical entity. It's just a group of people who have meetings together and sort of cooperate with each other from their various specialties."

Jill and Derek shot each other significant looks. Jill said, "Where does Bill Harrington live?"

"Birmingham."

"What about Rebecca Harrington?"

"Ferndale. Why?"

Jill got to her feet. "Do you have addresses for both of them?"

"No. Cassandra might—"

Jill held out her hand. "Thank you for your time."

Derek and Jill were heading out the door before the professor could say anything else.

# 14

*11:19 a.m.*

JILL HAD HER CELL phone in her hand and was punching numbers in as they left Taplin-Smithson's office. She frowned. "Dammit! The call won't go through. I can't tell if it's this building or there's too much caller traffic."

"Probably both. Try a land line," Derek said.

Jill stopped at the receptionist's desk and asked to borrow her phone. Derek frowned, thinking, and then turned and walked away. His gaze took in the names on each door. Finally he found the one belonging to William Harrington, PhD. He glanced at his watch. It was now 11:22 a.m. If the Serpent didn't get his money in twenty-three minutes, another group of people were going to get killed in thirty-eight minutes. He had absolutely no reason to doubt this guy's intentions or willingness to go through with his plans.

And he was pretty certain the university wouldn't be able to get the money moving that fast, even if they were willing to. It would have been time to negotiate under other circumstances. The FBI would contact the Serpent and tell him that there wasn't enough time to do this, but if he could just give them an extra hour, maybe two, they could get this done. They would try to negotiate the money, try to get him to decrease it. And all the while they would have people tracking the calls. But this guy knew that, didn't he? He was smart. He made the call through the media, gave his demands and his time-table, and hung up.

Derek was sure of it. Matt Gray would be scrambling. They'd be back-tracing that phone call just as fast as they could—if the media didn't stonewall them.

Was it traceable? Had the Serpent called from a cellular phone? Was it a cloned phone? A disposable phone? Had he called from a phone booth? From an office? A house?

And who was the next target?

What was the code this terrorist spoke in? What symbols were in his head?

Derek reached for the doorknob, pulse hammering in his ears. Suddenly he felt exhausted and dizzy. Bitter, metallic sweat seeped from his pores. His left knee throbbed with pain. All the squatting and kneeling necessary to go through the pockets of the victims at the Boulevard Café had aggravated his knee injury.

Around his neck were juju beads and a chain. Involuntarily he clutched at the steel four-leaf clover and the Saint Sebastian medal.

Behind this door was … what?

If Harrington was the Serpent, it was possible he could have booby-trapped his office.

Sweat beaded on Derek's forehead.

Taking in a deep breath, he closed his eyes, gripped the knob, and turned. Locked.

He glanced at his watch again. Thirty-seven minutes left. *Quit screwing around, Derek!*

He flung his shoulder against the door. It cracked with a loud bang but didn't open. Again, he slammed against the door. With a wood-and-metal shriek, the door burst inward. He stood there on the edge of the office, panting, relieved he hadn't been at the mouth of an explosion or a gas attack. *If Harrington was the Serpent, it was possible he could have booby-trapped his office.*

It was still possible.

The hallway was filling up with people. Across the hallway, a woman in a white lab coat said, "Who are you?"

He held up his ID, announced his authority, and stepped into the office.

Somebody else said, "Call security."

Even less time than he'd hoped for.

The office was less quirky than Taplin-Smithson's but about the same size. There was a large, round-edged desk, possibly made out of some sort of maple or bleached oak. A large computer monitor hulked on a corner. There was a high-backed cloth office chair and two other chairs in front of the desk. A credenza held a laser printer. Two matching bookcases contained medical reference books and bound copies of medical journals. There were two four-drawer metal filing cabinets. On the wall was a painting of a seascape that looked like it was painted with acrylics. On another wall were several diplomas and award certificates.

Derek sat at the computer and popped it on, waiting for the Windows desktop to come to life. When it finally did, he brought up Microsoft Outlook, clicked on Mail, and looked through the Sent file.

It was all correspondence with students and colleagues. He scanned as quickly as he could. One header caught his attention. It read: CHEM/SCENARIO 14.

Derek clicked on it. The body of the e-mail read:

*To: Bernard W. Schultz, PhD*
*Stanford University*
*SKOLAR MD/Biological and Chemical Terrorism database*

*B—*

*Attached is the latest chemical terrorism scenario to come out of the Working Group. I don't like their response—too optimistic. They don't understand friction. Still, it shows promise. Let me know what you think.*

*Bill*

Attached to the e-mail was a Word document. Derek clicked on it and read the title.

### Wayne State University Center for Biological and Chemical Terrorism Research

*Scenario 14: Chemical Terrorism Attack and Emergency Medical Response/Detroit, Michigan*

**Abstract:** *This document presents a fictional scenario of a chemical terrorism attack on the city of Detroit and the emergency, law enforcement, and public health response. This scenario involves a chemical terrorism attack at the North American International Auto Show, held annually in January at Cobo Center in Detroit, Michigan. The event draws in anywhere from 800,000 to 1,000,000 visitors each year, including, in 1999, President Bill Clinton. Media attention is very high, with over 6,600 journalists from 68 countries in attendance. The show runs for …*

It was all very interesting, Derek thought, but the auto show was held in January, and this was October. But if Harrington was involved in this, then maybe there was another scenario here somewhere. He fingered the row of computer CDs in a disk case, the sense of urgency weighing him down. Jill Church appeared at the door, her face white.

"Are you insane? What are you doing in here?"

He ignored her, continuing to search.

"We can't just go breaking and entering," she said, anger lacing her voice with tension. "We have procedures. We have the chain of evidence. Everything will get thrown out of court the way—"

He spun in the chair and reached for a filing cabinet drawer. "Feel free to tell the families of the next group of victims that you didn't stop things in time because you were waiting for a search warrant."

She still didn't enter the room. He stopped, his hand inches from the cabinet handle.

"What?" she asked.

Again, a wave of fear swept over him. He said, "There's some sort of Working Group here that puts together chemical and biological terrorism scenarios. I'm wondering—"

Suddenly she was next to him. "You're sure?"

He nodded and waved at the computer. "There's one there."

She glanced at it, her eyes opening wide. "Dear God! You don't suppose ... ?" She whirled and started to open the filing cabinet. His hand caught hers.

"What?"

"We have to be careful of booby traps."

"What?" Her face went even chalkier. "What are you talking about?"

Derek pointed to the floor. From behind the filing cabinet ran a wire. It looked like fishing line and was almost invisible. It ran along the crease between the floor and the wall, out of sight behind a bookshelf.

Voice low, Derek said, "You need to evacuate the building."

"I'll call the bomb squad," she said.

Derek nodded. He glanced at his watch. It was 11:29 a.m. They had sixteen minutes until their money deadline and thirty-one minutes until the next group died. He was going to have to take the chance.

# 15

As JILL MOVED DOWN the hallway, she spoke in a loud, authoritative voice: "Everyone must leave the building. I repeat: Evacuate the building. This is an emergency. Everyone calmly leave the building!"

A blond man in a white lab coat poked his wire-rimmed glasses up on his nose and stood in her path. "What's this all about?"

"FBI," she said, badge ready in her hand. "We have an emergency situation. Please evacuate—"

"What's going on?" someone else interrupted. Jill wanted to roll her eyes. Count on a bunch of doctors to stand around asking questions instead of getting their butts in gear.

"We have a bomb threat in this building," she said, hoping this wasn't the wrong approach. "You need to evacuate the building. Immediately!"

That got their attention. People began moving toward the door. Jill finally threaded her way to the receptionist's desk and was about to commandeer the phone when a uniformed security guard appeared. "There's a situation?"

Jill flashed her credentials. "There's a possible bomb in one of the offices on this floor. We need to evacuate the building immediately."

The security guard squinted at her, put the walkie-talkie to his lips, and moved away from her. She heard him say, "We have a Code Orange. I repeat: Code Orange."

A moment later a voice came over the loudspeaker requesting an immediate evacuation of the building. A Klaxon began to sound, and everybody hurried toward the exits.

Jill picked up the phone and dialed Matt Gray. He picked up after a single ring. "Gray, FBI."

"Jill Church. There's a possibility that an office here at the Public Health Building has a bomb in it. We've found evidence of chemical terrorism scenarios, and the office may be booby-trapped."

After a moment's silence, Gray said, "You are way beyond what I ordered you to do, Jill. Way beyond."

She ignored the comment. "I've got security involved. They're evacuating the building. Can you organize the bomb squad?"

More silence. Then, "We're on it. I ..." Gray trailed off. In the background, over the sound of the siren in the building, she heard a babble of voices. Finally Gray said, "I was going to send you over to the university president's office to discuss paying the ransom. He's expecting you—"

"We have a policy of not negotiating with terrorists," she said, mind momentarily blank. What was Matt talking about? She had a situation here.

"I know what our policy is," he snapped. "But it's not our decision, is it? We can only make recommendations. Meanwhile, we need to consider shutting down the university. They may be the target."

"We've got a bomb *here*, Matt."

More silence. "Where's Stillwater?"

Jill pressed the phone to her ear in amazement. "He's in the office. He's the one who uncovered the possible device."

Again that delayed silence, as if Matt Gray were running everything by someone else before responding. "You left him alone?" Gray's voice was incredulous.

That did it. "Call the bomb squad, Matt. Now!" She slammed the phone down and whirled, heading back toward Harrington's office and Derek Stillwater.

# 16

---

*11:37 a.m.*

DEREK SMELLED DEAD BODIES. He knew he wasn't really smelling them. Not here in Harrington's office. It was a hallucination his brain churned out for him when he was stressed. When Saddam Hussein had used biological and chemical weapons on the Kurds in northern Iraq, he had been part of a covert team that slipped over the Turkish border to investigate.

When Aum Shinrikyo gassed the Tokyo subway, killing twelve people and exposing over five thousand, he had flown in with a team of FBI, CIA, and military experts.

During the first Gulf War, he had been a frontline cowboy, creeping to within shouting distance of bombing targets, setting up laser-guidance systems, and evaluating the biological and chemical fallout from destroyed ammunition depots.

Derek knew the stench of dead bodies.

He knelt on the office floor beside the bookcase and slowly removed books from the bottom shelf. He moved deliberately, cautiously edging the books out one at a time. It was possible the books were wired for just such a situation. Or worse, they had been set on a pressure switch and removing them at any speed would set off an explosion or gas attack.

One book at a time. On the entire bottom shelf were bound copies of *The Journal of Public Health Policy*. From the looks of it, at least six years' worth. Each bound copy was about three inches thick and must have weighed close to a pound.

Once he had five of the texts removed and stacked neatly to one side, he could peer in. Unfortunately, he couldn't see a damn thing. He fished in his pocket and came up with his key chain, which contained a tiny flashlight. He had a much better set of equipment back in his Go Packs, but that was in Jill's trunk in the parking garage. A piss-poor place for it, under the circumstances.

He slowly stuck his head into the space left by the removal of the books and held the tiny flashlight in his teeth. He could see the wire continue along the wall. It didn't seem to be attached to any of the books.

"Didn't seem to be" were words he had been taught to be concerned about in his Special Forces demolition training.

Jill appeared at the doorway. "What are you doing?"

"What does it look like?" He didn't turn away from his work. With great care, he removed another bound journal.

"The building's being evacuated and the bomb squad's on its way."

He removed another book. Three more to go. "What time is it?"

"11:43."

"So in two minutes the university's going to wire three million dollars into a numbered Bermuda bank account and this whole thing will go away," he said. "Two minutes."

When Jill didn't respond, he tilted his head to look at her. "And in seventeen minutes, more people will die. And the only chance we have of stopping that might be in this room."

Jill swallowed.

Derek met her gaze before going back to removing the books. It was 11:45 according to his watch when he pulled the last book off and could see that the wire was tied to an eyebolt screwed into the wall. The line was drawn taut.

"Ever had demolition training?" Derek asked, reaching in his pocket for the Leatherman multi-tool he always carried.

"I spent five weeks at Redstone," she said. "How about you?"

He studied her for a moment. Redstone Arsenal was the army's demolition training grounds outside Huntsville, Alabama. He had spent a year there, though most of that year had been spent teaching biological and chemical warfare history for the Weapons of Mass Destruction course work. The FBI ran its Hazardous Devices School there with the army.

"I've had some training," he said.

He opened the scissors part of the multi-tool. "It's possible," he said, "that this wire goes to the back of the drawer and is connected to some sort of IED." IED stood for "improvised explosive device," a military acronym for non-military things that go boom.

"Are you sure?"

He had his scissors poised over the wire. "No," he said. "And my advice is to get out of the building with everybody else."

"Why don't you wait for the bomb squad?"

"Time?"

"11:47."

He glanced at her. "Husband? Kids?"

She swallowed again. "A son. You?"

"Divorced, no kids. Not even a goldfish." He nodded at the tool in his hand. "Last chance."

Jill said, "Wait for the bomb squad."

"Agent Church, I'm cutting the damn wire. If I were you, I'd take cover."

She scowled at him. "I'm ordering you—"

"I don't work for you."

She pulled her weapon, a Glock, and trained it on Derek. "Stand down, Stillwater. We follow SOP on my watch. Enough with being a cowboy. Stand down."

Derek shook his head. "Can't say I didn't warn you." He cut the wire.

# 17

*11:47 a.m.*

MARY LINZEY, THE WXYZ producer, stood with Steve Shay and Ed Wachoviak inside the Administration Building on the Wayne State University campus. It was a beautiful building, she thought. The outside was curved, mirrored glass. On sunny days, it reflected the sun and the blue sky. Today, on a grim, chilly October day, it appeared gray, the only reflection being low-hanging clouds, the barely green lawn, Gullen Hall, and the Student Center. The interior entryway was done in white masonry and rose four stories to a steepled glass ceiling. Marble tile floors and full-grown trees lined the entryway. It was currently jammed with members of the press, who had immediately rushed to the Ad Building to try to get a statement from WSU's president, Dr. Alicia Kramer.

Dr. Kramer was not available for comment, not surprisingly. She was locked away in her office with her cabinet, the Board of Governors, several FBI agents, and undoubtedly many, many lawyers. Campus security had even locked down the building to the extent that the press couldn't get past the atrium lobby.

Ed looked at his watch and said, "I'm gonna get in position. C'mon, Steve."

They jockeyed through the crowd to find a spot where they could get a shot of the president or possibly the university mouthpiece, Cassandra DiBiaggio, if and when they made an appearance.

Fred Ball, a reporter with WDET, the local National Public Radio affiliate, tapped Mary on the shoulder. "So you're at ground zero on this one," he said.

Ball was a pro, and Mary liked him a lot. He had broad shoulders and narrow hips and stood slightly over six feet tall. His shaved skull gleamed darkly, and his teeth flashed in a smile.

"Hi, Fred. Yes. My time up to bat."

"Would you care to make a statement for me?" Fred pushed a microphone toward her.

She shrugged. "I'd just as soon not become the center of this news story."

Fred had a very deep voice. "Mary, who are you kidding? This guy contacted you personally. You're news. The Serpent's in contact with you personally." He clicked on the tape recorder. "Why do you think the Serpent contacted you personally?"

"No comment, Fred."

"What did he sound like?"

She was getting a little annoyed. "You heard the tape, just like everybody else. He used something to change his voice."

"Do you think it was a man? Could it have been a woman?"

She hesitated. "The voice definitely sounded like a man, but that's a good point. I guess we really don't know. Now, Fred—"

"Did the Serpent say anything to you besides what was on the tape?"

She glared at Fred now. "No."

"How did the FBI deal with you?"

She stepped aside. Other reporters were looking at them now. She said, "The FBI special agent in charge, Matthew Gray, attempted to confiscate the recording and block us from airing it. He cited the U.S. Patriot Act, but the station's attorneys assured us that the Patriot Act does not inhibit freedom of the press or the First Amendment. We did, however, cooperate fully with the Bureau by turning over the original recording."

"What do you think the Serpent really wants?"

"You heard the tape. He wants money."

"So you believe he's doing this for money?"

"I can't really say, Fred. That's what he said."

"Do you think you'll hear from the Serpent again?"

"I don't know."

"Do you think the university will pay the ransom?"

She hesitated. "We'll know as soon as—"

Her cell phone rang. Fred's eyes widened in interest. "Excuse me," she said.

She stepped outside the building, but Fred followed her. "Turn that damned thing off," she snapped, glaring at his tape recorder. She hit record on her tape recorder and answered her cell phone.

Again she heard the mechanically altered voice in her ear. "Is this Mary Linzey?"

"Speaking. Who is this?"

"This is the Serpent. Are you taping?"

"Yes."

"Here is my statement. The university has failed to meet my demands. The Serpent will strike again. In five minutes. It is on their heads."

The phone clicked off. Fred looked at her curiously. "Was that him?"

She nodded and swallowed, her throat dry. She felt excited and sick, all at the same time. She snuck a peek at her watch. The digital readout clicked from 11:55 to 11:56.

"Four more minutes," she said. She scanned the crowd, looking for an FBI agent. Any FBI agent. Where the hell were they?

With Fred trailing behind her, she sprinted back inside the lobby, elbowing her way through the press, trying to force her way to the doors of the Administration Building, desperate to find Matt Gray.

# 18

*11:47 a.m.*

WHEN DEREK CUT THE wire, Jill flung herself sideways to the hall-way floor. She sprawled there for a moment, angrier than ever, and then got to her feet and stepped into Harrington's office. Derek still crouched before the bookcase. His face was gray and coated with sweat.

She slipped her gun back into its clip. "Get up," she said. "Get on your feet so I can kick your ass."

"Hear that?"

"*Hear what?!*"

He held up a finger. It was hard to hear anything over the clang of the alarm. "That hissing noise," he said.

Jill's heart dropped. "You think—"

Derek stood up, shaking his head. "No," he said. "I'd already be dead."

"I don't smell—"

"Sarin is odorless. But you'll feel a burning sensation in your nose and throat. If this was sarin, I'd already be dead."

He fixed his attention on the filing cabinet. "Still feeling lucky?" he asked.

"Don't—"

Derek pulled open the top drawer of the filing cabinet. With a *pop!* a plastic inflatable cobra sprang upright out of the drawer, bobbing back and forth. A tinny recorded voice said, "Ha ha! Ha ha! Ha ha!" over and over.

Staring at it, Derek turned to Jill. He looked pointedly at his watch. Without a word, he opened all the filing cabinet drawers. Every one was empty. Beneath the cobra was a familiar red canister. When he cut the wire, it triggered the canister, which filled the cobra figure with whatever gas was in the canister and set off the voice recorder. He didn't know what gas was in the cobra, and had no plans to cut it open and find out. Leave that for the lab boys or the bomb squad.

Derek turned to look at the computer. "Let's take the disks and get out of here. Let the—"

Jill set her jaw. "We're not doing any such thing. I want to make something perfectly clear to you. What I've seen in the last fifteen minutes makes me suspect that everything you're being investigated for might be justified. You don't follow procedures. You don't take precautions. You're a goddamned menace. You contaminated what could be the best evidence to this guy—none of it will be usable in court now—and you put both of our lives at risk. For nothing. Besides, you're not here to run an investigation—"

"Actually, I am," he said. "Evaluate, coordinate, investigate."

"Are you listening to me?"

He walked over to the computer, studied the menu, and tapped Print, so he could get a copy of the CBCTR's "Scenario 14." There was a peculiar click from the printer. Without hesitation, Derek launched himself at Jill. Almost simultaneously the printer exploded, a blast of heat and flame engulfing the office. From the floor, Derek felt the energy wave roar over them. The office was an inferno, crackling and roaring.

He rolled off Jill. "Dammit! Where's the exting—"

The sprinkler system in the office kicked on, drenching the space in water, further destroying anything that wasn't already charred or shattered by the blast.

Jill, next to him on the floor, shielded her eyes from the roiling black smoke and oily cold water. "Guess you forgot to check for secondary devices," she said.

Derek stared into the office. "At least you're alive. You can thank me later."

# 19

THE CLASSROOM WAS ON the second floor of Scott Hall, where the Wayne State University Biochemistry and Molecular Biology Department was centered. It was a medium-sized tiered lecture hall that could accommodate over one hundred people, though there were only about sixty today. IBS 7010, Molecular Biology, was an Interdisciplinary Biomedical Sciences class that the majority of graduate students in any area of biology had to take during the first term of their programs.

Dr. Isaac Tschevkov was a mousy gray man with a slight hunch to his shoulders. Pink scalp peeked through the white flyaway hair that he rarely combed. He stepped in front of the lectern and fumbled with the microphone. He had a wispy voice with a deep accent, and he used the microphone to project his voice throughout the auditorium. "Okay, okay," he said over the scratching, screeching sound of the microphone he clipped to his coat lapel. He wore black dress shoes, brown slacks, a white shirt, and a black tie, with a brown plaid sport coat over it all. "Let's get going," he said. "I am Dr. Isaac Tschevkov. I'll be covering unusual aspects of molecular translation and transcription. Presumably, since you are all graduate students, you will already be familiar with the basics. I will look at the exceptions. Today, we'll be covering A to I RNA Editing. Can anybody tell me what this is?"

A couple of students raised their hands. Tschevkov pointed to an Asian woman sitting toward the back of the room, wearing a white sweater. "During—"

"Speak up," Tschevkov said, amplified voice booming around the auditorium. "Speak up so everybody can hear you. Go ahead, stand up."

IBS 7010 was team-taught, professors from various departments taking a swing at their areas of expertise. Tschevkov was a molecular biologist; he had spent years studying the genetics of flatworms. Today was his first day of lecturing.

She stood up, looking awkward and uncomfortable. She tried to project her voice. "Before transcription, adenosine deaminases modify individual adenosines under certain circumstances."

"Modify them to what?" Tschevkov boomed.

"Um, inosine."

"*Ja.* A, for adenosine, to I, for inosine. Thank you, miss." Tschevkov walked over to the overhead projector and began to sketch out the molecular structures of adenosine and inosine. "This happens on particular spots of the—" He abruptly stopped speaking, his hand reaching for his neck. He coughed. "Excuse me. As I was saying…" He coughed again. Slowly, Tschevkov dropped to his knees, hand at his throat.

# 20

*12:14 p.m.*

MATT GRAY WAS ON a roll. The mobile command center was parked outside Scott Hall. Derek and Jill sat in chairs in the back while Matt paced in front of them. Gray's face was turning a dangerous shade of purple. Derek said, "You're going to blow a blood vessel at this rate. Why don't you calm down?"

Gray spun on him. "Why don't you shut the fuck up, Stillwater? As far as I can see, you've done nothing but cause trouble. You're here to observe and liaise with the office. So why don't you shut up and observe."

Derek gave Gray a flat, unemotional look. "Anything else?"

"Yes! Follow procedures. Even DHS has procedures to follow. When you think there's a bomb in an office, you call in the bomb squad. You don't try to defuse it yourself. Especially if there was no risk of it going off."

The bomb squad and the crime scene team, those not at Scott Hall, were going over Harrington's office. At Scott Hall, forty-three were dead, and twenty-one were injured and in the hospital. The university had been officially closed. Gray had called for reinforcements and had people coordinating with the Detroit PD. The mayor and the governor were on the phone constantly, asking for updates so they could talk to the press. Gray was having a meltdown, and he needed to focus his aggravation on somebody. Derek was handy.

"Did you hear me?" Gray demanded.

"Sure. I heard you."

"Then what are you going to do?"

"My job," Derek said. He stood up. "Which, if you'll get out of the way, I'll continue to do."

Gray shook his head. "You are not going into Scott Hall. This is my operation, Stillwater. I'm not giving you access."

Derek provided a tight smile. "Excuse me. I have work to do."

"I'm not finished, Stillwater. Sit your ass down."

Derek took a step inside Gray's personal space. "I'm not part of the Justice Department. I don't answer to you. Now, I've got a job to do. Maybe if you'd have done yours, those kids would be alive now."

Gray blocked Derek's path. "Okay, hotshot. You're done. Sit down."

"Out of my way." Derek moved around the FBI agent.

Gray reached inside his coat and yanked out a pair of handcuffs. "I'm done with you and your bullshit, Stillwater. Hands behind your back. I'm arresting you for obstruction of justice, for hindering a federal investi—"

Derek hit the FBI agent in a flurry of fast, short punches. Jill lunged to her feet, but before she could do anything, Derek was over the prone figure of Matt Gray and out the door. She crouched beside Gray. Gray's face was a mask of blood, mostly from a bloody nose that was spurting scarlet all over his face. He appeared dazed.

Jill helped him sit up. "Are you all right?"

Gray struggled to his feet, trying to shake off the assault. He staggered momentarily, then focused on Jill.

"He hit me," he said, his voice more puzzled than angry. "The bastard hit me. He assaulted me. You saw it."

Jill bit her lip.

"You saw it, right? He hit me. You saw it."

She nodded. It occurred to her that over the years she had wanted to do exactly what Stillwater had done herself—more than a few times.

"What are you waiting for?" Gray snarled, his voice nasal and choked, "Go get him."

"What about—"

"Don't worry about this Serpent crap. Go get Stillwater. It was your job to babysit him. Now you've got a real job to do."

She frowned, hesitating. "You want me to arrest him."

"Yes. For assaulting me. Arrest him. You get him in cuffs, and I want him locked up until this is over."

"Matt—"

He turned on her, spitting blood. "Do you want to be arrested with him? Do I need to sideline you for insubordination? This is a direct order, Jill. Go arrest Derek Stillwater."

"Yes, sir," she said, and left the command center.

When she got to the spot where she'd left her car, it was gone. "Derek! God damn you! You stole my car."

She rubbed her forehead for a moment and took in the ambulances, fire trucks, and press vehicles, debating what to do. She had no desire to go back to Matt Gray and tell him Stillwater had hot-wired her car. She would just have to improvise.

Also, she had a pretty good idea where Derek was headed.

# 21

*12:15 p.m.*

MICHAEL CHURCH AND RAY Moretti rattled down Crooks Road in Michael's old Honda Civic, Michael behind the wheel. It was lunchtime and they were headed for a McDonald's drive-through. Ray, short and swarthy with dark hair shorn close to his scalp, was jamming his finger down on the radio channel selector with his left hand while lighting up a joint with his right. He stopped for a moment as a radio announcer talked about the Serpent.

"... There has been a second sarin gas attack, this time at Wayne State University. The attack took place in a second-floor auditorium at Scott Hall. So far, forty-two students and a professor have been reported dead. Twenty-one students—"

Ray stabbed the seek button again. This time a rap tune by J Slim came up. "Hey, man," Ray said. "I can't wait till tonight. Wanna hit?" He held up the joint for Michael. Michael shook his head and pointed to the radio.

"Go back to that news story."

"What, you think your *mommy's* working that?"

Michael knew she was. And that scared him. He'd never admit it to anybody. Not to his mom. Especially not to Ray. He worried about her. His father had been killed in a terrorist bombing while working at the embassy in Dar es Salaam, Tanzania. That had been August 1998, and his father had been working for the State Department. Michael didn't remember his father that well—he'd only been a little kid—and didn't really remember Tanzania at all. What he remembered was a sense of loss and how his mother had changed afterward. He wouldn't admit it to anybody, but he no longer really remembered what his father looked like. His mother didn't keep any photographs around. He knew she hadn't thrown them away. But she had put them away and stored them out of sight...out of sight, out of mind.

A part of him, right now, was pleased that his mom was tied up in this investigation. It meant she probably wouldn't be home tonight. And that meant he could go to the J Slim concert and she'd never know about it.

He smiled at that thought and reached out for the joint. "Yeah," he said. "Gimme that. Mom's probably working this case. The Serpent. What an asshole."

"Yeah. *The Serpent.* This guy watches too much TV."

Michael giggled. "Maybe he's hoping he'll get caught and they'll make a made-for-TV movie about him." They both burst into laughter.

Michael's cell phone rang. He snagged it and clicked it on, not glancing at the caller ID. "Yo!" he said.

"Michael! It's Mom."

For a wild, panicky moment, Michael thought she knew he was smoking a joint with Ray. His heart thumping, he said, "Yeah?"

"Honey, I have an emergency. I need your car."

"What?"

"I need you to drive down into the city and pick me up."

"*What?*" He was stupefied. He felt like he had lost thirty IQ points in response to her statement. "I don't get it."

"Michael, listen closely. Are you in your car? Are you going to lunch?"

He glanced nervously at the joint Ray was holding to his lips. "Y-yeah."

"Then keep right on going. I'm going to walk to the Fisher Building. Do you know where that is? It's where we saw *Cats*. Remember?"

"Yeah." What a stupid play that had been.

"It's on West Grand Boulevard. Get on I-75 and go south to—"

"I know where it is," he said. "But I've got Ray with me—"

"Fine. Bring him along. Come get me."

"Mom—"

"Michael, this is an emergency. Just do it. Now. Can I count on you?"

He clutched the phone. "Yes."

"See you soon."

After she clicked off, Michael stared at the cellular phone. He looked at Ray, toking his brains out in the passenger seat. Michael rolled down his window, reached over, and snatched the roach from Ray's fingers and flung it out into space.

"Hey! What the fuck?"

"We've got to go pick up my mother. Roll your window down. Roll your goddamned window down. We've got to air this piece of shit out."

"Are you fuckin' nuts? Your mom's FBI. She'll bust my ass. Stop the car."

"Ray—"

"Stop the motherfuckin' car. Are you nuts? What's the matter with you? Where's your mom's car?"

"I don't know." Michael gripped the steering wheel, feeling oddly exhilarated at the same time he felt claws of fear tear at his spine. His mom said it was an emergency. She needed him.

"Stop the car. Dammit, Mike! Stop the fuckin' car."

Michael pulled onto the shoulder of Crooks Road. Ray practically exploded out of the car.

"What are you gonna do?" Michael asked, leaning down so he could look at Ray.

"Hitchhike. Walk. I don't fuckin' know. You've lost your mind. Fuck off, man. What's going on?"

Michael shrugged. "Hey, man—"

"Get the hell out of here, man. Go! Go rescue your *mommy*."

Michael swallowed. "Hey, Ray!"

"What?"

"Fuck you too!" He stepped on the gas, spraying gravel behind him and leaving Ray in his dust.

# 22

*12:22 p.m.*

FERNDALE WAS A SUBURB north of Detroit. It called itself "Fashionable Ferndale," and maybe the alliteration was appropriate. Ferndale was where the twentysomethings who couldn't afford the considerably more fashionable neighboring suburb of Royal Oak lived, at least those for whom shopping, nightlife, and overpriced upscale living relatively close to Detroit were a priority.

Derek had Rebecca Harrington's address, but it was proving to be a little harder than expected to actually find her house. Ferndale appeared to be a tidy little suburb with scads of cottages and bungalows, all of which seemed nearly identical—small two-story houses on small lots with a concrete porch, shrubs, sidewalks, and white aluminum siding. There were very few garages or carports. It was like every house had been built in the 1940s, which, he reflected, they probably had.

Finally he found her house on a cul-de-sac. It was a pleasant enough neighborhood, not unlike all the others he had driven through. Mature oak, sycamore, and willow trees. Small, fenced-in yards. There was an elementary school two blocks away. He parked on the street, considered his options, and then hunted through his Go Packs. While he was at it, he knocked back some Tylenol with tepid water from a bottle. He retrieved an electronic lock pick from one of his Go Packs with an additional set of small tools, as well as a small but powerful Maglite flashlight.

He strode up the walkway onto the front porch and punched the doorbell. As he expected, nobody answered. Nonetheless, he hit the doorbell again, then knocked with a good solid rap. Still no answer. Yet there was a car in the driveway, a maroon Jeep Cherokee.

He took out the electronic lock pick, inserted the thin rods into the keyhole, and tapped the activator button. Within seconds the door was unlocked, and he stepped into the house.

Immediately in front of him was a carpeted staircase rising to the second floor. Off to his right was the living area. Blue carpeting, sofa, rocking chair, love seat, maple coffee table, and TV. The wall decorations were framed quilts that he suspected Rebecca Harrington had done herself. They looked great.

He moved through the living room into a dining room and kitchen. There was an odd vibe in the house, one he didn't like. It didn't feel quite empty. He took his Colt out of its holster and held it down by his side, moving more cautiously than before.

"Hello?" he called out. "Anybody home?"

He listened. Was there a sound? Something from above? A muffled rattle or thump?

On the far side of the kitchen he found a back door and a landing and a staircase leading to the basement. Instead of searching the basement, he turned back to the front stairs and moved upward to the second floor, Colt held in both hands and pointing upward. He took each step slowly.

At the top of the stairs, his nose twitched. Whatever was setting off his Bad Vibe Alarm was up here. There were three bedrooms and a bathroom off a short hallway. He quickly entered the bathroom. Nothing.

The first bedroom he entered was the master bedroom, and that's where he found Rebecca Harrington. Her ankles and wrists had been bound with silver duct tape. And worse, so had her nose and mouth.

She had suffocated to death.

# 23

*12:33 p.m.*

JILL CHURCH WAS PACING in front of the entrance to the Fisher Building when Michael pulled up. All the windows were open in the Civic, which immediately caught her attention. It was not a particularly warm day. It was, in fact, a little chilly. She shoved the thought to the back of her mind for a moment and climbed in.

"You made good time," she said. "I'm really sorry about this, but I'm going to need your car."

Michael shrugged, the perpetual scowl firmly plastered on his face. "Where's your car?"

Jill settled back and buckled her seat belt, rolling up the window. "Can we close the windows?" she said. "Why are your windows open?"

Michael shrugged again and leaned over and cranked up his window. "Where to?"

"I'll drop you back at school. Where's Ray?"

Michael pulled forward into traffic on West Grand Boulevard. The gridlock had thinned over the last couple of hours. Of course, more people were leaving the city now than going in.

"I let him out," Michael said. He sniffed.

"Getting a cold?" Jill asked.

"What?"

"Sniffling?"

"No. Just … nothing. Where to?"

"Like I said, I'll drop you back at school."

"Okay. This about that Serpent thing?"

He took a turn from the Boulevard onto the northbound Lodge. "Don't drive so fast," Jill said.

"Mom, everybody's going seventy."

"Just go the speed limit. Can you get a ride home from school from somebody?"

He nodded. "What's this all about?"

"I can't talk about it, Michael."

He took his eyes off the road to glare at her. "No shit," he grumbled. "So what else is new?"

Jill clenched her fists in her lap and blinked away the tears that welled in her eyes. "I don't need this right now, Michael. I just need your car for the rest of the day."

"Yeah, right."

"Michael … you do understand that my job is important, right?"

"Sure."

She flinched at the lack of interest in his voice. "It's not just that it's what we live on," she continued. "What I do. It's important."

Michael didn't say anything. He got off the Lodge onto the Davison.

"You do understand that, right?"

"Uh-huh. So what's wrong with *your* car? Break down?"

Jill said, "Um, another agent . . . borrowed it."

Michael peered at her over his shoulder, then ducked back to watch the road. "What was wrong with his car?"

Jill kneaded her temples with her fingertips. "Michael, I really don't want to discuss this right now, okay?"

"Why should this be any different," Michael muttered.

They drove in silence as Michael maneuvered from the Davison to northbound I-75. Jill wrestled with her emotions. It was just policy. Don't talk about active cases with civilians. And that meant her son. It had cropped up from time to time in the past, but not lately. Lately he hadn't wanted to talk about anything. It was like sharing a house with a deaf-mute. A deaf-mute with an attitude. All of a sudden, today, he wanted to talk about her work.

Michael filled the silence by punching on his radio. A loud, belligerent voice filled the car interior:

*". . . Don' mess wit' J*
*He knows what to say*
*To the bitches that cum*
*On his face.*
*Yo, babe—"*

Jill jabbed off the radio. "That's . . . that's . . ."

"Mom! I was listening to—"

Jill's cell phone rang. She held up a silencing hand to her son and put the phone to her ear. "Jill Church here."

"Church, it's Stillwater. I've got—"

"You are in such serious trouble! Where are you?"

"Church, would you—"

"You know that Matt Gray wants me to arrest you? Look, just tell me where you are. I'll meet you, take you back to the Federal Building. If you want, I'll take you to the airport and you can just fly back to—"

"Agent Church, shut the fuck up! Rebecca Harrington's been murdered."

It felt like her throat was swelling shut. "What? How—"

"I'm leaving, but if you want to take control of the scene, you'd better get over here."

"Over where? Control of the ... Stillwater, you have to stay there. This is in Ferndale, right?"

"Yes. She's in her bedroom on the second floor of her house. You're going to have to bring the local cops, the Ferndale PD, into this, but you've got to make them understand—"

"Are you out of your mind?! You stay there! You stay right there until I get there! Don't contamin——"

He hung up on her.

With a frustrated shout, she slammed her fist down on the dashboard of the Civic. "God damn it! God damn it!"

Michael's eyes were wide. "Mom?"

She pressed her hand to her forehead, took a deep breath, let it out. "We're going to Ferndale. We're going to a murder scene. Right now."

"Cool."

"It's not cool!" she snapped. "This isn't a game, Michael!"

"I know." He turned to look at her, ripping down the left lane of northbound I-75. "My father died as a result of a terrorist attack. Remember? I know it's not a game."

# 24

*12:35 p.m.*

THE MAN CALLING HIMSELF the Serpent stood outside Scott Hall with the rest of the spectators, taking it all in. It gave him a thrill to watch the chaos. It was a particularly exciting feeling to watch a plan as complicated as this one come to fruition.

So far, events had gone pretty much the way he'd hoped they would. He was surprised by this, actually. There was a concept called "friction," which meant, basically, that things did not go according to plan. It was a military term, first coined by Carl von Clausewitz in his *On War*, and it referred to physical impediments to a military campaign. Clausewitz's prime example of friction was the weather.

The Serpent reflected that maybe he had been lucky. He remembered thinking about the wind just before detonating his gas device in the Boulevard Café. He remembered questioning whether he should have considered the weather in his planning. But his attacks all involved interior sites, and the temperatures were all moderate. Sarin reacted faster in warmer environments, but it seemed to be working fast enough for his needs.

Things had worked out so far, and he knew it was because he had planned carefully, because he was smarter than they were, and because he was keeping several steps ahead while at the same time setting up his master plan. But his plan was moving into its most complicated phase, and the risks were going to get very high.

He smiled, heart beating hard in his chest. *You will know who I am, father. I will be as famous and as revered as you are. And as feared.*

Moving slowly through the crowd, he acted like any other rubbernecking spectator. The Detroit Fire Department had set up an inflatable tent off to one side to use as a staging area for moving people in and out of the building in their hazardous materials suits. It was here that he was headed, but part of his plan required a slightly different approach.

Two yellow Detroit fire trucks were parked along with several ambulances, police cars, medical examiner vans, and other vehicles. The Serpent walked toward them, everybody's attention focused on the building and the removal of the bodies. Nobody guarded the vehicles.

He walked right up to one of the fire trucks, eyes scanning it. He saw what he was looking for—a dark windbreaker with DFD stenciled on the back. Without breaking stride, he snatched it up and slipped into it, heading toward the containment tent.

At the tent, a uniformed Detroit cop stood lackadaisically to one side, his job primarily to keep the media away. With a DFD baseball cap pulled low over his forehead and his hands stuffed into the pockets of the windbreaker, the Serpent nodded at the cop and walked into the tent as if he had every right to be there.

Once inside, he saw that the various agencies had clustered into their own corners, segregating themselves. He found what he was looking for—where the FBI had congregated. Each bag was stamped with a name: Smithson, J.; Corrigan, W.; McMillan, F.

That was the one. Frank McMillan. Kneeling down, the Serpent took out his cellular phone, made certain it was turned on, and dropped it to the bottom of Frank McMillan's duffel bag beneath his street clothes.

Mission accomplished.

The Serpent, job completed, turned and walked out, nodding to the Detroit cop on his way out. This had been the riskiest thing he had done so far, and it had gone without a hitch.

The Serpent smiled, enjoying the nearly sexual flush of adrenaline. Yes, everything was going just fine.

# 25

*12:41 p.m.*

DEREK PARKED OUTSIDE WILLIAM Harrington's house in Birmingham. Birmingham was a little farther north, straight up Woodward Avenue from Ferndale. Birmingham was trendy in a way that Ferndale could only dream of being. Birmingham was where old money lived, but not old money like the Pointes on the northeast side of Detroit. Birmingham had a population just under twenty thousand people, but the median income level was slightly over $100,000, with a 3 percent poverty rate; the average home went for more than $360,000. Looking at William Harrington's house just off Main Street, Derek doubted the numbers he was pulling off the web via his tablet computer. It appeared to be a small Cape Cod on a tiny lot. It was beautifully maintained, and the yard seemed well-manicured, but it was not a large, elaborate house. None of the houses on this street appeared large, but they all seemed older, well cared for, and richly appointed. The house had a one-car garage, which was closed.

He dialed Harrington's telephone, but nobody answered. An answering machine picked up, with a male voice saying, "You have reached the Bill Harrington residence. I can't come to the telephone right now. Your call is important to me, so leave your name and phone number and I'll get back in touch with you as soon as possible."

The voice was deep, with careful, formal diction and enunciation.

Derek needed to take a minute. He felt like he was being spun a bit, that events were controlling him instead of the other way around. He had moved his Go Packs to the front seat, and he reached into one of them and took out the special phone the Department of Homeland Security assigned their troubleshooters. They weren't cellular phones, but rather hand-held modified Iridium satellite phones with a scrambler function. In theory, he could use it from anywhere on the planet due to a series of geosynchronous satellites scattered around the globe. The scrambler was state-of-the-art as well, having little or no obvious distortion.

He speed-dialed number 1 and held the phone to his ear.

"Derek? It's about time you called with an update," growled the voice of the secretary of DHS, General James Johnston.

"I've been a little busy."

"I just heard there's been a second attack."

"Yes."

"Will there be more?"

"I haven't heard any news of a threat, but I doubt this guy will quit until he gets whatever he wants."

"What does he want?"

"According to the first call, he wants money, but I doubt if that's really what he wants."

"Fine. Update me."

Derek ran it all past him. Every bit of it.

There was silence on the phone until Johnston said, "You punched out the SAC?"

"Yes, sir, I did. I'm surprised you haven't heard about that yet."

"Not yet. Derek, was that necessary? Or are you just trying to get me to pull you off this assignment?"

"I wouldn't come off it now if you ordered me to."

Johnston sighed. "That doesn't surprise me much. I'll call him, see if I can smooth things over."

"I need something, sir."

"What's that?"

"I need you to get somebody over to a guy named Bernard Schultz at Stanford. He's involved in something called SKOLAR MD. That's spelled S-K-O-L-A-R-M-D. It's a database. Anyway, Harrington was sending him chem-terrorism scenarios that this think tank was putting out. We never got a chance to track down the people here who were writing these things, but Schultz had at least one of them. Can you handle that?"

"I'll get somebody on it."

"Good. And e-mail them directly to me once you do."

"Will do. Anything else?"

Derek hesitated. "Yes. Two things. See if you can track down all the names of the people involved with the Center for Biological and Chemical Terrorism Research here at Wayne State. Names, contact information, CVs if you can get them. It might be tough. The U's closed down because of the second attack."

"Can do. I'll e-mail that to you as well. What's the second thing?"

"Run a background check on an FBI agent named Jill Church."

"The one who's babysitting you."

"Right."

"You have doubts about her?"

"No, not really. But I feel like I've met her before, and I don't know why. She spent five weeks at Redmond. That might be it. But my gut tells me it's something else."

"Is this a priority?"

"No. The other data's top priority. Especially the information from Schultz, if you can get it."

"I'll take care of it. Anything else?"

"No. Not yet."

"All right, Derek. Good work so far. But try to be more diplomatic with the authorities."

"That never seems to get me anywhere."

"That's because you've never tried it. What's next?"

"You don't want to know."

"Derek—"

"What you don't know can't hurt you, General. Goodbye." He hung up and stared at Harrington's house. He needed to go inside the house. He remembered going into Harrington's office all too well. He hoped the Serpent hadn't booby-trapped his house as well.

# 26

*12:45 p.m.*

MARY LINZEY WAS STARTING to get nervous. After the second call from the Serpent, she had tracked down the FBI SAC, Matt Gray. During the Detroit terrorism trials post-9/11, she had dealt with Gray, and she understood him to be a by-the-book kind of FBI agent with some problems distinguishing between civil rights and criminal procedure. Since 9/11, of course, that was hardly unusual. The government had made it possible to call damn near anybody in the War on Terror an enemy combatant, ignore their civil rights, and throw them in a cell for as long as it wanted.

There had also been hints and rumors about a possible sexual harassment lawsuit against Gray by one of the female agents, but nothing had come of it. Nothing official, anyway.

After Mary explained the last call, Gray confiscated her phone and turned her over to another agent, who took her to an empty room in the WSU Administration Building, asked her to sit down, and then disappeared. It occurred to her that being locked in a room anywhere at Wayne State could be deadly, and her unease grew. Who knew she was here? Well, Fred Ball did. He'd been taping the entire exchange. Figures. How would he report it?

"... *representatives of the Federal Bureau of Investigation detained a local ABC journalist, WXYZ producer Mary Linzey, after she was contacted by the terrorist calling himself the Serpent...* "

She checked the door. It was unlocked. She opened it and peered out. The FBI agent who had delivered her there was in the hallway, yammering away on a cell phone. He looked a little young, the prototypical Fed, with dark hair cut short and parted on one side, chiseled features, blank eyes, and a dark suit. He pulled the phone away from his ear. "Yes?"

"What am I doing here?"

"Please be patient, ma'am."

"Where's my phone?"

"Laboratory," he said.

"I want it back."

"I'm sorry, ma'am. That's not possible."

"What if the Serpent calls me back?"

"I sincerely hope he does, ma'am. Now, please return to the room and wait until I can—"

She started walking down the hallway away from the agent. "Hey!" he shouted at her back. "Where are you going?"

She broke into a run. Enough of this. She wasn't under arrest. She wasn't going to be detained while the biggest story of her career passed her by.

She ducked into a stairwell and ran down three steps at a time, hearing the door slam above her. She was staying just ahead of him, and she knew this was crazy. Where the hell did she think she was going to go?

Then she was out on the main floor, sprinting out of the building. She stopped. The crowd was gone. The FBI agent stepped out from behind her and grabbed her arm. "What do you think you're doing?"

"Am I under arrest?" she asked.

"No. You're a witness. Please—"

"Let go of me," she snarled, pulling her arm away from him. "Are you familiar with freedom of the press? I want my phone back."

"That won't happen, ma'am," he said with a shake of his head. "They're going to use it to track down his cellular phone. If . . . what are you doing?"

She had her tape recorder in her hand. "I'm taping this."

"Ma'am—" He reached out for the recorder, and she snatched it away from him.

"And what?" she said. "Is the FBI capable of tracking this guy down using his cellular telephone?"

"If it's on, yes. We can track a phone to within one hundred yards if it's on."

"Do they have to be calling?"

"No."

"And that's what's happening now?"

"Yes, ma'am."

"Your name, sir?"

He seemed to take a deep breath. "Agent Roger Kandling."

"Why didn't you confiscate my phone for this after the first call?"

Kandling blinked, his eyes a deep blue, almost gray. "No comment."

"Somebody screwed up?" she said.

"No comment."

She turned off the tape recorder. "Off the record."

He eyed the tape recorder, reached out for it. She handed it to him. He confirmed that it was off, and said, "Matt Gray fucked up. He should have locked you in a box and waited for the next call and had everybody ready to track it. We would have been able to cordon off the area, and this whole mess would be over."

"Why do you think he screwed up?"

"Because he won't listen to anybody else. He's got his undies in a bunch about this troubleshooter from DHS, who frankly is about three steps ahead of everybody else."

Her attention sharpened. She took her tape recorder back. "Tell me about this troubleshooter."

"His name is Derek Stillwater. He's ex–Army Special Forces, an expert on biological and chemical weapons."

She blinked. "The Chimera guy?"

"Yes. He's the one."

"I thought he was under investi—"

"The Bureau *is* investigating him. The attorney general has warned Secretary Johnston that Stillwater should not be actively working. Frankly, most of us think he went off the edge a long time ago."

"Yet he's here," she said.

"Yes, ma'am. And he was here at the university when this happened."

She inhaled sharply. "There were rumors that he may have known more about the attack at U.S. Immuno, that he might actually have been an inside man."

"No comment."

"It is true, is it not, that Derek Stillwater was once a friend and team member with the terrorist behind the attacks on the White House and U.S. Immunological Research?"

"Yes, ma'am. That is correct."

"Derek Stillwater is under investigation by the FBI for the torture and murder of a Russian citizen. Is that correct?"

"That is correct."

"How did Derek Stillwater allegedly torture and kill this Russian citizen? It was a woman, correct?"

"He suffocated her using plastic bags," Kandling said.

"Why is this man running around loose?"

"That's a good question, ma'am. A very good question."

She stared at him. "Do you think Derek Stillwater might have some inside information regarding the Serpent?"

Kandling swallowed hard. "Ma'am, I wouldn't be surprised if Derek Stillwater *was* the Serpent."

# 27

*12:52 p.m.*

Agent Roger Kandling watched Mary Linzey hurry away. When she disappeared from sight, Kandling whipped out his cell phone and placed a call.

"Gray here."

"Sir, it's Kandling."

"Did she buy it?"

"All the way, sir. She's working on the assumption that Derek Stillwater may actually be the Serpent. If she doesn't swallow that, she at least is suspicious of his involvement here."

"Good," Gray said, his voice sounding muffled and nasal. "Good job, Kandling. Anything else?"

"Just a suggestion, sir."

"What's that?"

"Alert the local police that Stillwater is a 'person of interest' and should be detained," Kandling said.

Over the phone Matt Gray laughed low and soft. "I like that. Yes. Good job. I don't want to spread my resources out any more, but get the local cops on it. Good. Take care of it. And Roger?"

"Yes, sir?"

"We never had this conversation."

This gave Kandling pause. Was he being hung out to dry by the SAC? "Yes, sir," he said. "Understood."

"Soon as you're done, get your ass back over here."

"Yes, sir."

They clicked off and Kandling took a second to think through his approach. Gray was playing games with Stillwater and with inter-department turf feuds. That was fine by him. He had no love of the Department of Homeland Security. The Bureau was still the top anti-terror cops, as far as he was concerned.

But he saw no reason why he should be taking the Fifth during the inevitable congressional investigation. He wanted his neck kept out of that potentially ugly noose.

It was a classic CYA procedure—cover your ass—and he took a moment to figure out exactly how to cover his own for when this thing blew wide open. When he figured it out, he dialed the Detroit FBI office and set things in motion.

# 28

*12:56 p.m.*

JILL AND MICHAEL CHURCH pulled up in front of Rebecca Harrington's Ferndale house. Jill sighed, "Thank God."

"What?"

Jill looked at her son. "The Ferndale police aren't here. I was afraid—"

"Mom? What's going on?"

She frowned. "I can't talk now, Michael. Please stay right here. I have to go in that house."

"Mom—"

"Stay!" she said, climbing out of the car. She hurried up the steps to the front door. She paused, looking around. Michael was slumped behind the wheel, glaring at her. *Lord, what a mess!* she thought.

The front door was unlocked. She opened it and stepped in. Derek had said Rebecca Harrington was upstairs. But it was bad procedure not to secure the house, so she did a quick recon of the main floor and slipped into the basement to make sure she had the house to herself. Then she went to the second floor and found the body of Rebecca Harrington. She studied the scene for a moment. Rebecca Harrington had not died easily. It had been a horrible way to die, she thought, suffocating like that. The woman's eyes were wide open, the whites speckled with pinpoints of blood. Her face, strained in agony, rigid in death, also had red spots, called petechiae.

"Who did this to you?" Jill murmured.

She scanned the room, wondering if Derek had found anything here and taken it with him. He was a menace, and she was getting ever angrier with him. There was a way to do these things. A proper, procedural way to handle cases.

A tiny, quiet voice in the back of her mind said, *His only priority is stopping the next attack. That's all.*

"Mom?"

She spun, letting out a gasp. "Michael! What are you doing here? I told you—"

He stood in the doorway, staring past her at Rebecca Harrington.

She rushed over and spun him around. Her tone was gentle. "Go back to the car. I have to call the Ferndale police. Please, Michael."

"She's ... dead."

"Yes. Go on, Michael. Please. Wait for me. I'll be there in a minute."

He seemed to float as he left. She pressed her palms to her forehead. Then she took out her phone and got hold of the Ferndale PD. She also called the office and asked that a crime-scene specialist be sent to supervise the local police. Then she went back to talk to Michael.

He was leaning against his car. She gave him a hug and was surprised when he hugged her back. He said, "Who would do something like that?"

"A very bad man, Michael. Probably the Serpent."

"Did … did he torture her? She suffocated, right?"

Jill doubted if there was an innocent sixteen-year-old in the country, what with all the exposure to the world by TV, movies, and the Internet. Still, seeing a murder victim was traumatic—not just the first time, but hopefully every time. It wasn't something one wanted to get accustomed to.

Keeping her voice level, she said, "The police are going to question you now. They're going to give both of us a hard time about why you went in there and why I let you." She paused. "They're going to give me a lot of … oh hell, Michael, they're going to give me a lot of shit about even having you along. It's going to make me look like some sort of amateur. They're going to separate us, or try to. I might be able to control that because you're a minor, but if they do, either way, you have to tell the truth. Understand? You have to tell them *exactly* what you did and why. Don't lie. Tell the truth."

"Am … am I going to be arrested?"

She smiled. "No, Michael. But it might be unpleasant. But you're smart and you're level-headed. Don't be cute or tricky or be a smart-ass. This isn't the time for that. Answer clearly and to the point. Only answer what they ask. Don't volunteer information, and don't add to what they ask for. Don't clarify unless they ask for a clarification. Understand? Just tell them what they want."

He nodded, a short head bob.

"Are you going to be okay?" she asked. "That was … that was pretty bad up there."

He swallowed hard. "The Serpent did that?"

"Probably."

"What does he want?"

She sighed. "He's making ransom demands. Maybe it's about money."

"But her..." He shook his head.

She thought for a moment. "Michael, if I tell you this, then you're going to have to tell the Ferndale cops when they ask you. This way, if I don't tell you, then you can just say you don't know. They may ask you a dozen different ways why she was killed, and all you can say in all honesty is, 'I don't know. I think it has something to do with the Serpent.' It's better for you. It's better for me. It's better for the case. Understand? I can tell them what I need to tell them because I'm an agent. I can decide what they are qualified to hear. But you need to tell them the truth. So I'm not going to tell you."

He opened his mouth to protest, but she raised her hand. "I'm not going to tell you *now*, Michael. But when we're done with the police, I *will* tell you. I'll tell you as much as I can. All right?"

He stared at her.

She held out her hand. "Deal?"

His expression was hard to read. A complicated range of emotions flitted across his face. Then he shook her hand. "Deal," he said.

# 29

*1:03 p.m.*

DEREK FELT LIKE HE had wasted enough time. Despite his trepidation, he had to enter William Harrington's house. He climbed out of Jill's car and proceeded up the driveway, jumping when his satellite phone buzzed. Relieved to have an excuse to wait, he clicked it on. It was Jill Church.

"Where are you?" she asked.

"Did you find Rebecca Harrington?"

"Yes, Stillwater. I did. And by the way, punching Matt Gray was just about the stupidest thing you could have done."

"Oh, I don't know. I've done a lot of other stupid things. Why are you calling?"

"Because I have a question I want you to answer."

William Harrington's driveway was shaded by mature trees—oak, birch, maple, and poplar—their leaves beginning the fall color tour. If Harrington's trees were any indication, it was going to be a good year for it. They were a good 60 percent changed, blazing yellows, reds, and oranges. Derek scanned the street, noticing a blue car that looked like a cop cruiser turning the corner.

"Are you tracing this call?" he asked.

"No, why?"

"Huh," he said, eyes on the police car. "Are you lying to me?"

"What's going on, Stillwater?"

"What's your question?"

"Irina Khournikova."

Derek's blood ran cold. "That's not a question. That's a name."

"A Russian national that you are reputed to have tortured to death. By suffocation. And now we've got somebody else here suffocated to death."

"Get your facts straight. Irina Khournikova is alive and well and working in Moscow, last we heard. She's a Russian anti-terrorism expert. What's your question, Agent Church?"

The Birmingham police cruiser slowed down as it approached. Derek smiled and waved. *Hey*, he tried to project. *Just some guy coming home for lunch. Hi, officers! How are you today?*

"Stillwater—"

He sighed. The cruiser stopped, and two cops climbed out. The closest one said, "Sir, is there a problem?" He was tall, broad-shouldered, looking trim and fit in his uniform. Probably in his thirties, he had sandy brown hair, clear brown eyes, and a square jaw. One hand was on his gun.

"No, no problem," Derek said. He didn't like the hand on the gun. The other cop came around the cruiser, keeping Derek in view. They had their procedure down. They didn't bunch together. They both came at him at angles, able to cover each other and keep an eye on Derek. *They have no reason for this*, Derek thought. Somebody had sicced the cops on him. Had it been Gray? Or Jill?

"Honey," Derek said into the phone, voice sweet, almost saccharine. "There are a couple police officers here. Did you call them?"

"Cute," Jill said. "No, Stillwater. I didn't. What do they want?"

He clipped the phone to his belt without shutting it off and turned to the cops. "Is there a problem, officers?"

"We'd like to see some ID," the second cop said. He was older than his partner, maybe around fifty. Balding, he had clear blue eyes, a jowly red face, and a thick mustache. He wasn't as fit as his younger partner, but he still looked strong and tough despite the paunch. It was that kind of "strong fat" look that some big men have.

"Sure," Derek said. He reached for his back pocket. Both cops tensed. "Hey, easy now. I'm just getting my identification." He moved slowly and deliberately. "My name is Derek Stillwater. I'm an agent with the Department of Homeland Security. I'm here—"

As soon as he said his name, the younger cop pulled his gun. "Hands out. Hands out where I can see them. Get down on your knees, hands on your head."

"I can't get down on my knees," Derek said, which was true. His knee throbbed and wouldn't bend that much. "Look—"

The second cop moved very fast for his size. He moved in toward Derek's right. "Get down! Do it—"

Derek was all too aware of the first cop and his gun. He tried to protest, but the bigger cop moved in, a tonfa swinging. The baton struck the side of Derek's bad leg. With a scream, he collapsed to the ground, hands pressed to his knee. Then the cops flipped him over on his back and secured his wrists with flexicuffs. A quick pat-down came up with his gun, his ID, the electric lock pick, and the satellite phone. The younger cop said into the phone, "Hello? Who's this?" He listened, then said, "That may be, ma'am, but we have to take him in. He'll be at the Birmingham Police Department." He clicked off. The two cops dragged Derek to his feet and, before he could protest, flung him into the back of the squad car.

The older cop went through Jill's vehicle, collected Derek's bags, and put them in the trunk of the squad car. As soon as they had secured Jill's car, they drove away.

# 30

*1:07 p.m.*

MATT GRAY, NOW WEARING an FBI windbreaker zipped up over his shirt and tie to cover the blood, was in the mobile command center discussing events with his superior in Washington, D.C. A slim, blonde female agent was on a phone at the other end of the RV. She suddenly sat up and called out, "Lab's got this guy's number. They're tracking now."

"Sir," Gray said, "things are breaking here. I'll…yes, sir. Thank you, sir." He clicked off and spun. He jabbed his finger at another agent, a wiry Latino with soulful dark eyes and curly black hair. "Are you in contact with the Nighthawks?"

"Yes, sir."

"Get them scrambling."

Agent Cortez settled into a radio command post and began to talk to the group of fixed-wing and helicopter air support that patrolled the area. Ever since 9/11, the FBI had increased its air coverage, especially in high-risk areas and at borders. Detroit not only had the busiest international border in the country at the Ambas sador Bridge to Windsor, Ontario, but nearby Dearborn had the largest Shiite Muslim population outside of the Middle East. The Detroit FBI had a large group of technical support to draw on.

The other agent, Sugarman, said, "Cell tracking…" Her eyes widened. She turned to Gray. "He's here, sir."

"Here? What the hell are you—"

Sugarman said, "They've tracked his cellular signal to within one hundred yards of this area, sir. The Scott Building."

Gray's jaw clenched. "In the crowd!"

Agent Cortez, talking to the planes and helicopters, ordered, "Triangulate in this area. I repeat, triangulate to the Wayne State University campus and the Scott Building. Yes, right here!"

Gray leaned out the door and shouted to his liaison officer. "The Serpent's in the crowd. Get everybody mobilized. We're triangulating the phone now! *Now*, understand! Nobody leaves the area! Nobody! Shut this area down!"

The agent screamed into his cell phone, dashing toward the communication post for the Detroit Police Department liaison. The DPD had more manpower present than the FBI did.

"We've got him!" Gray snapped, thinking that he'd be working in Washington by the end of the year if they nailed this guy this fast. "We've got him!"

# 31

*1:11 p.m.*

JILL WAS FRANTICALLY TRYING to decide how to respond to Derek's arrest when the local police showed up. She figured Derek would just have to sit tight until she got her own mess straightened out. The detective who approached her from the Ferndale Police Department studied Jill's identification closely before turning to frown at Michael. "Who's this?"

"My son. Michael Church. Before you ask—"

"You bring your son along on investigations?"

*Damn*, Jill thought. *He asked before I could explain.* "It's a little complicated."

"I just bet it is."

Jill took a deep breath. Detective Wayne Bezinski was short, balding, and slight. He wore wire-rimmed glasses that magnified his blue eyes. Dressed casually in khaki slacks, a dress shirt, and a windbreaker, he nonetheless carried himself with confidence. Bezinski was accompanied by another detective, a woman. She was broad-shouldered and stocky, probably in her forties, with steel-gray hair that she wore to her shoulders. She wore a dark pantsuit with no-nonsense rubber-soled shoes. She kept very quiet and stood aside, keeping an eye on Michael.

"Detective," Jill said, "take one more look at my identification and then stop interrupting me."

Bezinski tapped his finger on her ID folder. "Fine, Ms.— "

"That's *Agent* Church. Federal Bureau of Investigation. Are we clear on that?"

Bezinski frowned, then handed back her identification. "We've got a body upstairs?"

"Yes. I've also called in a Bureau evidence specialist from downtown."

"What's this all about? Murders aren't your jurisdiction."

"This is related to the sarin gas attacks in Detroit."

Bezinski's eyes widened. He shifted his gaze to Michael, who stood nervously next to his car. Bezinski's expression shifted and his eyes narrowed. He turned back to Jill. "Why's he here?"

"Someone else needed my car, so I called Michael to come get me, and I planned to use his car. On the way back to Troy, I received a call about the body here." She gestured at Rebecca Harrington's house.

"Uh-huh," Bezinski said. "Okay. Kind of inconvenient. Who called you about the body here?"

She hesitated. "An agent with the Department of Homeland Security."

Bezinski looked up from his notepad. His expression became even more inscrutable than before. "His name?"

"Derek Stillwater."

Something flickered in Bezinski's face. "And your relationship with Derek Stillwater?" His pen was poised over the notepad.

"I'm acting as the FBI liaison with the Department of Homeland Security. Agent Stillwater is a specialist in biological and chemical warfare. He flew in with the Bureau's Hazardous Materials Response Unit."

Bezinski's left eyebrow raised just a fraction of an inch. "What time was this?"

"What?"

Bezinski focused on her. "What time did Agent Stillwater fly into town with the Bureau people?"

This question caught her more than a little off-guard. "Why?"

"Why what?" Bezinski countered.

"Why do you want to know?"

"Just tell me, please."

"Right around nine o'clock."

Bezinski wrote that down and looked up at her. "You're sure of that?"

"Yes. I was waiting at the helicopter pad at Henry Ford Hospital when they arrived."

"Where did they come from?"

"They?"

"The Hazardous … what was it again?"

"HMRU," she said. "They're out of Quantico, Virginia."

"And Stillwater?"

"Baltimore, Maryland."

Bezinski's eyebrow rose again. "What time was the attack at that restaurant?"

Jill put her hands on her hips. "What is this all about?"

Bezinski met her gaze. "Clearing something up in my mind, Agent Church. And it seems to me that a few facts I can verify would help."

"It was at eight o'clock. Almost exactly eight."

"Is there any chance whatsoever that Derek Stillwater was here in Detroit at eight o'clock this morning?"

"No."

Bezinski nodded. "Agent Church, I'm not entirely certain what's going on here, but all local law enforcement agencies have been notified to be on the lookout for Derek Stillwater. He has been classified as a 'person of interest,' whatever the hell that means, and it was hinted that he might be behind these attacks."

Jill stared. "*What?!*"

"You heard me. But the time frame doesn't seem to work right. Of course, perhaps he set it up earlier and triggered it from a remote location."

"Where is this coming from?"

"Your office."

"The FBI?"

Bezinski nodded. "Yes, ma'am."

*Well,* thought Jill, *that explained the Birmingham cops.* And it smelled to her like something Matt Gray might be behind. "I believe Stillwater's in custody in Birmingham," she said.

"I see. How do you—"

"He just called me only a few minutes ago. And I can assure you, Detective, that I was with Agent Stillwater at the time of the second attack. He's not responsible for it. Now, the woman here, however, is directly involved. In fact, her ex-husband is our prime suspect. She was supposed to be at the site of the first attack today. And in her ex-husband's office at Wayne State University, we found evidence that causes us to believe he's the prime suspect—not Derek Stillwater—in these attacks. The office was also booby-trapped."

"That explains the eyebrows," Bezinski said.

"What?"

Bezinski ran a finger over his eyebrows and then pointed to hers. She ran her fingers over her own eyebrows. They felt short and spiky. Like they'd been fried. "I didn't even notice," she said.

"So there was an explosion?"

She nodded.

"Two mass killings, an explosion, and now a corpse." Bezinski glanced over at Michael. "This just isn't your day, is it?"

"No."

"Let's go in and look at our scene. You have a warrant?"

"No."

He studied her. "Probable cause?"

"A tip."

"From?"

"Stillwater."

"He have a warrant?"

"You'd have to ask him," she said.

Bezinski eyed her and sighed. "Shit. Let's go in. Tell you what, Agent Church. I was having a much better day myself before you showed up. Son," he said to Michael, "stay right here with Detective Standish. She'll have some questions to ask you. That okay with you, Agent Church?"

Jill nodded, giving Michael a significant look.

"Fine," Bezinski said. "Let's get down to business."

# 32

AGENT FRANK MCMILLAN RINSED off under a safety shower, still wearing his biocontainment suit. Once it was certain he had gotten any residue of sarin off the suit, he was allowed to strip it off and hang it up to dry, changing into street clothes. It was hot, exhausting work, cataloguing and securing a scene of this size. There was an emotional toll to be had as well. None of them wanted to stop and take a break, but they were all professionals. They wouldn't do anybody any good killing themselves working without a breather now and then. In this case, McMillan followed the lead of the HM-RU's protocols, taking a break every hour to get out of the suit, go to the john, have something to drink to rehydrate, and get away from all the death.

He moved into the tent and slipped into the pair of surgical scrubs he kept in his duffel for just such an occasion. He needed to carry his gun, but the Glock was heavy. He usually wore it on a belt clip, but wearing scrubs, he couldn't. His damn pants would fall down around his ankles, and wouldn't that be a pretty picture on the six o'clock news? So he took out the gun and carried it. Pain in the ass. The whole back-and-forth, in-and-out thing was a pain in the ass.

It was too big a hassle to pull his street clothes back on, take a walk, knock back some Gatorade, maybe a PowerBar, find a bathroom nearby, then go back, change out of his clothes, back into the space suit, back into the crime scene. Oh well. What was he going to do? So he slipped into the pajama-like scrubs, pulled on his shoes, picked up his duffel, and headed out for a stroll and a smoke. *And maybe*, he thought, *I should find a john soon.* His bladder felt uncomfortably full. But his nicotine craving was stronger. Smoke first.

McMillan was a lanky redhead, hair clipped nearly to his scalp on the sides, worn short but curly on top. He stood about six-three. He'd played forward at Seton Hall but hadn't been quick enough or accurate enough to go pro. He still played ball at the gym when he could, keeping in shape. For a guy in his forties, he thought he was in good shape. He could keep up with the twentysomethings, even occasionally show them a thing or two. Right now, though, he felt drained and exhausted. Maybe it was the cigarettes. He should give the damn things up, he knew. But they helped with the stress.

The Detroit cop guarding the tent was looking up at the sky. "How's it going?" Frank asked.

"Something's up," the cop said. He was a short, muscular man, and acne scars pocked his face, giving his coal-black complexion a lumpy appearance, like the surface of the moon.

McMillan looked up and noticed helicopters. There were a couple of TV choppers, but he also recognized at least three Bureau copters. Farther off he saw two circling airplanes. "They've got a lock," he murmured.

"On the Serpent?"

"I bet. They're triangulating. Bastard was hanging around to watch the excitement."

"Sick fuck," the Detroit cop said.

"Got that right. I'd better go check what's going on." He loped off toward the command center with his duffel.

# 33

*1:15 p.m.*

IN THE COMMAND CENTER, Agent Cortez communicated with the helicopters and airplanes triangulating on the Serpent's cell-phone signal. Matt Gray paced as best as he could, a walkie-talkie in his hand. He had set up sharpshooters all around the perimeter of their one-hundred-yard area, which encompassed part of the University Health Center, Detroit Receiving Hospital, and the Medical Library. He was in direct communication with Agent Samuel Woldencourt, who was coordinating the takedown with the Detroit PD, his agents, and the SWAT team.

Cortez said, "The Serpent's on the move."

"Where?" Gray rushed to Cortez's shoulder.

"Still in our area—"

"You got it?"

A voice came over the radio. "Signal is moving in a southwesterly direction within the grid. I repeat, southwesterly direction. We have eleven targets, I repeat, eleven targets in that grid. Locking on."

"Request a visual," Gray said.

"Nighthawk 6," Cortez said. "This is LFA 2. LFA 1 requests a visual."

"Locking on, LFA 2. Nighthawk 6 out."

"LFA 2, this is Nighthawk 3. Coordinating ... five, four, three ... Nighthawk 6, this is Nighthawk 3. Do you have lock?"

"Target is in muted green, carrying red duffel bag. Confirm. Nighthawk 6 out."

"Nighthawk 3 confirms. Target is wearing green and carrying red duffel bag, moving in a southwesterly direction. I repeat, moving in a southwesterly direction. Nighthawk 3 out."

"Nighthawk 1 here. Target is confirmed. Triangulation locked on."

Matt Gray, voice tense, clicked the walkie-talkie. "This is LFA 1. We have a confirmed lock. Target is wearing green and carrying a red duffel bag, moving across grid in a southwesterly direction. Do you have a visual?"

"LFA 1, this is Blue Team leader. I have a visual. Green scrubs. Red duffel bag. Moving in a southwesterly direction across grid. Subject is armed. I repeat, subject is armed."

Gray nodded. "Blue Team leader, take him."

"LFA 1, this is Blue Team leader. I confirm. Subject takedown. I repeat, subject takedown."

# 34

*1:17 p.m.*

MARY LINZEY, ED WACHOVIAK, and Steve Shay were camped out in front of the Detroit Medical Center, as close to Scott Hall as they were able to get, since the Detroit police had cordoned off the area. Something was going on. Something big. Mary, who had spent the last half an hour trying to track down information on Derek Stillwater by working Ed's cell phone just as hard as she could, said, "Something's going on. You see that? Up there? I think I saw a sniper or something. And all the helicopters ..."

Ed was already bringing the camera up on his shoulder. Steve Shay took a look at himself in their truck's mirror, brushed back a lock of hair that didn't want to stay in place, and said, "Got me in?"

"Over your right shoulder," Ed said.

Steve Shay, microphone to his mouth, said, "This is Channel 7 Action News reporter Steve Shay, reporting from the Detroit Medical Center. Above us are a number of Federal Bureau of Investigation helicopters. Behind me, you can see, the Detroit Police

Department has cordoned off an area in the vicinity of Scott Hall. The Bureau's Media Relations Office won't comment, but there is clearly an ongoing—"

Mary Linzey gasped. Steve Shay broke off, spinning, promptly picking up where he left off. "As you can see, a number of Detroit Police and FBI agents have converged on … are you getting this, Ed? Oh my God—"

# 35

*1:18 p.m.*

Trotting toward the command center, Frank McMillan sensed something was wrong right away. The Bureau helicopters shifted lower, for one, and he wasn't oblivious to the fact that the news helicopters were staying away from the immediate area. Which meant the Bureau was keeping them out of their airspace. Frank also noticed a lot of movement in the surrounding area. What had before seemed to be a random conglomeration of law enforcement and emergency medical personnel now seemed both more organized and segregated. The Detroit PD and the FBI were on the move, operating separately but in concert. It was all there for a trained observer to see. Out of the corner of his eye, atop the Scott Building, he noticed a camouflaged figure with a rifle ducking out of sight. The Bureau had put snipers around the area. Something was definitely going on.

Then Frank noticed a man running off to his left. The figure wasn't clear, but Frank saw he carried a gun and was moving very quickly.

Dropping the duffel, Frank yanked out his Glock, flinging the holster to the ground next to the duffel. "Hey!" he shouted, bringing up his weapon. "You! Don't move!"

The first bullet struck Frank McMillan on the left side, about four inches left of his navel, along the floating ribs. It spun him around, but McMillan, reacting as he had been trained to do, dropped into a classic Weaver stance, both hands on his gun, and returned fire.

Then all hell broke loose.

# 36

*1:19 p.m.*

MARY LINZEY STOOD FROZEN, watching as literally dozens of people with guns opened fire. Steve Shay nearly dropped the microphone, then seemed to catch on to the notion that he was standing on top of a major career-maker and got a grip. He turned to Ed and said, "Focus on the guy they're shooting."

Ed was already on the move, trying for a better angle. He wasn't the only one, Mary saw, watching as the other stations' cameramen jockeyed for position. With a grimace, she watched a cameraman from CNN sprint toward the battlefront. *Cowboy*, she thought.

Steve Shay raced after Ed, microphone to his mouth, keeping up a running commentary as Ed took in the carnage.

"...As a man ran across the street from the direction of the Scott Building, shooting broke out. The figure, presumably the man calling himself the Serpent, returned fire. But the entire area...Ed! Over here!"

Ed ducked behind a parked car, aiming the camera at where dozens of cops and other people were firing at the lone man, who fired back.

Shay continued, "The Serpent is returning fire—oh God!"

A high-velocity round fired by one of the snipers struck Frank McMillan in the side of the head. The entire opposite side of his skull exploded outward in a spray of scarlet blood, white bone, and gray brain matter.

"Ed, did you catch that? Oh God!"

Ed looked away for a moment, about ready to vomit. "We'll never be able to use that," he said. He looked a little green. "I had it on close-up."

"Start practicing your Pulitzer acceptance speech, Ed. This is fucking fantastic!"

Ed stared at Shay. "We're still hot, Shay."

"Oh … sorry. We'll edit it out."

Silence abruptly dropped over the area. The only sound was the rotors of the helicopters beating the air.

Steve Shay turned so he was again in front of the camera. "This is Steve Shay, Channel 7 Action News reporter, in Detroit. Just behind me you can see that the alleged terrorist calling himself the Serpent has been brought down in a hail of bullets by the Detroit Police Department and the Federal Bureau of Investigation."

Mary Linzey appeared at their side. Quietly she said, "You get all that, Ed?"

"Yeah. Every bit of it."

"Let's get the feed going. CNN's …" She trailed off. "Something's wrong."

They ran toward the scene, just like all the other journalists in the area. Mary let Ed shoulder his way through the crowd that was gathering, leading the way.

Steve Shay stuck his microphone toward a man Mary recognized as Matt Gray, the SAC. "Is this the Serpent, Agent Gray?" Shay asked.

Gray stared blankly at him, his eyes dull, expression perplexed. "No comment."

"Special Agent Gray," shouted a reporter from Fox News. "Is this case over? How did you know—"

An FBI agent in blue coveralls knelt next to the figure of Frank McMillan. "Oh Jesus! Oh no! Jesus Christ!" The agent looked up at Matt Gray. "It's Frank McMillan! It's McMillan!"

The reporters shouted questions, but Gray's face turned the color of moldy cheese. Suddenly he said, "We're clearing the area! This is a crime scene! I want everybody but essential Bureau personnel to clear the area. Samuelson, Tittaglio, Johannsen—get them the hell out of here. Get everybody the hell out of here!" The three FBI agents began coordinating the movement of everybody away from the body of Frank McMillan.

Mary Linzey scanned the crowd, looking for someone, anyone, who might be able to give her a clue as to what had just happened. She searched for Roger Kandling, who had been so forthcoming about Derek Stillwater, but he was nowhere in sight. Her gaze landed on another agent she occasionally dealt with, Simona Toreanno. Toreanno, in a gray pantsuit, seemed to be wandering aimlessly away from the site of the shooting, her expression shocked.

Mary ran over and tapped her on the arm.

"Agent Toreanno? Simona."

Toreanno turned. Relatively young for an FBI agent, she was in her mid-thirties and had dark, curly hair she wore to her shoulders, an oval face with large, almond-shaped brown eyes, long black eyelashes, and a dash of ruby lipstick on her full mouth. Tears filled her eyes.

"What?"

Mary held up her hands. "I don't have a camera or tape recorder on me, Simona. I'm not taping. This is off the record. Who's Frank McMillan?"

Simona blinked and shook her head. She seemed to take in the crowd with a little more focus, looking for somebody.

"Who's Frank McMillan, Simona? Who was he?"

"FBI," Simona whispered. "One of ours."

# 37

*1:35 p.m.*

JILL CHURCH STOOD IN the hallway outside Rebecca Harrington's bedroom, watching the Ferndale Police Department's crime-scene technician work the room. She wasn't happy. She had called in a Bureau tech, who hadn't shown up yet. Trying to control the scene—as Stillwater had suggested—wasn't really all that easy a thing to do. It wasn't actually the Bureau's jurisdiction, though she could argue—and had been arguing—that because this was directly tied into the terrorist attacks that day, it *was* her jurisdiction. The problem was, she couldn't get corroboration for it. Who was she going to refer the Ferndale cops to? Matt Gray?

"Anything interesting?" she asked the technician, a Latino who looked about twelve years old. He'd been introduced as Officer Gomez. He wore a navy blue windbreaker, faded jeans, and hiking boots. Half-rim glasses perched on a blunt, broad nose, and spiky black hair jutted off the top of his head like a hedge.

"Like what?" he asked, crawling around the floor with a pair of tweezers in his hand.

"Physical evidence," Jill said. "Some indication of who might have done this." Her money was on the husband, Bill Harrington.

"You mentioned the ex-husband, right?" Gomez said. He looked up at her, light flashing off his glasses.

"Yes."

Detective Bezinski, standing next to Jill, said, "Don't get distracted by the case, Joe. Just get the evidence."

"Where's the ex-husband live?" Gomez asked.

"Birmingham," Jill answered.

Bezinski rolled his eyes. "Oh jeez. Look, Agent Church. One case at a time, all right? Or Joe's gonna want to get a warrant for the ex-husband's house and run that scene and spend the rest of the day comparing his lint collection to try to tie the ex to this scene."

"What's wrong with that?" Jill asked.

"Nothing's wrong with that. But we got a scene here to process first. Let's do it."

"We *are* doing it," Jill said, exasperated. She was starting to understand Stillwater's impatience. Homicide cops didn't spend much time preventing crimes. They came in after someone was already dead and methodically tried not only to solve the case—if it needed solving—but to build a case to take to court. Unless they were dealing with a serial killer or somebody ready to flee the country, they could take their time.

When you had someone like the Serpent threatening to kill a bunch of people every four hours, you didn't have time to waste.

"I'm going to look around some more," Jill said.

"Hey, don't contaminate anything," Gomez called.

It was Jill's turn to roll her eyes. She checked the next bedroom. It was set up as a guest room: a queen-sized bed made up with a blue-and maroon-checked comforter, an empty dresser with a few knick-knacks scattered across the top, and not much else. On two walls were the kind of paintings that sold by the foot at starving-artist sales. They were fine, nothing wrong with them, but they lacked some sort of spark that would make them remarkable. One was a seascape, the other a painting of a birch forest along a stream in the winter.

Jill went through the closet and found a few dresses that seemed decidedly unfashionable, a couple of pillows and folded blankets. As she'd thought, it was a guest room.

The next bedroom had been converted to a sitting room/office. There was a computer desk, a filing cabinet, a rocking chair, and a TV set and portable stereo system. Next to the rocking chair was a basket of yarn, knitting needles, and a partially completed sweater. *Rebecca Harrington liked to knit to relax*, Jill thought. She wondered why she did it up here instead of the living room, pondering the juxtaposition of the office and the knitting area.

Jill sat down at the computer and punched the power on, waiting for it to boot up. Idly, she fingered through the disk holders. Rebecca Harrington apparently was some sort of research coordinator at the Barbara Ann Karmanos Cancer Institute in downtown Detroit. All of the disks seemed to be articles related to ongoing clinical trials.

Once the Windows desktop appeared, she found the Microsoft Outlook icon and clicked on it. She started with the calendar. Interestingly, Rebecca had planned on being at the Breakfast Club that morning. There it was, listed at eight o'clock. The rest of the day also listed meetings and deadlines. It looked like Rebecca had missed all of them.

Jill's phone buzzed. She clicked it on. It was Eleanor Mancuso, the Bureau evidence technician she had called. Eleanor sounded breathless. "Jill? It's Eleanor. I'm turning around. I won't be in. Have you heard?"

"Heard what?" Jill's heart sank, thinking the Serpent had struck again.

"There was a big shooting down at Wayne State. They were triangulating the cell signal, and it targeted Frank McMillan. Then all hell broke loose and Frank got shot to pieces and a Detroit cop got killed and two others—Detroit Fire Department, I think—got wounded in the crossfire. I'm going back."

"Eleanor ... Frank? Why did it triangulate on Frank?"

"I don't know," Eleanor said. "*I don't know*. But he's dead. They're saying he might have been the Serpent. Can you believe that?"

Jill sat with the phone in her lap, thinking about it. *Can you believe that?*

Jill had worked closely with Frank McMillan on anti-terror initiatives in Michigan, though not recently. She had largely been sidelined since her abortive sexual harassment suit against Matt Gray. Not sidelined in any way that could be used in a court, as her attorney had told her. Nothing obvious. But moved into liaison roles and support positions rather than operational or investigative roles. Otherwise, her attorney had said, it was largely a case of his word against hers. The threat of the lawsuit had backed Gray off, but it hadn't helped her career much.

McMillan would have had the inside knowledge to understand how the various law enforcement groups would interact in this type of a crisis. He would have been able to plot something as elaborate as this.

But she didn't think he could manufacture sarin gas. Frank had a legal background and a law enforcement background, not a chemistry or science background.

Even assuming he was capable of going bad and committing mass murder, she didn't think McMillan had the technical expertise. Like most FBI agents, Frank hated terrorists. Like most FBI agents, he had known many people who had died in terrorist attacks—at Oklahoma City, at the World Trade towers, at the Pentagon, at a number of embassies around the world. He didn't give terrorists noble but misguided motives. He called them what they were—thugs, murderers, and criminals. He had once given a talk on terrorism—at Wayne State, she remembered—on how terrorists could cloak their actions in moral imperatives and reasoning, but that's all it was. A cloak. Something to mask that they liked violence. They liked chaos.

He had quoted Lenin: "The purpose of terrorism is to terrorize."

Eleanor had said, *"Can you believe that?"*

No, she couldn't.

Bezinski stuck his head in the door. "Find anything?"

Jill stared into space, her mind grabbing at an elusive memory, something else Frank McMillan had said in passing.

"What's wrong?" Bezinski asked.

Jill held up her hand, cocking her head. Thinking. Trying to snag the memory. Bezinski waited patiently.

Suddenly Jill sat upright. "That can't be a coincidence!" she said.

Bezinski stepped into the room. "I don't really much believe in coincidences. At least not in a criminal investigation. What's up?"

Jill jumped to her feet, unsure of what to do next, of where to go. "What's going on, Church?"

She looked at Bezinski. He didn't know about Frank McMillan. He didn't know about the shooting incident in the city. He didn't know about the terrorism scenarios that the Working Group of the Wayne State University Center for Biological and Chemical Terrorism Research had written.

So he sure as hell wouldn't be able to connect the dots the way Jill did when she remembered Frank McMillan slipping into his coat two years ago and saying, "I'm heading over to Wayne. I'm consulting with this terrorism research group over there."

"Sounds like fun," Jill had teased him.

McMillan had shrugged. "They work out scenarios for various attacks and then develop training programs and response plans for public health and emergency medical teams. I go in and tell them how we'd respond in any given situation."

Bezinski was now trying to get her attention. "Agent Church? Jill? What's going on?"

Jill stared at him. "I've … I've got to …"

Bezinski waited.

"I've got to get going. I've got to hook up with …"

Bezinski said, "Who?"

Jill took a deep breath. "This guy from Homeland Security. I think he was on to something. I've got to get going."

# 38

*1:52 p.m.*

DEREK SAT SPRAWLED OVER two chairs in what passed for the interrogation room at the Birmingham Police Department. Overall, he thought Birmingham had just about the nicest interrogation room he had ever been in. The entire department seemed more set up as a tourist bureau than for real law enforcement. Derek figured that was part of their charter—don't scare the locals with anything gritty.

He had ignominiously taken his pants off, propped up his left leg, and demanded an ice pack, which was now resting on his knee. They had stuck him in here and disappeared, probably to make phone calls to the FBI and whoever else they felt inclined to consult.

Derek tried to be patient. He reminded himself that he had been fighting this assignment in the first place. If he were to be completely consistent, he should be happy getting sidelined so he could fly to Mexico in pursuit of the terrorist calling himself the Fallen.

Instead, he felt the weight of forty-some college kids whose lives he had been unable to save.

Thinking that way did no good. His thoughts kept returning to William Harrington's house. He felt fairly confident that William Harrington was the Serpent. The booby trap in the office, the murdered ex-wife, the overall skill set. A biochemist with a background in chemical terrorism scenarios and an ax to grind. He'd gone off his nut. Now all Derek had to do was either prove it or convince somebody else, like Jill Church or Matt Gray, that they had to do something about it.

Derek picked up the ice pack and studied his knee. It was swelling, although he hoped the ice pack would help cut that down. It also throbbed, and he had made the mistake of putting his full weight on it shortly after being dragged from the police car. He wasn't entirely sure he would be able to walk for a while. What he really needed was ice, rest, and some Percocet.

Someone knocked at the door. Then it opened and Jill Church walked in. She paused for a moment to take in his leg and the fact that he was sitting there in his white Jockey underwear. Her expression grim, lines radiated out from her eyes and the corners of her mouth. She seemed to have aged a few years in the last hour.

"You've looked better," she said.

He cocked his head. "I've already been detained. What are you going to do, drag me back to the city and turn me in to Gray for assault?"

She shook her head. "As hard as this is to believe, Stillwater, things have gone totally to hell since you stole my car."

"Borrowed. I *borrowed* your car."

"Speaking of my car, where the hell is it?"

"At Harrington's house, unless the cops impounded it," Derek said. "What do you want, Church?"

"I'm getting you out of here. Come on."

He shook his head. "That might be a problem."

Hands on her hips, she stepped closer to him. Her voice was a menacing hiss. "Stillwater, I'm not in the mood. One of our agents was killed in the city. They suspect he might be the Serpent. Everything's gone to shit and I think it's all a diversion. Now is not the time for you to be an asshole."

Derek couldn't stop his grin. He waved at his knee. "Uh, the problem is I don't think I can support my weight. I need a crutch or something. And, um, I might need help getting my pants on."

She glared at him, then turned and stomped out of the interrogation room, leaving the door open.

Derek felt unreasonably merry. "And if you could get me a sandwich or something?" he called after her. "I'm hungry."

# 39

*2:06 p.m.*

DEREK HOBBLED OUT OF the interrogation room using a cane one
of the cops had found for him. He discovered a uniformed cop
studying his Go Packs, which had been taken from Jill's car and delivered to the Birmingham Police Department. The cop had blond
hair so white it seemed practically transparent. His eyes were a gla-
cial blue, his skin the color of bone. Derek wondered briefly if he
was an albino.

Derek moved to the table and unzipped the packs.

Jill, behind him, said, "We don't have time for this."

"Yes, we do," he said. He glanced up at the albino cop. "Everything had better be here."

"It is," the cop said. His badge said Officer Blackburn. "Here's
your phone. That's an Iridium, right?"

Derek took it from him, checked the charge, and clipped it to
his belt. "Yes."

"I couldn't access it."

"That's right," Derek said. "You couldn't. It's password protected."

Blackburn reached into the bag and pulled out a device about the size of a Magic Marker, with a double cartridge. "Sir, we were wondering..." The cop suddenly looked a little nervous. "What is this, sir?"

Derek took it from him and held it up. It read:

**Pralidoxime chloride injector**
**For use in nerve agent poisoning only**

"You have problems reading?" He placed it carefully back into the duffel bag. "It's an atropine injector. If you get exposed to nerve gas, like VX or sarin, you can give yourself an injection with this."

"Does it work?" The cop licked his lips.

"Yes, it works. Hope you never have to test it."

Derek made sure everything was there, and then he looked at Jill. "Will you carry these, please?"

She grudgingly hefted the Go Packs with a grunt and led the way out of the Birmingham police station. Michael paced nervously in front of his Civic. A gust of chill wind blew the hair off his forehead, and he crossed his arms over his chest to stay warm.

Derek froze, leaning his weight on the cane. "Jesus Christ!"

Jill turned to look at him. "What?"

Slowly, Derek turned back to Jill, reluctantly taking his gaze off Michael. "Is that your son?"

"Yes. That's Michael. It's a long story. He wouldn't be here if you hadn't stolen my car."

"Borrowed."

Derek shuffled after Jill, eyes fixed on Michael.

Jill threw the bags into the back of the Civic and turned once again to Derek. "Derek, this is my son, Michael Church. Michael, this is Agent Derek Stillwater. He's a troubleshooter for the Department of Homeland Security."

Derek shifted the cane to his left hand and held out his right. "Hello, Michael. I knew your father. You look just like him."

# 40

*2:07 p.m.*

AGENT MATT GRAY WAS back in his office on the twenty-sixth floor of the Patrick McNamara Federal Building on Michigan Avenue. He had changed out of his bloody shirt but kept the combat boots on. He paced back and forth in front of the window overlooking downtown Detroit, the river and Windsor beyond.

Two other agents sat at a round conference table, watching him. Gray said, "What's the lab say about the phone?"

Agent Simona Toreanno said, "No fingerprints, but they're otherwise working on it."

Gray stopped his pacing and looked at his two top agents. "I would like to know why Frank McMillan would be behind these attacks. Ideas?"

Simona Toreanno's face grew red. "It was a setup. There's no way Frank was the Serpent."

Gray skewered her with his flat gaze. "Then how do you explain him having the phone in his duffel bag?"

"The Serpent put it there," she said.

Gray jabbed at her with his index finger. "Right! Sure, Toreanno. The Serpent slipped into the area with the highest concentration of cops and agents looking for him, snuck inside the biocontainment tent, and dropped it in Frank's duffel bag. Why? Why take the risk?"

"He would know we would track the call," she said. "So he knew it would cause problems. I doubt he could have predicted just how many problems. But we *are* running around chasing our tails instead of chasing him."

"That's bullshit." Gray went back to his pacing. "This is a PR nightmare. A mass murderer in the middle of the Bureau. On my watch! I was much happier believing Stillwater was behind this."

"He might be," Roger Kandling said.

Gray turned to look at him. For the benefit of Agent Toreanno, he kept the look of pleased expectation off his face. "How so?"

Kandling, as if walking through a mine field, carefully said, "Stillwater had easy access in and out of the tent. The credentials to move among us. He was even in the MCC with you." Kandling paused. "Sir, if I may suggest…"

"Go on," Gray urged.

Toreanno watched Kandling intently.

"If Frank McMillan was actually this guy, the Serpent, he would know we were going to triangulate on the cell signal once we got the TV producer's cell phone."

"Which we probably should have confiscated immediately after she let us know about the call," Toreanno said. She said it carefully as well, not wanting to suggest that Matt Gray had screwed up, though that's what she thought. Gray hadn't even demanded her phone. He

147

had said Mary Linzey would never give it to them because of First Amendment considerations. At the very least, Toreanno thought, if he hadn't wanted to battle WXYZ's lawyers, he should have demanded that an agent stay with her in case the Serpent tried to call her again. It was only one of several major oversights that had occurred under Gray's command. Toreanno felt that Gray was now busy trying to cover his ass and point the blame, rather than figure out what had really happened. And Gray was acting as if this entire deal was over. The Serpent had made a ransom demand, it hadn't been paid, he'd killed people, and now he was done.

Agent Toreanno didn't think the Serpent was done. She had told the lab people to keep that cell phone on and wait for the next call. To be prepared to track the incoming call.

Gray fixed his gaze on Toreanno, shifted to Kandling, then swiveled back to her. His eyes narrowed. "You're saying that Frank wouldn't have left that phone on if he were the Serpent."

"Exactly," said Kandling.

"So Stillwater could have put it in McMillan's duffel bag and left it on, knowing it would be tracked and it would make McMillan and the Bureau look bad."

"Exactly," said Kandling again.

"Give me a break," said Toreanno.

Gray spun on her. "You were just saying that the cell phone wasn't Frank's, that he couldn't possibly be the Serpent. Now you're changing your mind?"

"No," she said. "I buy the scenario, just not that Derek Stillwater is the Serpent."

Gray ticked off on his fingers. "One, Derek Stillwater is an expert in chemical warfare and terrorism. He has the expertise to set these sarin gas bombs. Two—"

"He was in Baltimore at the time of the first attack at the Boulevard Café," Toreanno said.

"It was set off by phone. That cell phone. Which Stillwater could easily have—"

"This is bullshit!" Toreanno burst out. "You've got some sort of personal vendetta against this guy. It's clouding your judgment, which hasn't been ..." She trailed off.

"*What?*" Gray growled.

"Nothing, sir. I'm sorry. Derek Stillwater may work outside strict investigative procedures, but that's his job, sir. He's supposed to observe outside the chain of command and make suggestions. I agree that the Department of Homeland Security is an unorganized mess, but this notion of placing experts in specific types of terrorist situations to advise and suggest alternative avenues of response is a good one. If you really believe Stillwater set the bomb off from Baltimore using that phone, it's a simple matter to track which Baltimore cell it was called from—right before an entire Bureau team flew in and picked him up."

He stared at her for a long moment. Finally, "Agent Toreanno, I believe we're through here. I suggest you go back over to the MCC and coordinate with Agent Cortez."

She stood up. "Sir, for the record, I don't believe the Serpent is done. If the pattern continues, he'll strike again at four o'clock. And he may very well contact us with a ransom demand or warning an hour or an hour and a half before then. We should be ready for that possibility."

"Thank you, Agent Toreanno. That's all."

Toreanno blinked, then turned and walked out of Gray's office.

Kandling said, "I think she's right."

Gray waved his hand in a dismissive gesture. "All the more reason to lock Derek Stillwater up. Have you heard from Jill Church?"

Kandling hesitated.

Gray wheeled on him. "Have you?"

"It seems," he said slowly, "that Derek Stillwater found Rebecca Harrington murdered in her home in Ferndale. Last I heard, Jill was at the murder scene."

Gray looked puzzled. "Who the fuck is Rebecca Harrington?"

"It's in the update," Kandling said, pointing to a file on Gray's desk. "She's the ex-wife of Dr. William Harrington."

Gray still wore a blank expression on his face. "Who is?"

Kandling took even longer to answer. "There were nine people at the Boulevard Café this morning, sitting right at ground zero, right on top of the gas canisters. They were regulars. Every Wednesday morning at eight. Usually there were ten of them, the tenth being Rebecca Harrington."

"There were over fifty people there. What makes them so special?"

"It's all in the update," Kandling said evenly. "But I'll recap. One of them, John Simmons, was a professor at Wayne State University, the assistant director of the Center for Biological and Chemical Terrorism Research."

Before he could continue, Gray waved him off. "It sounds like a smoke screen. Why kill fifty people when you want to kill just one?"

"Or nine," Kandling said. "Maybe that was just convenient. Why blow up the entire Oklahoma City Federal Building when you just wanted to hurt the FBI?"

Gray frowned and turned back to pacing in front of the window. After a moment, he said, "I want you to provide a press statement."

"Me, sir?"

"Yes, you," Gray said, back to Kandling. "It will say that our investigation is ongoing, that Agent Frank McMillan had in his possession the cellular phone that made the original call from the Serpent. We have no reason to suspect Agent McMillan was the Serpent, and that we are leaving the investigation open, including looking at a number of potential suspects, including Derek Stillwater, with the Department of Homeland Security. Got that? Be vague, diffuse some of the—"

"The press isn't going to let me get away with that, sir. And shouldn't this come from you or Sheridan?"

"I want it to come from an agent."

Kandling said nothing for a long time. So long that it caught Gray's attention and he turned to look at Kandling. "Do you have a problem with that, Agent Kandling?"

"Yes, sir, I do."

"Are you being insubordinate?"

Kandling shook his head. "I don't mean to be, sir. But I think you—if I may be candid, sir—I think you need to back off Derek Stillwater and try to figure out who the hell the Serpent really is. I agree with Simona. The Serpent's not finished yet, and we're running out of time. This lead with William Harrington and Rebecca Harr—"

"Fine," Gray snapped. "In your statement, include that along with Stillwater, we are looking at one or more Wayne State faculty members who may have the motive, means, and opportunity to commit these crimes. That way we've covered our asses sufficiently. That work for you?"

"I would be happier if Tabitha Sheridan did it. She's the media rep."

"I want you to do it, Kandling. Understand? You. Consider it an order."

Kandling nodded, slowly rising to his feet. "Yes, sir."

# 41

MICHAEL CHURCH STOOD UP straight, his expression shocked. "You knew my father?"

At the same time, Jill Church exhaled so deeply it sounded like a snake hissing. Derek tilted his head and looked at her, amused, then went back to Michael. "If your father was Steve Church."

Michael glanced nervously at his mother, then back at Derek. "Yeah. My dad was Steve Church. You really knew him?"

"Sure. Good man," Derek said, and gestured at the car. "I've got to get off my leg." He moved toward the back seat, struggled into the small car, and sat with his back to the door, his leg propped alongside the seat. When Michael and Jill settled into the front seats, Derek said, "I was working with a CIA team in Dar es Salaam, investigating terrorist activity in Tanzania. I was still loosely attached to the army, and your dad ran the CIA team."

Michael jerked his head. "Dad was in the State Department. He worked in the embassy."

Derek raised an eyebrow. He turned to study Jill, who watched her son with a set, grim expression on her face. "Jill?"

She shook her head.

"We've met before, haven't we?" Derek said.

Slowly, she nodded her head.

"After the bombing, right?"

Again she nodded her head.

"Mom?"

"Your father," Derek said, "worked out of the U.S. embassy in Dar es Salaam, but he wasn't with the State Department. He was a case officer with the CIA. Do you know what that means?"

Michael looked bewildered. "A case officer? Mom?"

Jill Church, voice flat, said, "A case officer is sort of a spy. They run spies, basically. They recruit people to spy for them, to provide them information. That's what your father did."

"Why didn't you tell me?"

Jill turned so she was staring out the windshield.

"Mom? Why didn't you tell me?"

"How old are you, Michael?" Derek said.

He turned. "Sixteen. Why?"

"If you had been ten and told people your dad was a spy, what would people have thought?" Derek asked him.

Michael opened his mouth to speak, and closed it again. He seemed to think about it. "They would have thought I was lying." He turned back to Jill, who sat rigidly in the passenger-side seat. "But why didn't you tell me? I . . . I'm old enough to know this now."

"We really have work to do, Michael. Will you please drive us back to my car. We'll talk about this later."

"That's what you always say." He turned away but didn't put the Civic into drive.

Derek said, "Michael—"

"Was my mom a spy too?" Michael asked, still facing forward.

Derek waited to see if Jill would respond to that. When she didn't, Derek said, "Your mother, if I remember correctly, was an FBI agent then as well. Doing security things for the embassy, probably."

"I was with the Legat." Jill paused, thinking. "I was the assistant legal attaché. That means part of my job was to liaise with the local and governmental law enforcement. I was the communication between Tanzanian law enforcement and the Bureau." She turned to her son. "And yes, your father, Stephen Church, worked for the CIA, not the State Department. I'm sorry I never told you. But I guess you're old enough to know. Now, Michael, please put the car in drive and let's go."

Derek provided directions, and they quickly found William Harrington's house. Jill's car was still parked in front. She got out and transferred Derek's bags to her car, then leaned down to talk to Michael.

"Go on back to school," she said. "I'll call and explain to them. I doubt if I'll be home on time tonight. Can you handle things by yourself?"

Michael shrugged. "Yeah, but are you sure you don't need my help?"

Jill smiled. "I'm sure."

"Actually," Derek said, limping over, "do you have a cell phone?"

"Yes."

"Good. I'm worried that the Serpent might have booby-trapped this house. Your mother and I need to reconnoiter the perimeter, then go inside very slowly and make sure it's safe. I would really appreciate it if you stayed here and waited for us to give an all-clear before you left." Derek paused. "You know, in case the house blows up, it would be kind of nice if you called 911 for us."

Michael's eyes widened. "You think—"

"And, uh, you know, if we're like, um, on fire or something," Derek said, a smile on his face, "it'd be good if you, you know, put us out."

Jill sighed. She patted her son's arm. "We'll be fine."

"But wait for us," Derek said.

"I'll give you five minutes," Michael said. "Should we, like ... synchronize our watches?"

Derek looked at his watch. "I've got 2:18."

Michael checked his watch and adjusted it. "Check."

"We'll give you a signal before we go in," Derek said. "We're just going to walk around the house and check things out from the outside. But when we go in, we'll start the clock running. Got it?"

"Got it," Michael said.

"Good man." Derek reached out his hand. "Nice meeting you, Michael."

Michael shook Derek's hand. "Nice meeting you too. I'd like to ... I'd like to know more about my father."

Derek nodded. "When this is over, I'll tell you what I know. Deal?"

"Deal."

"Don't go anywhere until we give you the signal."

Derek returned to Jill's car and pawed through his Go Packs until he came up with the electric lock pick, a pouch of tools, and a flashlight. He paused before picking up the atropine injector the

Birmingham cop had asked him about. He limped back over to Michael and handed it to him.

"This is in case we get exposed to sarin gas. It's pretty straight-forward. You yank this cap off here and slam it into the thigh or butt. Right through the clothes. Read the directions." Michael looked frightened. Derek added, "It's just a precaution, Michael." He leaned down, "There's only one dose. So if you have to decide, do your mother."

"Y-yes, sir."

"Don't worry," Derek said. "We'll be fine." He turned to join Jill.

# 42

*2:20 p.m.*

As they approached the front door, Jill Church said, "I was wondering why you were familiar."

Derek nodded, studying the front door of William Harrington's Cape Cod. "I thought we'd met before. I don't specifically remember you, but Michael sure looks like his father."

Jill bit her lip and stayed silent.

Derek cocked his head. "Sorry about the CIA thing."

"It's okay. It's time he knew, I guess." Jill turned back to the door. "You have a plan?"

"I would like to avoid getting blown up again today."

"That's a *goal*. Now, a plan?"

Derek reached out and knocked on the door. He waited.

Jill had her hand on her gun. Derek did too. Nothing happened.

"Okay," Derek said. "Nobody's home. At least nobody alive. It's been that kind of a day." He pointed. "I'm having problems kneeling. Would you take the flashlight and light up along the edges of this door, see if you notice anything unusual?"

She took the flashlight and scanned the door, then clicked it off with a shrug. "Nothing unusual. Let's walk around the house, like you suggested."

They moved slowly around the perimeter, studying the ground, the base of the foundation, the windows. Whenever they came to a window, Derek approached without touching anything, turned on the flashlight, and attempted to peer into the dim house. Whenever he was done, he handed the light to Jill, who double-checked. The interior of the house appeared empty. Nothing stood out.

Finally they worked their way around the whole house, back to the front door. Derek glanced over at Michael in the Honda. "Seems like a good kid."

"He is, generally. He's at *that* age."

"What's he into?"

"Girls. Video games. Girls. Karate. Girls. Rap and heavy metal and hip-hop."

"And girls," Derek said.

"You were probably just like him when you were sixteen."

"Not the rap, heavy metal, or hip-hop. And the karate came later for me. I was into track and cross-country. Good grades. I was a grind. Straight As. Big into chemistry and biology. The girls, though ..." He sighed and turned to the door. "Nothin' but trouble. Some things never change. Here we go. Said your prayers?"

"We're going to feel foolish if we take all these precautions and there's nothing here."

"Not nearly as foolish as we'd feel if our body parts were scattered over downtown Birmingham." Derek reached out and opened the screen door. He sighed. "One down." He retrieved the electric lock pick from his pocket and gestured for Jill to examine the interior door. She did, finally saying, "Nothing obvious."

Derek inserted the pick carefully and clicked the button. After a second, he gripped the knob and said, "Ready?"

"Ready."

He opened the door. Again, nothing happened. Derek swung the door wide but didn't step inside. He played the flashlight around. The front door opened into a foyer with hardwood floors. A Navajo rug covered most of the entryway in muted reds, oranges, and yellows. Together they studied the rug.

"Should I try lifting it up?" Jill asked, gesturing.

"I don't see anything that could be a tripwire. Lift just a corner." She did, then lifted it all. Nothing.

"In we go, then." Derek turned and waved at Michael. He raised an open hand, all five fingers displayed. *Five minutes.* Then he and Jill entered the house.

It was neat and clean and seemed entirely empty. Sticking together, they moved through the house, looking for tripwires or anything that seemed remotely suspicious. Finally Derek said, "Tell Michael he can go back to school. And tell him thanks."

Jill nodded and slipped out of the house. She returned a few minutes later with the atropine injector in her hand. She gave it to Derek, who slipped it into his pocket. "Okay," Derek said. "What are we looking for?"

"Evidence that William Harrington is the Serpent."

"You think he maybe left a signed confession?"

"No."

"Upstairs?"

They climbed the stairs to the second floor. Like Rebecca Harrington's house, one of the bedrooms seemed to be a guest room, and another appeared to be an office. Derek stood just outside the office/bedroom. There was a desk with a computer, a small table with a printer, an office chair, filing cabinets, and two bookshelves filled with textbooks. There was a big lounge chair with a good reading lamp next to it. Piled next to the chair was a two-foot-tall stack of technical journals.

Derek studied the room. "Could you give me a hand, please?"

Jill approached him. "What do you need?"

"I want to get down on the floor. I need your help."

She met his gaze. "Okay."

"And I'll really need your help getting back on my feet."

A smile flickered across her face. "Oh, I don't know. Leaving you lying on the floor might move things along smoother."

"Ha, ha. Very funny, Agent Church." He held out his hand.

She helped him to the floor, where he sprawled on his stomach. With the flashlight in hand, he scanned the floor. He blinked.

"See anything?" Jill asked.

"Yes," he said.

"What?"

He waved her down to his level. She joined him on the floor. He pointed the flashlight and aimed it into the footwell of the desk. From this vantage point they could just see what appeared to be the bottoms of two red metal canisters.

Derek rolled over and sat up, breathing in deeply. Jill sat up, studying him. "You going to be okay?"

Sweat had broken out on his forehead, and his complexion had turned gray. He held up a hand, leaning forward so his head was close to his knees. He inhaled deeply. His hand crept to the throat of his shirt and clutched a medallion around his neck.

Jill reached out and pulled up the chain to look at the medallion, a four-leaf clover, and juju beads. "Saint Sebastian?" she asked.

"Supposed to help protect against the plague," he said, voice muffled. "My patron saint of choice. Might work better if I were Catholic."

"Can you defuse it?" she asked.

He nodded. "Yes. I should be able to." He panted slightly, sounding strangled. "Just as soon as this panic attack passes."

Jill studied him. "Maybe you should get into another line of work."

"Yeah," Derek nodded. "Why didn't I think of that?" He reached into his pocket and retrieved the set of tools. "Here's the thing," he said. "After this morning, I'm worried about a secondary device. It's not the kind of mistake you get to repeat. But I've got another concern. If he set this to go off when a desk drawer or filing cabinet drawer is opened, great. But I'm worried about a pressure switch."

Jill's eyes widened.

"Yeah," Derek said. "Like underneath the carpeting somewhere." A smile tweaked his lips. "You want to go in first, or shall I?"

# 43

*2:32 p.m.*

INCH BY INCH, DEREK crawled across the floor toward the desk. As he moved, he gently ran his hands across the carpeting in front of him, feeling for any bump or irregularity in the floor. Nothing. Finally he made it to the desk. He slowly rolled over onto his back so his head was in the footwell and he could look up at the metal canisters.

Jill crouched in the doorway. "Well?"

"It looks straightforward," Derek said. "There's a wire here that's attached to a trigger switch. The wire goes into the desk. So it looks like if you pull at least the top drawer of the desk out, it'll trigger the canisters."

Derek continued to lie there studying the device.

"Do you want me to come over there?"

"Actually," Derek said. "I want you to be here and me to be in another state."

"That's not—"

"I know what you meant. No. Not yet. Stay right where you are."

Derek scooted farther into the footwell, using the flashlight to try to peer behind the desk.

"See anything?"

"Dust bunnies."

Jill made a disgusted noise. "Anything important?"

"No."

Derek edged out of the footwell and sat up. He looked around the room, taking everything in. He stared at the desk and frowned. "I've got a problem."

"What?"

"I want to stand up and look at the stuff on top of the desk, but in order to stand up I'm going to have to use my cane or lean on the desk. And I really don't want to lean on the desk."

Jill held up the cane. "Here I come."

Taking careful, small steps, she walked across the room until she stood next to Derek. She held out her hands. Derek grasped them and allowed Jill to help him to his feet. He took the cane and leaned on it, studying the surface of the desk. It was a big, rectangular desk made out of highly polished oak. There was a computer on top, a desk lamp, a beer stein filled with assorted pens and pencils, a yellow legal pad, a pad of pink Post-it notes, a diskette holder, and a day planner.

Derek glanced at his watch. "I wonder if the Serpent called in another threat."

"Want me to call in?"

He looked at her over his shoulder. "And Matt Gray will order you to put me in protective custody, right?"

She didn't answer.

"Why don't we concentrate on what we've got here," Derek said. He raised an eyebrow. "If that's all right with you?"

"That's fine."

Derek looked at the printer on an end table. "You suppose this guy is a one-trick pony?"

"Don't move," Jill said, and knelt on the floor. She slowly moved across the room the same way Derek had, testing the carpeting as she moved, until she was next to the end table holding the printer. It was a Canon laser printer. She held out her hand, and Derek dropped the flashlight into it. She popped it on and focused the beam on the tray where the printer paper fed in. "In his office, you triggered the explosion when you hit Print, right?"

"Yes."

"But we don't know if it was the print command that set it off or the paper coming out that actually triggered the switch."

"Or the roller moving. That would probably be the easiest way to set it up."

Jill thought for a moment. "As simple as gluing a stick or rod to the roller so when it moved it moved the trigger. A simple mechanical switch."

"Maybe."

Jill leaned to the left and looked toward the wall, then leaned right and did the same thing.

"What?" Derek asked.

"I'm wondering if unplugging the printer would be a good idea or a bad idea."

They stared at each other. Derek said, "I'll do it. You leave the room."

She shook her head. "No. You leave the room."

165

"I'm not—"

Jill crouched down and said, "I'm counting to three."

"Jesus," Derek said, dropping to the floor. "A little fucking warn-ing!"

"One. Two. Three." Jill yanked the plug.

# 44

*2:39 p.m.*

FRED BALL, THE WDET National Public Radio news reporter, was still at Scott Hall, interviewing anybody who would talk to him. Several FBI agents who knew Frank McMillan personally told him flat out that the man was definitely not the Serpent. He was inclined to believe them. The entire situation had taken on a kind of surrealistic FUBAR quality, FUBAR being the old military acronym for Fucked Up Beyond All Recognition.

He was talking to a Detroit cop, Officer Tom Medina, who had been guarding the tent where the FBI and Detroit Fire Department guys staged their entries and exits into Scott Hall. "Yeah," Medina was saying. "I saw McMillan leave. We talked for a minute about how we thought something was going on. 'Cause of the helicopters and all the activity. Shit. I was watching him when he took the round in the head."

"What was your job, exactly?" Ball asked.

"Mostly to keep civilians out of here. Just stand outside the tent and make sure that reporters and civilians don't get in."

"Did you check identification or have a checklist?"

"What? No. There was only a handful of people working inside. They were either Detroit FD or FBI. There was that one guy at the other site, Stillwater, with Homeland Security, but I never saw him here. Heard a rumor Gray wouldn't let him in."

Fred Ball, keeping the microphone of his digital recorder pointed toward the cop, said, "Did anybody you didn't recognize go in or out?"

Medina shrugged. "I mean, I didn't notice anybody. Well, there was that one fire guy. He just popped in and out."

Ball paused. "When was this?"

Medina thought for a minute, scratching his chin. "Well, let's see. That would have been twelve-thirty or so. I think the only reason I remember was, you know, these guys pretty much work in cycles. Forty-five minutes on, fifteen off. More or less. They stagger it, but it's pretty regular. So they all pretty much went in at the same time, a little after twelve, and nobody came out for a while. Then this guy comes in, nods, goes in, then comes right back out."

Fred Ball was getting an idea. It was a pretty exciting idea, and there wasn't much fact to hang the idea on, but he had an idea nonetheless. "You said this guy was with the fire department?"

"Yeah."

"How did you know?"

"Uh, he had the windbreaker and hat on."

"Hat? He wore a fire hat?"

"No. He had a blue windbreaker, the one that says Detroit Fire Department on the back, and he had a cap, like a baseball hat, with the DFD on the front."

"You see him before?"

"No."

"What'd he look like?"

Medina shrugged. "I don't know. Why?"

"I'd like to talk to him, that's all," Ball said.

"Just ... just a guy."

"Young, old, what?"

"I don't know. I was thinking he was fairly young. I don't know why, though."

"What color hair?"

"All I saw was the hat."

"Skin?"

"What?"

"Black, white, pink, gray? What? Is he a white guy? An Arab? What?"

"Oh. You know, he might've been Asian. Or Hispanic. Brownish skin, but not, you know, black."

Ball asked a few more questions and clicked off his tape recorder. He had a feeling Medina had seen the Serpent. But how to follow up on it?

Suddenly Ball's telephone rang. He clicked it on. "Fred Ball here."

"Fred Ball with National Public Radio?"

"Yes." Fred tensed. There was something odd about the voice. Then it hit him. It was distorted. "Who is this?"

"This is the Serpent. I want you to take down a message."

# 45

WHEN JILL CHURCH PULLED the plug on the printer, nothing happened. Derek, lying on the floor with his arms over his head, looked up. "Agent Church, you're getting reckless."

Jill breathed a sigh of relief and held out her hand, which shook slightly. "You're wearing off on me. Now what?"

"Dismantle these gas canisters and get into this desk. And I'd like to get into this computer."

Jill nodded. Moisture dampened her forehead. She wiped her brow with her sleeve and said, "What can I do to help?"

Derek rolled over on his back, placed his tools on his chest, and held his hand out for the flashlight, which Jill gave him. In exchange, he handed her the atropine injector. "Familiarize yourself with this thing. Just in case."

Lying on his back, Derek studied the switch to the gas canisters. It seemed straightforward. In fact, he thought, it seemed too straightforward. If you pulled the wire, it triggered a switch that opened the regulator on the canisters. There didn't seem to be anything more complicated than that to it. The canisters had been attached to the desk with a metal bracket screwed to the wood.

"Can you lean over the desk and look behind it?" he asked. "Without putting any weight on the desk?"

Jill gingerly did as he asked.

"What do you see?"

"An extension cord and dust. What am I looking for?"

"Something that might trigger the device or some other booby trap if I take this damned thing off the desk."

"I don't see anything like that."

"Okay. I'm cutting the wire. You read the directions on the atropine injector yet?"

"Just cut it," Jill said.

He cut the wire. The wire sagged, and nothing hissed or exploded. Derek, who had been holding his breath, let it out in a rush. "You dead?"

"I'm fine."

"Good. Glad to hear it. Okay. I'm going to unscrew this thing and hand it out to you."

From his tool kit, Derek took a small battery-powered screwdriver. He adjusted the bit and cautiously unscrewed the bracket. When the screws were about halfway out, he said, "Problem."

"What?"

"I don't want to drop this thing. You're going to have to climb in here with me and hold it while I do the, uh, screwing. It's going to be, um, cozy."

Jill maneuvered to the floor and slithered in next to Derek. It was more than cozy.

Derek grinned. "If we die like this, we'll never live it down."

"Shut up."

"Watch the knee."

"Just start screwing."

Silence.

"Don't. Say. A. Word."

Derek reached up and completed unscrewing the bracket. Jill slowly pulled the canister away. Derek, lying on his back, was nose to nose with her, pressed against her, toes to chin.

"It's not just a job," he said. "It's an adventure."

"Shut the fuck up. Hold this." Jill handed him the canister. Once he had it in his hands, she slipped back out of the footwell, reached in, and took it from him.

"Now what?" she asked.

"Take that thing out of here."

"Don't do anything while I'm gone."

"No problem," he said. "The next thing we have to do is open the drawers. I'm going to spend the time you're gone asking forgiveness for my sins."

Jill hefted the canister and picked up the diskette case. "I'm sure I won't be gone nearly long enough, then."

# 46

*2:41 p.m.*

FRED BALL GRIPPED THE phone and waved to get Officer Medina's attention. He mouthed, "The Serpent's on the line! FBI!" and started walking in the direction of the mobile command center. Into the phone he said, "How do I know this isn't a prank? Everybody thinks the Serpent was that FBI agent that just got killed."

"Then the FBI is just as stupid as I think they are," the Serpent said. "I'm going to make a statement. Are you prepared to take it?"

Moving quickly now, Medina racing on ahead, Ball said, "I'm recording. But why don't you tell me what this is all about?"

The Serpent continued. "There will be another attack—"

"Where?"

"There will be another attack," the Serpent repeated. "If five million dollars is not wired into account number 84 532-68873-23 at the Bank of Bermuda Limited by 3:45 today, Eastern Time, I will set off another attack."

"Can you repeat that number?" Ball asked desperately. His heart raced, and his hands were sweaty. Ahead, he saw Medina come out of the MCC truck with a female FBI agent and point to him. She sprinted over.

Fumbling in his pocket, Ball yanked out his wallet and flipped it open, showing it to the agent. She looked blankly at it. He tapped the business card. She took the wallet, slipped out the card, and held it up, pointing to the cellular phone number printed there. Ball nodded. She disappeared into the van.

"It's the same account as earlier," the Serpent said.

"Why are you doing this?" Ball said, hoping he could keep this nut on the line long enough for the FBI to triangulate.

"Five million dollars in that account. By 3:45. Or more people will die at 4:00."

"Who's supposed to pay the ransom?" Ball asked. "Before, it was Wayne State University. Is that who you want—"

The connection ended.

Ball stared at the phone in his hand. Agent Simona Toreanno appeared at the door of the MCC, eyes wide. "He disconnected?" she asked.

Ball nodded. "Did you get him?"

"Not live," she said with a shake of her head. "But we're locking in." She held a radio to her lips. "Do you have the—"

She listened. "Go!" she said. "Go!"

Above them, the helicopters moved away, heading south. Ball stared at her.

"Somewhere around the Ren Cen," she said. She held out her hand. "I need your phone."

He handed it to her.

"And the tape."

Ball shook his head. "Sorry. I don't—"

Toreanno stepped forward. "We'll make a recording of it for you. But we need that right now. Right now."

Ball swallowed. He nodded and handed over the recorder, wondering if he'd ever get it back.

# 47

*2:43 p.m.*

ONCE HE WAS CERTAIN Jill was out of the house, Derek turned back to the desk. They could go on like this forever, taking precautions for every single aspect of the office, then every other part of the house if they came up dry here. But time was running out. William Harrington was the Serpent, that much seemed clear. And the bastard was playing tricks with everybody, setting up the cops and investigators who might follow up on him.

All Derek wanted was a clue. One clue that would point to the next target, so they could evacuate. So they could save some lives.

Reaching out, he slowly pulled open the top desk drawer.

Nothing. Inside was the usual desk detritus: pens, business cards, a stapler, a pair of scissors, a ruler, miscellaneous bits of paper and notes—office supply clutter.

Leaving it open, he turned to the other desk drawers. There were three, the bottom being a large drawer that could double as a filing cabinet. He slowly opened the top right drawer, careful to pay attention to any resistance.

Nothing. Inside was a ream of printer paper.

Derek left that open, then pulled open the second drawer. Slowly.

Old diskettes. Frowning, Derek scooped them out and stuffed them into his coat pockets.

The third drawer. He gripped the handle and slowly pulled. Was there resistance? Just the tiniest bit?

Derek hesitated. His pulse pounded in his ears. A bitter, metallic taste filled his mouth. Adrenaline, he knew. Now or never.

He pulled.

*SSSSSSSSSSSSS!* Suddenly an inflatable serpent popped up, bobbing as it filled.

Derek stepped back, heart in his throat.

The recording started. "Ha ha! Ha ha!"

He relaxed. Just like in the office at the university. A trademark. A joke.

The recording changed. "Better run! Better run! Three. Better run! Two. Better—"

Derek leapt toward the nearest window, arms over his head.

# 48

*2:44 p.m.*

AGENT ROGER KANDLING STOOD outside the McNamara Federal
Building. Off to one side was a hideous piece of sculpture made
out of junked cars. He had carefully set up the location for the
press statement so the sculpture wasn't in the background. There
were about a dozen reporters and TV cameras present, all trained
on him. Kandling liked that he was going to be seen on TV. He
thought it was possible the publicity might help his career. He only
wished the information he was going to give wasn't so dicey. He
wished he didn't have the feeling Matt Gray was covering his own
ass and tossing him a political anchor to swim with.

Kandling held up his hands. "I'm Special Agent Roger Kandling with the Detroit Field Office of the Federal Bureau of Investigation. I have a statement to make regarding the sarin gas attacks, the pursuit of the terrorist calling himself the Serpent, and
the shooting at the Medical Center earlier. Then we'll have time
for questions."

The reporters focused on him. He cleared his throat. "As you know, a terrorist calling himself the Serpent has conducted two separate attacks on civilians using sarin gas. The first was at 8:00 a.m. at the Boulevard Café on West Grand Boulevard. There was no warning or provocation. At 10:30 a.m. the Serpent contacted a producer with WXYZ-TV, channel 7, who was on site at the Boulevard Café. Using an electronic device to modify his voice, the Serpent demanded that three million dollars be wired into a Bermuda bank account by 11:45 a.m. or he would set off another gas attack at noon."

"Has the Bureau contacted the Bank of Bermuda Limited and discovered anything about who opened the account?" shouted a reporter with NBC. A clamor of questions from everybody else followed.

Kandling held up his hands for quiet. "As I said earlier, I will make a statement—"

"Was Agent Frank McMillan the Serpent?" shouted a CNN reporter.

More shouts. Kandling felt like things were getting out of hand. Tiny claws of panic gripped his heart and squeezed. He had to get this back under control. Somebody else shouted, "Does the Bureau have any other suspects beside Frank McMillan?"

He seized on the question, pointing to the reporter, a blonde woman with Fox. "The Bureau has a number of 'people of interest' that it is investigating. One of those is…" He hesitated. This was bad. He'd known it before and he knew it now. But they were all watching him so closely. "One of those is Agent Derek Stillwater with the Department of Homeland Security. As some of you may know, Agent Stillwater was involved in the White House attack last month and in the U.S. Immunological attacks. He is currently under investigation by the Bureau and the Justice Department for questionable behavior during those events. Stillwater is an expert in biological and chemical warfare and terrorism and is considered by many in these areas of expertise to be a loose cannon."

They began to shout, but everybody suddenly looked skyward as helicopters swooped overhead. In the near distance, sirens grew louder. The cameramen lost their interest in Kandling and focused on the helicopters, which were circling the area.

A dozen squad cars appeared from every direction, lights flashing, sirens blaring, and screeched to a halt in a wide perimeter around that part of the downtown area. Cops began to flood the streets, shouting into walkie-talkies.

"Agent Kandling!" shouted Steve Shay, with WXYZ. "Do you know what's going on?"

Kandling could only stare dumbfounded, unsure how to react as a SWAT cop in full combat gear carrying an assault rifle raced toward them.

# 49

*2:45 p.m.*

JILL CHURCH, LUGGING THE gas canister and the computer disk case across William Harrington's lawn to her car, was distracted, looking down the street. Was that...?

Behind her, she heard a crash. Spinning, she saw Derek burst out of an upstairs window in a shower of glass. He skidded on the steeply pitched roof, tumbled to the edge, and grabbed onto the rain gutter as he went over.

She dropped the canister and disk case, running toward the house. Derek dangled from the gutter, feet kicking. With a muffled *ker-whump*, an explosion blew out all the windows on the second floor. Flames flickered behind the windows. With a cry, Derek dropped into the bushes alongside the house.

Jill rushed over to him. His arms were covered with small cuts despite his coat, and a jagged gash on his forehead oozed blood.

"Are you all right?" she gasped. "What happened?"

Derek seemed slightly dazed. He reached out a hand and she gripped it, helping him to his feet. "I am having a really shitty day," he said.

"Where's your cane?"

He jerked a thumb toward the house.

"Lean on—"

A Honda Civic skidded to a halt behind Jill's car. Michael Church leapt out and sprinted toward them.

"Michael! You were supposed to go back to school!"

"What happened? The house blew up?"

"Michael—"

Michael moved next to Derek and helped support him. "Come on, lean on me. Let's get you away from the house."

"Thanks," Derek muttered, and let Michael assist him across the lawn to Jill's car. Michael opened the front passenger door and helped Derek sit down.

Jill stood, arms crossed, glaring at the two of them. To Michael she finally said, "You were supposed to go back to school."

"Mom—"

"Michael!"

"Mom, by the time I got there school would be over."

Jill threw up her hands. "You need to leave," she said. "I'm going to have to call the Birmingham police and the fire department and I don't want you here. *You weren't here.* Understand?"

"You want me to lie?"

Jill scowled. "I want you to get in your car and go. Now. I'll talk to you later. Go."

Michael's scowl matched her own, but he made a half-wave gesture to Derek, slouched over to his car, and, with a growl of the starter, kicked it into gear and peeled away.

Jill punched 911 into her cell phone and called the fire department and the police. When she was done, she turned to Derek, who leaned over the back seat to scrounge through one of his Go Packs.

"You opened the damned desk, didn't you?"

"Yes," Derek said, finally finding a bottle of water and a packet of pills. He downed one of the painkillers.

"Dammit, Stillwater. Why? Why didn't you wait?"

"We're running out of time. And I didn't want you to take the risk." He gestured in the direction Michael had gone. "You've got a son. I've got no one."

Jill turned to stare at the house, now engulfed in flames. Neighbors had begun to gather, watching the fire.

Derek, talking to her back, explained what had happened. She didn't respond. Finally she said, "I'm going to ask the neighbors what they know about William Harrington."

"Good idea," Derek said.

She turned to study him, looking him up and down. "Your head's cut pretty bad. I've got a first-aid kit in the trunk."

Derek held up the small kit he had retrieved from the Go Pack. "I've got one."

She snatched it from him and opened it. It was extensive and specialized. She held up a container. "Potassium iodide pills?"

"In case of a dirty bomb or nuclear attack. For the thyroid."

"Ciprofloxacin?" She held up another container.

"Anthrax."

Jill took out an alcohol wipe, a Betadine wipe, and a bandage. She dropped the first-aid kit back in Derek's hands, studied his forehead, tore open the alcohol wipe, and swabbed the gash.

"Ow!"

"Stop being such a wimp. You deserve this."

Jill smeared the yellow Betadine wipe on the gash, tore open the bandage, and affixed it over the wound. She crumpled the wrappers and tossed them angrily to the ground. "I'd ask you to help, but you're no help at all. You're a train wreck. Do you have a death wish?"

Derek didn't answer.

"Do you?"

He looked up at her. In a low voice, he said, "Go question the neighbors. I'll be right here."

With a frustrated groan, she backed away and went to interview the onlookers. Sirens were fast approaching. She glanced over her shoulder and saw Derek retrieve a tablet computer from one of his duffel bags. *Good*, she thought. *Maybe that'll keep him out of trouble.*

# 50

*2:46 p.m.*

AGENT ROGER KANDLING MOVED toward the SWAT cop, who slowed. Kandling held up his Bureau ID so the man wouldn't freak out with the assault rifle. "What's this all about?" he demanded.

A wiry black man, face barely visible beneath the helmet, the SWAT cop seemed to stand up a little straighter. "Sir," he said, dark eyes taking in the crowd of reporters, "the Serpent made contact with a reporter just minutes ago, and a trace indicated—"

"Wait a minute," Kandling said. Behind him, the reporters edged closer. Dozens of microphones and cameras swung their way. He grabbed the arm of the cop and pulled him farther away from the crowd. "What do you mean the Serpent made contact with a reporter?" He glanced over, searching for Mary Linzey. She stood next to her cameraman and the reporter Steve Shay.

"That's all I know, sir. Your field commander contacted us. The Serpent was calling from this area, sir." Suddenly the SWAT cop tilted his head, hand to his ear. Kandling realized the guy didn't have a walkie-talkie but rather a radio patched directly to an ear bud.

"What now?" Kandling snapped.

The SWAT cop said, apparently to whomever he was in communication with, "Yes, I'm speaking with ..." He gestured for Kandling's identification. Kandling handed it over. "... Special Agent Roger Kandling. Yes." The cop looked at Kandling. "Your phone—"

It buzzed. Kandling snapped it on. "Kandling here. Who is this?"

"Simona Toreanno. Roger, the Serpent just made a phone call to a reporter's cell phone. It wasn't from a cellular, though. We got a line trace. The Serpent called from the Federal Building."

# 51

*3:03 p.m.*

Jill Church finished talking to the Birmingham Fire Department chief and walked back to the car, where Derek had remained the entire time. She felt exhausted and stressed. She didn't want to talk to Derek, find out what he was planning next. It was time—way past time, probably—to check in, so she pulled out her cell phone and dialed Matt Gray's number. She was routed through the switchboard.

"It's Agent Church," she said. "I need to talk to Agent Gray."

"Just a moment."

It seemed like a long moment. Too long. While she waited, she watched the firefighters douse William Harrington's house with water. There were two trucks, lights still flashing red, coils of hoses, the smell of smoke. The house was a disaster. It had been a large enough explosion with enough heat generated to engulf the entire second floor within seconds. By the time the firefighters showed up, the house had been completely involved, and the roof collapsed not long afterward.

The Birmingham PD were not pleased that she and Derek had done their own illegal search, resulting in triggering an incendiary device. The Birmingham police chief himself, Chief Walter D'Agosta, had pulled her to one side to hear her story and to make sure she knew just how much trouble she was in. He was a heavyset, balding man in a navy blue three-piece suit, wrinkled white shirt, and blue patchwork tie. Mostly bald, he had a classic combover that threatened to lift all at once like a lid whenever the wind blew. He chewed gum and acted like he wanted to take a bite out of Jill at any moment. He'd probably figured he was intimidating, but Jill hadn't felt very intimidated.

"I should lock you up, you and that asshole Stillwater. I went over there to talk to him and he slammed the damned door in my face, said he was busy. I don't appreciate this, Church. You had no warrant. That's going to be very nice for the DA. And the only person who was in the house when this bomb went off won't talk to me. I think you'd better go over there and make sure your partner gives us a statement."

"Sure," she'd said, placating him, knowing by now that Stillwater didn't give a rat's ass what the Birmingham chief of police wanted. "I'll talk to him."

"And you—you should know better. And by the way, you're aware that the media is buzzing about Stillwater? That your own people are suggesting that he's this guy, the Serpent?"

"Do you trust everything the media says, Chief D'Agosta?"

Chew, chew, chew. "I do not. I'm not a fool. But maybe if he's working with you guys, you should get your story straight."

"I couldn't agree with you more."

"I should lock him up."

"It's the Bureau that wants to talk to him, Chief D'Agosta. I'm the Bureau. Consider him to be in my custody."

D'Agosta chewed some more, staring at her disbelievingly. "Where the hell's the owner of this house?"

"We don't know."

"Is he the Serpent?"

"Possibly."

D'Agosta chewed some more, then swore and stomped away. He turned around and jabbed his thick finger at Jill. "No more of this in Birmingham. You hear? No more. You step foot inside my jurisdiction, you drive *through* my jurisdiction, you alert me. We'll have you escorted by one of my officers. You understand me?"

"Yes," Jill said. *Putz*, she thought.

Now Matt Gray finally came on the line, sounding breathless and angry. "Church, where the hell are you?"

She gave him a synopsis. Gray was silent for a moment. "Were you there with him?"

"No."

"Why the hell not?"

"There was a canister of what we assume is sarin gas and a bunch of computer disks and CDs. I was taking them out of the house. Because of what happened at Harrington's office, we were aware of the possibility the office might be booby-trapped. We wanted to get evidence out of the house, just in case."

"Tell me this, Church. Is there any possibility that Stillwater is in cahoots with this guy, the Serpent? That maybe Harrington's the Serpent, but Stillwater's along to muddy things?"

"No, sir. I don't think so. Agent Stillwater is righteous."

"Don't give me that 'righteous' bullshit, Church. He's under investigation for a reason."

"His entire focus is stopping the next attack, Matt. Not building a case or going to court. He could care less what happens, as long as he stops more people from dying. That's why he cuts corners. You don't have to agree with the approach—I don't—but you need to understand it. It's our job to build a case and go to court. That's not his agenda whatsoever. We don't have to like it. He doesn't work for us. What's going on at your end?"

Gray was silent for a long moment. Then, "The Serpent called a reporter with NPR and said there's going to be another attack if somebody doesn't put five million in that Bermuda bank account."

"What time? Four?"

"Right. Four o'clock. And here's the odd thing. He didn't specify who was to pay the five million."

They were both silent. Jill said, slowly, "What do you think that means?"

"I think it means the money is bullshit. That's what I think. I don't think this asshole is doing this for money. I think he's doing it to jerk everybody around. He's doing it because he *likes* doing it. And you know what? He's great at jerking people around. We've got everybody and their brother here at the Federal Building *because he placed his last call from the Federal Building*. And get this, from the Department of Veterans Affairs on the twelfth floor. They think somebody waltzed right in, sat down at an empty cubicle and made the call, then walked right back out."

"Surveill—"

"We're stripping the tapes now, Church. But it makes us look bad, that's for sure." More silence. Then Matt said, "Jill."

"What?"

"This guy, Stillwater ... he know what he's doing?"

"Yes, I think so."

"Are you making any progress? Because I got to tell you, Jill, I don't want another attack on my watch. I'm serious."

"I know. Yes, he knows what he's doing. One thing you can do is try to track down names of everybody involved with writing scenarios for the Center for Biological and Chemical Terrorism Research."

"I'll get ... I'll get Agent Toreanno on it."

"Good. That's good. And get Wayne State to track down a photograph of William Harrington. Security should have it in a database or even on the university website. Get it to the media. Be on the lookout."

"Good. Good. That's good. Very good. Anything else?"

Jill hesitated. She knew at some level that Matt Gray was a good agent. A politician, an ass coverer, a careerist, but a good agent. He sounded a little desperate. Another successful attack today would kill his career. Maybe he was trying to get on the ball and make sure that didn't happen, no matter what his motivation.

*Or maybe,* she thought, *he's exploring ways to pin the blame on other people if everything goes to hell.*

She said, "Anything on the bank account?"

"No. Not yet. They're stalling us."

"Okay. We're working our end. We'll get back to you as soon as possible."

"Good. You do that."

Jill hung up, swallowed, and walked past the firefighters and onlookers to her car. She tapped on the window. Derek glared at her, punched a button on his tablet PC, snatched out a disk, and flung it into the back seat. He reached over and punched another disk into the slot.

"Open up," she said.

Derek leaned forward and unlocked the door. She pulled it open and looked in. The back seat was covered with a scatter of computer disks. "Any luck finding anything?"

Derek scowled. "So far, every fucking one of these things is blank. The floppies look like they've been run over with a magnet, and every damned CD is unformatted. This is all bullshit. *Bullshit!*" he yelled. "The bastard's playing games with us!"

He pounded his fist on the dashboard, voice rough with emotion and frustration.

"Okay," she said. "Okay, Stillwater. Take a second. Think. We've got an agent trying to track down the rest of the scenario writers. What else—"

Derek snapped his fingers, reaching for his Iridium phone. "I've got to get back to the boss. He's got somebody trying to track down the guy in California. The guy with SKOLAR MD."

"Call," she said.

And then, wondering if she was being set up to take a fall by Matt Gray, she said, "And Stillwater?"

He looked at her.

"No more mistakes. We can't afford them."

# 52

*3:07 p.m.*

MICHAEL CHURCH WAS FUMING. Back in his car, he cranked the stereo, an MP3 of J Slim rattling the windows. He guessed he would just go home. He didn't want to go home. He didn't actually know what he wanted to do. The day had been so full of revelations, his head was spinning.

*My father was a spy.*

He felt something that might have been pride. His mom had never wanted to talk about his dad, never wanted to talk about how he died. Just that they had both worked at the embassy in Tanzania and he had died in a terrorist attack. Everything about her attitude when Michael brought up the subject had indicated to him that she didn't want to talk about it. Maybe didn't want to think about it.

A part of Michael, the more grown-up part, realized that, to his mother, those must have been hideously bad memories. You couldn't have your husband die in a terrorist bombing, leaving you to be a single parent to raise a son, and not be messed up by the trauma in some way.

But Michael was a sixteen-year-old male, which meant he was largely addled by hormones and self-involved to an unhealthy degree. His physicality and size made him look like an adult, but his judgment and hormones hadn't caught up yet.

He sort of knew that too. Sometimes Michael felt like he did things his body wanted to do while his brain told him not to. It was like there was a gremlin living inside his head, or a poltergeist.

And right now, the poltergeist was dancing up a storm. Michael kept flashing on the body of that woman, the one who'd suffocated on her own bed because this guy, the Serpent, had duct-taped her nose and mouth shut.

He shivered, thinking about it. What kind of person would do that?

J Slim screamed profanities, talking about the unfairness of the world, about giving the world back some of that unfairness by living with attitude:

"... *You give it back,*
*Don't take no shit, Jack,*
*Life ain't no fair,*
*Nobody give you the time a day,*
*Nobody help you make your way ...*"

Michael bobbed his head in time to the rap, trying to take his thoughts away from the dead woman. Away from the little bit of fear he felt for his mom, about her chasing the Serpent, chasing someone who would suffocate someone else on purpose.

And he felt a glow of pride about the way Derek Stillwater had treated him. Stillwater had treated him like an adult. Had been straight with him. Honest with him. Asking for his help, even if it was acting as a watchdog in case something went wrong, which it had. Handing him that injector thing, telling him to read it, just in case. Stillwater had acted like he was up to the task, up to the responsibility.

Michael swung by Ray Moretti's house, figuring Ray would probably be home by now. He parked out front of the house, a big two-story modern thing with a small, well-manicured yard. Ray's sister, Ann, was home. She was two years older than Ray and Michael, and though Michael would never admit it to Ray, she was hot. Long black hair, big eyes, and those tight cropped T-shirts and low-rise jeans. Man, she made him sizzle.

"Hey," he said, when she answered the door.

Ann smiled. She was a senior, planning on going to U of M next year, pre-med. A serious student, in the National Honor Society, on the track team, and she played flute in the band. "Hi, Michael. Ray's upstairs."

"Hey," he said again, avoiding her eyes. "Uh, how's it goin'?"

"Okay. You hear about this guy, the Serpent?"

He smiled at her. Man, he got a rush just looking at her. She watched him, her expression serious. God, she was hot.

"Yeah," he said. "Psycho."

"Is your mom working that?"

Michael blinked. "Uh, yeah, but, you know, I can't talk about it."

"Ray said you ditched him, went to pick her up. Did she tell you what was going on?"

He froze. He wanted to tell her everything, to try to impress her. But he couldn't, could he? He really wanted to. He knew his mom wouldn't approve, and he could live with that. But he thought

Derek Stillwater wouldn't approve, and for some reason he didn't want to disappoint Stillwater. Michael took a deep breath. He wondered how Derek Stillwater would handle this situation. Stillwater seemed like a cool guy, someone who had a handle on things. What would he say? Probably something funny and charming.

"Only a bit," Michael said, feeling a little flood of confidence. "It's important ... you know, it's important that rumors don't go around. I mean, I know more than I can talk about." His face burned, especially at the way Ann was watching him.

"That's so cool," Ann said. "Your mom is so cool. An FBI agent. Not like my parents. I mean, Mom's a banker and Dad's, you know, he works at Chrysler."

"Hey, your parents are okay. Mom's just ... she's just Mom."

Ann blinked and smiled. "Well ... Ray's upstairs." She walked back to the couch, where she had been sitting with a notebook and chemistry textbook in her lap.

He watched her as she sat down and curled on the sofa. He watched the curve of her thigh in the tight jeans, the way the pink T-shirt rode up, the soft flatness of her stomach. He wanted to say something to her, make her see him as somebody besides her dummy brother's buddy. He opened his mouth and was surprised to hear himself say, "You know anything about sarin gas? I mean, you're real smart and you want to be a doctor."

Ann's face burned a little pink, and she smiled at Michael. "Thanks. Um, no, not really. We could look it up. On the computer. I bet there's a lot there. That's what the Serpent's using, isn't he?"

"Yeah. In gas canisters that he sets off using a cell phone."

"Wow! That's ... your mom tell you that? Wow, that's really scary."

Michael shrugged.

"C'mon," Ann said, jumping up. She waved for him to follow her. "C'mon, let's check that out on the computer."

He followed her up the stairs, unable to keep his eyes off her ass. She was so hot. She looked over her shoulder and saw him watching her. She flushed a little darker. "The computer's in my room. C'mon, Michael. This is exciting."

Her room was across the hall from Ray's. He'd never been in there, though he'd seen inside before. It was kind of a girly room. The drapes had big sunflowers on them, as did the comforter on her bed. Dark blue with big, bright, cheerful sunflowers on it. There were photographs in frames on her wall. It kind of surprised him. He'd expected her to have posters of rock bands or something. He studied one of the photographs while she booted up her computer.

It was of a sunset reflected across the glass panels of Chrysler World Headquarters. It was shot at an odd angle, so the big Chrysler star was isolated, refracting colors in a thousand shades.

"That's pretty cool," he said.

"You like that? I took it myself."

"Cool."

"I like photography. For a while I thought I wanted to be a photographer, but I think I'd rather be a doctor. What about you?"

"Huh? I like it."

She turned to him, brushing her hair over her shoulder. "What do you like?"

His mind went blank. "What?"

"You don't seem much like Ray. I think Ray's smoking dope. If Mom and Dad catch him, they'll kill him. But Ray's really not into anything. Video games, I guess. How 'bout you?"

"I . . . I like karate," he said. He hoped she'd be impressed.

Her eyes grew big. "Really? Are you a black belt?"

"Yeah," he said automatically.

"Are you any good?"

He nodded, knowing that he was.

"Do you, like, break boards and stuff?"

He smiled. "Better to use a saw. Most people don't get in fights with boards. We don't do that in the style I study, Sanchin-Ryu."

"Wow. Have you ever, like, gotten in a fight or anything?"

"Just in class. We call it *kumite*. It's like sparring. You know, fighting, but you don't hurt each other."

"Cool."

Ray's door opened, and he sauntered across the hallway. "Hey, what's going on? You finished bein' taxi driver for your *mommy*?"

"Shut up, Ray," Ann said.

"Shut up, yourself. C'mon, dude. Tell me what happened. Shit, man, lucky you missed history. Binks just 'bout put us all to sleep."

Michael stayed rooted to his spot, not wanting to leave. "I . . . Ann and I are checking something."

Ray rolled his eyes. "Jesus, you boner. Get a fuckin' life." With a shrug he wandered back to his room and slammed the door.

Ann looked at Michael. "You can go on."

He shook his head, jaw locking into a stubborn expression. "Nah, he's bein' a jerk. Hey, can you, you know . . ."

"What?"

"There's something else I want to check, once you're online."

"Sure." She clicked on the Internet icon. "What's that?"

He leaned over to the computer, very conscious of how close he was to her, how shiny and soft her hair was, how she smelled, which was wonderful. "Um...well, let's Google Tanzania and U.S. Embassy. There's some stuff I want..."

She leaned back, looking at him up close. She had such big eyes. And her mouth looked so—

"Michael?"

"Huh?"

"What's this about? You look a little..."

He turned to her. "I, uh, lived there when I was a kid."

"Really? In Tanzania?"

"Yeah."

"I didn't know that."

He shrugged.

"Was this an FBI thing? I mean...maybe you can't talk about it and stuff."

"Mom was with the FBI then, yeah."

She turned and typed it into the computer. When the entries came up, he pointed to one: "CNN.com—Embassy Bombings." News reports of the terrorist bombings that killed eleven. "That one," he said.

She rested her hand on his arm. "You okay?"

He nodded. "Yeah. I'm okay."

# 53

*3:15 p.m.*

DEREK'S CALL TO SECRETARY Johnston was answered by his personal secretary, Roslyn German. She was a brusque woman with a nasal Brooklyn accent, and Derek didn't know her very well. She was a recent addition to the staff.

"Secretary Johnston is not available, Dr. Stillwater," she said. "He's in a meeting with the president."

"I asked him to track down some information for me," Derek said, desperation seizing him once again. What would he do if they dead-ended?

"Yes, I have a note about that. He has a message for you. First, he says the FBI is stalling on the Jillian Church request."

"Screw that, it's not important."

"Sure, but you did ask for it."

"It's irrelevant now. Forget about it."

"I'm just saying—"

*"What's next?!"*

"I've heard about you, Dr. Stillwater. This is exactly what I was warned about."

"Then don't act so fucking surprised. What else does the general have for me?"

"I'll be discussing your attitude with the general, you know."

"Knock yourself out. The sooner you cut through the shit and tell me what I need, the sooner I'll be out of your hair."

"Fine. Secondly," German said, "there has been a problem with Dr. Bernard Schultz at Stanford. Let me check this. I'll read it to you. Are you still there?"

Derek controlled his desire to reach through the phone and pull Roslyn German's lip over her head. "I'm still here."

"First, Dr. Stillwater, there's a three-hour time difference between us and California."

"I know."

"So, the first point Secretary Johnston wanted to make sure you understood was that it was five a.m. for Dr. Schultz when the first attack in Detroit occurred."

"Get to the fucking point!"

"There's no reason to use that tone of voice or that type of language with me, Dr. Stillwater."

"Like hell there isn't." He clamped the phone to his ear, willing himself to be calm. "People are dying here."

She ignored that and continued on in her implacable way. "Secondly, Secretary Johnston wants you to note that it was only nine a.m. in California at the time of the second attack."

"What does this have to do with anything?" Derek clenched his hands into fists, glaring at Jill, who watched him without emotion.

The wind shifted and blew a cloud of oily black smoke their way. Derek shut his eyes, trying not to cough.

"Quite a bit, Dr. Stillwater, if you would be patient."

"I'm trying to be patient."

"You're not very good at it, are you?"

Derek didn't comment. He waited. He watched a firefighter run through the front door with a hose, determined to put out the fire for good.

"Dr. Stillwater, are you still there?"

"Yes," he said through clenched teeth. "Still here."

"Yes. Well, it seems, then, that Dr. Schultz did not hear about any of the sarin gas attacks until nearly 9:45 a.m. Pacific Time. He apparently had just arrived in his office at Stanford University when he was told about it."

"Fine. Does he have the—"

"Dr. Stillwater, Dr. Schultz suffered a massive heart attack this morning, shortly after 9:45 a.m."

Derek was speechless. He sat there in Jill's car, his stomach churning.

Jill must have sensed something was wrong. "What?"

He shook his head.

"Dr. Stillwater. Are you still there?"

"Yes, I'm still here. I can't believe this. That's a hell of a coincidence."

"Secretary Johnston has underlined *strong history of heart disease* here in his notes. Apparently Dr. Schultz has had several heart attacks before, is quite overweight, and had very high blood pressure. At least, that's according to the field agent we've got there in San Francisco."

"Who's that?"

"Janice Beckwith. She's at the hospital."

"Hospital?"

"Yes, Dr. Schultz was admitted to the Stanford University Medical Center."

"He's alive?!"

"Yes, though unable to—"

"I need Janice Beckwith's number."

"That's—"

"Now!"

"Dr. Stillwater, I really—"

"Now!"

Roslyn German was quiet for a moment, then rattled off an Iridium phone number. "Now, Dr. Stillwater, I really think you owe me an—"

Derek didn't hear the last thing Roslyn German wanted, which was apparently an apology. Instead, he was punching Agent Janice Beckwith's number into his phone.

# 54

Scott Abrams walked through the slots room of the Greektown Casino, part of his routine tour of duty. As casino manager, Abrams regularly toured the facility to keep staff on their toes and get a feel for the mood of the gamblers. He thought the mood was a little edgy today, though there didn't seem to be any real change in the buzz, clank, and clink of the slots. Maybe he was just projecting the day's events onto the casino.

The Greektown Casino—the original one, not the new one being built on the corner of I-375 and Gratiot across from Comerica Park and Ford Field—was 75,000 square feet of gaming area with over 2,400 slots. It was in the heart of Greektown, across from Trappers Alley, one of the more vital entertainment districts in Detroit, and it was one of three casinos in the city.

Abrams's assistant, Lisa Mobly, appeared around a corner. He smiled and joined her. "Everything seems to be going well."

Lisa Mobly was an elegant Native American woman, the assistant casino manager. The Greektown Casino was 90 percent owned by the Sault Tribe of Chippewa Indians, and Mobly had come down from Sault Sainte Marie, where she'd grown up. Looking at her in her gray suit, Abrams would never have guessed her for Chippewa, except for her dark hair. And it didn't really matter. She was his right hand.

"I was afraid with all these attacks going on in the city that business might drop off," she said. "But if anything, the numbers are up a little."

Abrams surveyed the room. There were easily fifty or sixty people in this room alone, and the casino had seven floors. His estimate was close to six hundred, which for a weekday afternoon wasn't bad at all. "Not our usual afternoon crowd," he said.

"Fewer retirees," Mobly agreed. "More shift workers. And the university's shut down. I think a lot of city businesses closed down too, in response to the attacks. There are more college kids here than usual."

"Maybe everybody feels lucky today," he said. "What's the news, anyway?"

She shook her head. "Still got the Feds chasing their tails. Let's hope this ends soon."

Abrams nodded, satisfied. Time to move on and check out other areas. "I have a feeling it will." He clasped his hands, looking at the gamblers feeding the machines. "Something tells me it's just about over."

Mobly cocked an eyebrow and soaked in her boss's good mood. "I hope you're right."

"Yeah," he said, heading toward the poker room. "I bet it's just about over."

# 55

*3:17 p.m. Eastern/12:17 p.m. Pacific*

AGENT JANICE BECKWITH PACED nervously around the waiting area at the Stanford Medical Center, keeping an eye on the television set. She was an athletic woman in her forties, a former military anti-terrorism investigator who had made the move to the Department of Homeland Security. Right now she wore a gray pantsuit, but she was just as comfortable in fatigues. Her hair was short, dark, shot with gray, and her angular face was unadorned by makeup. She was a tough broad, a term she used to describe herself without apology.

She had received a personal call from Secretary Johnston telling her to track down this college professor and providing some minimal background. But when she arrived at the university, the place was in an uproar. Professor Schultz had come in to work and had had a heart attack shortly after hearing news of the sarin gas bombs in Detroit.

She had gleaned enough information to understand that Schultz had been asking for another heart attack. She'd managed to get a look at the man and his chart. He weighed 402 pounds, his blood pressure was routinely about 155 over 140, and the man ate anything and everything he pleased.

Schultz was a professor of epidemiology at the Stanford Medical School, associated with UC-Berkeley, and was a consultant for some medical Internet company spun off from Stanford called SKOLAR MD. He might know something about these killings going on in Detroit.

She had a bad feeling about this, because nobody she talked to gave Schultz much chance of surviving this heart attack, his fourth.

She watched the news coverage on CNN like everybody else in the waiting room. The shit was definitely going down in the Motor City.

Her Iridium phone buzzed. She checked the incoming number and frowned. "Beckwith, DHS."

"This is Derek Stillwater, DHS. I'm working the Detroit case. How is Dr. Schultz?"

"I need your confirmation number."

Stillwater made a frustrated noise and read off a ten-digit number. She nodded. "Do you want mine?"

"I received your number directly from Johnston's secretary. We're pressed for time."

Beckwith had heard about Dr. Derek Stillwater, though their paths had never crossed. He was famous for his tirades, his clockwork letters of resignation, and his absolute disdain for protocol and procedures. Beckwith came from the military herself—in her case, the navy—and she couldn't fathom how this guy had survived a career in the army.

"We always are, Doctor," she said.

Several of the people waiting had shifted their attention from the TV to her. One guy nodded his head toward a sign stating No Cellular Phones.

She turned her back on him. "It doesn't look good."

"Can you talk to him?"

"He's in surgery. He has been for a couple hours. I don't think he's talking to anybody but God anytime soon."

There was silence. Then, "Okay, here's what I need. This guy received at least one e-mail from William Harrington, a professor here at Wayne State in Detroit. Harrington's the Serpent. He's a professor of biochemistry and the director of the Center for Biological and Chemical Terrorism Research. This place wrote terrorism scenarios. We know that at least one e-mail was a scenario. I need you to get back to Schultz's office and check his computer for these scenarios. Send all of them to me. Here's my e-mail." He read it off.

She jotted it down. "I may need a warrant for this. I'll—"

"Beckwith, listen to me. It's what, 12:20 or so there in California?"

She checked her watch. "Yes."

"The Serpent's going to strike again at one o'clock your time. You understand? You've got forty minutes to get to the office, get that information if it exists, and get it to me in time for me to evacuate wherever this guy plans on striking next."

She hesitated and nodded, already moving out the door. "Understood. I'm on my way."

# 56

*3:22 p.m.*

STILL SITTING IN THE passenger seat of Jill's car, Derek clicked off the phone and sat with it in his hand, frowning. Jill said, "We're working on it from our end too."

"That's good, because I'm out of options."

Jill studied him. He seemed distracted. He was looking at the house. The fire department had done a decent job of controlling and stopping the blaze. None of the neighbors' homes had been affected, but Harrington's house was a mess, just a shell with a partially collapsed roof, no windows, the walls of the second floor charred and skeletal.

She followed his gaze. "You're lucky to have gotten out of there."

He didn't seem to hear her. He was staring at the house, lost in his own thoughts.

A little frustrated, she waved her hand in front of his face. "Let's think, Stillwater. First a restaurant, then the class. What would your third option be?"

He shrugged. "Could be anything."

"But it'll be bigger."

"It'll be inside," he said. "There will be more people than there were in the last attack. My gut tells me it might be someplace public."

"In the city?"

Derek frowned. "The university's shut down. He had to know that was likely to happen. The city makes sense just because that's been the center of the attacks so far."

His expression went blank again, and he turned to stare at the house, now soaked and smoldering.

Warily, Jill crouched down in front of him. "Come on, Stillwater. We've lived through two explosions together. What are you thinking?"

Derek scratched his chin, closed his eyes, and took in a deep breath. "Let's head back into the city. I think we're done here."

"The Birmingham PD wants statements."

Derek's expression was wry. "I bet they do. So it would be better if we got the hell out of here before we spend the rest of the afternoon typing up reports. Save that for when this is done."

Jill scanned the crowd, saw that Chief D'Agosta appeared to be deep in conversation with the fire chief, and thought Stillwater might be right. If they didn't get out of here soon, they never would. She crossed around the car, slipped behind the wheel, and fired up the engine. "Hang on," she murmured, and squeezed the car up onto the grass and around the fire truck, scattering a handful of firefighters who were putting away their gear.

Behind her she heard D'Agosta shouting, but she decided now was an excellent time to develop hearing problems.

Derek studied the house the entire time, frowning.

Once they were away from the scene, he leaned over, retrieved an MP3 player from one of his Go Packs, popped on earphones, and clicked it on. He leaned back in his seat, crossed his arms over his chest, and closed his eyes.

"What're you listening to?" she asked.

He didn't move or open his eyes. He said, "J. S. Bach. Mass in B Minor."

She blinked, surprised.

A moment later, she pulled onto Woodward and headed south, back into the city. Derek had not moved or said a word.

Then, without warning, he said, "Kind of strange he was willing to torch his own house."

She thought about that. "Not if he expected to have several million dollars in a bank somewhere."

Derek didn't reply. They passed the Detroit Zoo, its water tower painted with animals. Derek, eyes still closed, finally said, "You said he didn't say who should pay in his last phone call."

"That's what Gray said. He doesn't think the Serpent's doing this for money."

Derek's expression, eyes closed, was pensive. "Probably not," he said.

"Then why let his house go up in flames?" she said, almost to herself.

The only sound was the wheels on the road and, faintly, violins and a soprano singing in what Jill thought must be German. They were just crossing 8 Mile Road into the city when Derek said, "He didn't plan on coming back."

"He has an escape plan," Jill said.

Derek opened his eyes and turned to her. "Or it's a suicide run."

# 57

*3:27 p.m.*

FBI AGENT SIMONA TOREANNO waited in her car outside the University Health Center. The majority of the university's campus had been evacuated. The exception had been the Detroit Medical Center, including Grace Hospital and Detroit Receiving, though security had been stepped up and the Detroit PD bomb squad was doing sweeps for explosive devices. The University Health Center, however, was as quiet as ... *Well*, she thought, *as quiet as a tomb*.

A black Lincoln Town Car pulled up near her, and a stocky black man in an elegantly tailored gray suit approached. In a deep, mellifluous voice, he said, "Are you Special Agent Toreanno?"

"Yes. Are you Dr. Nolan Webster?"

"Yes."

Agent Toreanno stepped out of her car. She realized that Webster wasn't just stocky but tall, standing nearly six-feet-five at least. She had to crane her neck to look him in the eye. Despite her instincts, she did not step back from his physical presence.

"I will need to see identification, Doctor."

Webster looked briefly amused before a grave expression crossed his face. "Yes, of course. I'd like to see yours as well."

They exchanged identification, and Webster waved for her to follow. "I'm not entirely sure what you need, Agent Toreanno, but I'll help in any way I can."

"I need as much information about the Center for Biological and Chemical Terrorism Research as you can provide. In particular, we want the names and contact information of everybody involved."

"Ah, I see. And this has to do with William Harrington?"

"And John Simmons."

Webster paused in his stride toward the building's front doors, a set of keys in his hand. He looked at her over his shoulder. "John died in the first attack."

"Yes, sir. We know that."

"He was my friend."

"I'm sorry, sir."

He nodded thoughtfully, inserted a key into the lock, and opened the door for her. She stepped in before him and he followed, locking the door again after them.

"Was William Harrington also your friend, sir?"

Again the over-the-shoulder glance. "We were colleagues. I didn't know him very well."

Toreanno wondered if that was true, or if, given the likelihood of Harrington being a mass murderer, Dr. Webster, dean of the medical school, was intentionally keeping his distance.

"That sounds like you didn't like him, sir."

Webster stopped and turned to look down at her. "Agent Toreanno," he said, "if you are asking me if I think William Harrington is this murderer calling himself the Serpent, I can't help you. The fact is, I do not know. I hope it's not true. I have met Dr. Harrington, and we interacted occasionally at university social events and at meetings, but our interactions were not regular or in-depth. On the surface, Dr. Harrington seemed to be an intelligent, capable man with no obvious evidence of mental illness. He was polite and collegial. As far as I know, there were never any complaints filed against him. That is all I know."

"Thank you," she said.

Webster seemed about to say something else, but instead he turned and strode toward the elevators. Over his shoulder, he said, "I have a list of all the faculty involved with the CBCTR. You will find contact information there."

They rode up to Webster's office, on the top floor. It was large, with a view of downtown only partially blocked by the Medical Center. His furniture was blond oak, modern, his diplomas and other accomplishments framed on his walls. Webster crossed to a large filing cabinet, unlocked it, and thumbed through several files until he found what he was looking for. "I'll copy this for you," he said. "It'll take a few minutes to warm up the Xerox."

When he returned with the warm copy, she studied it. There were nine names on the list. Two of them, John Simmons and Brad Beales, had died at the Boulevard Café. Subtract William Harrington and she was down to six.

"Thank you, Doctor. Now I'd like access to John Simmons's office." *And hope like hell it wasn't booby-trapped*, she thought.

# 58

*3:37 p.m.*

THE SERPENT PULLED THE car into the parking garage of the Greek-town Casino and drove to the top floor, where there were the most open spots and the fewest cars parked. He circled twice, studying again the security cameras and what he perceived to be the blind spots. He especially liked one dark area in the center, blocked by a support column. It was available, which seemed especially fortu-itous. The gods were indeed smiling on him today.

That thought amused him. By birth, he was divine, a child of a god. Soon, he would be recognized for who and what he really was. Soon.

The radio played WDET, the local National Public Radio sta-tion. They had shut off all music programming and were covering the Serpent. He felt thrilled by that. The focus of so much atten-tion. So much fear.

It felt powerful.

For a moment, or maybe it was longer, the Serpent lost track of everything—of the mission, of the tasks ahead, the challenges—and reveled in the destruction he had caused.

Suddenly jolting back to the present, the Serpent studied the dashboard clock, trying to figure out how much time had passed. Five minutes? Ten?

It was now 3:47. Had he been sitting here in the car all this time? For a moment, panic gripped at his heart. What was happening to him? Was he blacking out?

Shaking his head, he scanned around the structure, looking for any witnesses. It was nothing. Just the stress of the day. It was tiring, being a god of chaos.

A smile played at his lips. The Serpent. He was already famous. And by the end of the day, everybody in the world would know the Serpent. And the Serpent would be the head of Aleph. Today he would show the followers and the hidden the way to salvation. It would be like a second coming.

When he saw no one, he set about preparing for the next phase of his operation.

# 59

THE PROFESSOR AT STANFORD was being a dick, thought Agent Janice Beckwith. He was a near stereotype of the arrogant college professor, with a thick beard and brown hair swept off his forehead and worn a little long. He had an attitude that left *arrogant* in the dust, well on its way to *megalomania*. He wore college-professor clothes as well: khaki slacks, a white button-down shirt, a brown corduroy sport coat with patches on the sleeves. But even more than that was his posture, which was so upright he practically leaned backward, the better to peer down his nose at her. This was a guy who took himself entirely too seriously.

"I'm not sure I understand what you want. And you said you were with the FBI?"

"Department of Homeland Security," Agent Beckwith said, pleasantly enough. "And I felt I was very clear. I need access to Professor Schultz's office."

Dr. Jameson Lloyd, the bearded professor, shot her a knowing look. "And you have a search warrant?"

"I don't need one," she said. "You, as an educated man, are certainly aware of the provisions under Statute 831C-3 of the Patriot Act allowing for non-warranted searches under two provisions, the first being, and I quote, 'instances of imminent national security.' The second provision is known as the 'hot-pursuit proviso.'"

Dr. Lloyd blinked. "I see ..."

Agent Beckwith met his gaze unflinchingly. "You are familiar with these statutes, correct?"

"Of course," Lloyd said. "Of course. Yes. Well, then, yes, let me find someone to take you to Dr. Schultz's office."

"I've been there. I can find the way. Thank you very much."

"Of course. Please proceed."

She shouldered past him, not letting a smile mar her face. Dr. Lloyd wasn't much of a poker player, but Beckwith was. She had just bluffed him—not the first time she had used the fictional Statute 831C-3 to convince people to give her permission to do what she pleased.

She found Schultz's office, which was unlocked. She pushed her way into a large room piled with loose papers, books, folders, and technical journals. It was as if somebody had taken the contents of a Dumpster and shaken it out over the room. Yet it wasn't like the office had been ransacked. There was a sort of organized feel to the mess. She didn't doubt that Schultz knew exactly where everything was, that he had some sort of system for organizing things.

She was thankful she didn't have to find what she was looking for among the papers. Beckwith glanced at her watch. It was

12:52 p.m. Pacific Time. The Serpent was going to strike in eight minutes.

Without wasting another second, she settled into Schultz's old, battered desk chair and punched on his computer. From her briefcase, she withdrew her tablet computer, a disk, and a flash drive. Sure enough, it was as she suspected: Schultz had password-protected his computer.

She slipped the disk into the drive and waited. After about thirty seconds, the program had located the password and opened the computer files. She scanned the programs, checking My Documents. Despite all the paper scattered about the office, Schultz had placed a lot of his work on his computer. She quickly searched through over a hundred files in My Documents alone, not including hundreds of photographs and music files.

She clicked on the search option and typed in "Center for Biological and Chemical Terrorism Research." The computer began to churn through the hard drive.

"Agent Beckwith."

Professor Lloyd had returned with another faculty member, a severe woman in a flower-print dress, iron-gray hair pulled back in a bun, glasses on a cord dangling from her scrawny neck.

Beckwith glanced at the two of them, took in the time—12:54 p.m.—and pulled her handgun out of its clip and pointed it toward the ceiling. In a flat voice, she said, "Step back. Close the door."

The woman gasped. "I'm calling security."

The clock turned to 12:55 p.m. A computer window opened: *Search Completed*.

On her feet in one fluid motion, Beckwith kicked the door shut and locked it. She popped the flash drive into a USB port on

Schultz's computer and downloaded all the files to it, then transferred the files to her tablet computer.

*Good to go*, she thought, reaching for her phone.

# 60

*3:57 p.m.*

DEREK AND JILL HAD worked their way slowly into the downtown
area. It felt like they had caught every stoplight, which meant every
block. Derek had taken off his earphones and booted up his tablet
PC, and he'd been checking his e-mail every few minutes. His spir-
its drifted near rock bottom. They weren't going to make it. Again.
He smelled dead bodies. His mind flashed on scenes from northern Iraq, women and children gassed to death by Saddam Hussein.
He closed his eyes, willing the memories away, praying to God he
wouldn't add more to his morbid collection of mental images today. He felt ill, stomach churning, head pounding.

Derek's phone buzzed. He snatched it up. "Beckwith?"

"Beckwith here," she said. "I'm uploading all these files now.
There are a lot of them."

"Thanks." He clicked off and said, "Pull over."

Jill slipped the car into a spot on Woodward Avenue in front of a restaurant called Union Street Station. Derek already had his tablet computer up and running and was downloading the files.

"How—"

"Satellite link-up," he said. "Okay, here we go. Christ, there are seventy-three of them." He started clicking on the attachments, all scenarios created by the Working Group of the Wayne State University Center for Biological and Chemical Terrorism Research. Click, click, click. One after the other, just as fast as he could.

"What time is it?" he snapped.

"3:59," Jill said, voice hollow.

"Shit. Shit. Shit ... There—"

The file read:

### Wayne State University Center for Biological and Chemical Terrorism Research

*Scenario 27: Multiple Timed Chemical Terrorism Attacks and Emergency Medical Response/Detroit, Michigan*

*Abstract: This document represents a fictional scenario of multiple timed chemical terrorism attacks on the city of Detroit and the emergency, law enforcement, and public health response. This scenario involves multiple sites attacked using sarin gas [See Weapon Analysis, section 2-1] at four-hour intervals in various locations around the city. The initial site is a small restaurant in the New Center Area, the Boulevard Café. It is attacked at precisely 8:00 a.m. [See Site Analysis, section 3-4A]. Exactly four (4) hours later, at 12:00 p.m., a second site is attacked, a classroom at Wayne State University in Scott Hall [See Site Analysis, section 3-4B]. Again, exactly four (4) hours later, at 4:00 p.m., the third and final site is attacked ...*

# 61

*4:00 p.m.*

SCOTT ABRAMS, THE GREEKTOWN casino manager, picked up his
phone. "Yes?"

"Sir, we've got a phone call from the FBI. They...we need to
evacuate, sir. Right now!"

Abrams was a little slower on the uptake than desirable. "Ben?
What's—"

"Right now, Scott! I'm pulling the plug. Right now!"

Abrams noted the urgency—almost panic—in his chief of security's voice. "Do it!" he snapped.

Almost immediately, an alarm sounded. *Man,* thought Abrams.
*Ben must have literally had his hand on the alarm.*

Lisa Mobly pushed through his door without knocking. "What's
going on?"

"I don't know. Ben said the FBI called."

Her face paled. "It's four o'clock."

"So?"

"The Serpent…"

Abrams's eyes went wide. "Let's go. Get everybody out. Everybody!" They raced from his office, yelling for everybody to evacuate immediately. This was not a drill.

Out on the main casino floor, people reluctantly left their money and headed for the doors. Security guards, faces tense, directed people, hurrying them out. Teams of security moved quickly from floor to floor, making sure people were headed for the exits.

Abrams, pushing through the crowd and trying to locate Ben Lewin, heard a cry and spun, fear flooding his senses unlike anything he had ever experienced in his entire life.

# 62

*4:11 p.m.*

JILL PULLED HER CAR to the curb of Monroe Street. A Detroit cop, expression grim, hurried over to her. "You'll need to leave the area," he growled.

Jill flashed her ID. "Where can I put the car?"

The cop squinted at her ID and gestured toward the corner. "Somewhere over there. This is a major clusterfuck."

Jill nodded and did a U-turn, double-parking on Brush Street. The streets of Greektown were mobbed with people, cars, fire trucks, and ambulances. She looked over at Derek. "Can you walk?"

"I'll try."

He opened the door but found that he couldn't put his full weight on his left leg. He shook his head. "No."

"Hang on."

Jill raced off, reappearing a few minutes later with a pair of crutches. Derek raised his eyebrows. "Where the hell did you find these?"

"Ambulance."

"Ah." It took him a moment to get his balance, and once he found that he really only needed one, after a bit of adjustment, he was able to keep up with Jill. They pushed themselves through the crowds, moving from Detroit cop to Detroit cop, getting directions to where Agent Matt Gray was talking into a walkie talkie. He turned when they appeared. He looked at Jill before turning to Derek.

"What happened to you?"

Derek ignored him. "Were we in time?"

Gray cocked his head. "In time for what, Stillwater?"

"Did we warn them in time?"

"That was you, huh?"

"I made the call," Jill said. "We found a scenario— "

"This is all very interesting, Jill," Gray said. "I'm sure we'll need to get everything in writing. But right now I don't want to hear it."

Derek moved past Gray, hobbling with the crutch, but Gray snapped, "Where the hell are you going, Stillwater?"

"Were we in time? *Did we get them out in time? How many died?*" He couldn't keep his anger under control any longer. He moved toward Gray as if to attack, a ludicrous idea, balanced on a single crutch.

Gray smirked. "Go ahead, Stillwater. Try it again. I'll beat you with your own crutch."

Derek grimaced. "You've screwed this up from the beginning, Gray. The second attack should never have taken place."

"Sure. And your involvement's been a big help. Just like the U.S. Immuno debacle. Saved a lot of lives there, didn't you? How's that helicopter pilot? Able to walk yet?"

227

Derek lunged at Gray, who stepped aside and kicked the crutch out from under him. Derek flailed and slammed to the pavement.

"C'mon, Stillwater," Gray said, standing over him. "Get up so I can kick your ass."

"Enough!" Jill jumped between them, helping Derek to his feet.

"Oh, are you on his side, Jill?"

Jill, not looking at her boss, said, "That looked real good, Matt. Turn and smile at the cameras. I bet you'll make the national news for that one."

Gray paled. He didn't turn to look at the TV cameras, which were indeed focused in their direction, but his posture went rigid. His Adam's apple bobbed so hard it looked as if he were trying to swallow a live cat. He held a hand out to Derek. "Hey, no bad feelings. We're even now."

Derek glared at him. "Were we too late? Did we get them out?" His voice was low, harsh, as if squeezed through a tiny hole.

"Yeah," said Gray, suddenly conciliatory for the cameras. "You two were in time, all right. Nobody died here, Stillwater. There was no gas attack. The only people hurt here were three old ladies who wouldn't leave their slot machines and got knocked down by the crowd rushing for the doors."

Jill pressed her hand to her forehead. "Matt..."

Gray shrugged. "I'm sure you two have a good story, but the fact is, there was no gas attack here."

"Is the HMRU here?"

"Sure, Stillwater. They're going over the place inch by inch. I was just talking to Fitzgerald. So far, nothing."

Derek stared at the long, low building. It felt so wrong. *What... what happened? It made sense. The scenario...*

He moved toward the front doors.

"Derek!"

He ignored Jill, heading forward. He was stopped by one of the HMRU agents, who wore a contamination suit, the hood dangling down his back, a radio in his hand.

"Hey, Derek." It was Andrew Calloway, the lanky FBI agent Derek had teamed with at the Boulevard Café. He looked exhausted, face pale, red hair damp, shoulders slumped. "You look like shit. What happened to the leg?"

"No gas?" Derek looked at the casino again.

"Nope," Calloway said. "And I'm glad, man. This has been a rough day. What have you been doing?"

Derek swung back to Calloway. "Chasing down leads. I've been in two explosions set by this guy. He likes to booby-trap things." He described the collection of terrorism scenarios they uncovered.

Calloway scratched his head and sighed. "Derek, I don't know what the fuck to say. Maybe he chickened out. Maybe somebody dumped money into that account. You know, paid the ransom."

"Who?"

Calloway shrugged. "Beats me."

Derek studied the doors. "I'm going in."

"I'll help you with your suit. Come on, we're set up—"

"Screw the suit," Derek said. "I'm going in." He shuffled toward the doors.

# 63

*4:15 p.m.*

Agent Simona Toreanno sat in John Simmons's office. Even though the building and this office had been swept by the bomb squad, she had taken no chances on entering. She had borrowed Dr. Webster's master key and asked him to move down the hallway. Every step of the way, she took whatever precautions she could to make sure she wasn't at the center of an explosion or gas attack.

It seemed damn near anticlimactic when nothing happened. Webster shot her a curious expression, but she did not apologize for her caution. Better safe than in pieces.

He watched her carefully sift through Simmons's office before asking if she still needed him. She assured him she did not and said she would let herself out. He paused for a moment, no doubt wondering if he should leave her alone in the building. Finally he agreed and left.

Silence fell with his departure. It was a little disturbing being alone in the building. It felt empty. And there was still the smell of smoke. She could hear the sounds of the ventilation system, the whir of generators, the whisper of computers. Otherwise, it had the peculiar feel of an abandoned building.

She studied Simmons's office. Prominent on the desk was a photograph of Simmons with another woman, presumably Rebecca Harrington. They were a nice-looking couple. Probably in their forties somewhere, fit, wearing casual clothes, arms around each other, smiling. The background was a sunset over a lake—possibly Lake Michigan, based on the distant horizon. A romantic trip somewhere? She felt a pang for them, for their deaths.

Agent Torcanno wondered if this entire disaster with the Serpent had been sparked by their affair. If William Harrington had snapped and decided to take out hundreds of people along with his ex-wife and her lover. She shivered, thinking of *her* ex-husband. At one time or another, she would gladly have put a bullet in the bastard's head … but not really. He was Bureau too, now working in D.C. His affairs had put an end to their marriage, and her humiliation had almost ended her own career. It probably was true that the spouse was always the last one to know.

But she had worked her way high in this branch of the Bureau. She and Roger Kandling had a friendly competition for promotion, either here or elsewhere. She respected Roger, though he was almost as political as Matt Gray. She was much more cautious in her politics, preferring to do good, hard work and accomplish things, trying to stay on everybody's good side without compromising herself with politics. Maybe she was just an idealist. She preferred to focus on the job, not on personal advancement. Sure, she wanted to succeed and she hoped to work out of D.C. someday, but it wasn't her overall ambition. In her job, the wrong focus could cost lives.

She scanned the office, taking in the details, hoping to get a sense of its occupant. Simmons kept a neat office, clean, not too messy. It looked like a working office. Files were piled neatly on a folding table along one wall. It also held his laser printer, a scanner, and boxes of computer disks. The bookcases were utilitarian, everything aligned and upright; photographs of a number of people, many who looked like graduate students, decorated the walls and the bookcases. Simmons, she thought, had been a people person.

She reached over and picked up one photograph. It was of ten people sitting at tables in what she recognized as ground zero of the Boulevard Café. There were varying expressions on their faces, but they all seemed to be in a good mood, enjoying each other's company. There was William Harrington, sitting across from Rebecca Harrington. Simmons next to Rebecca—friends, maybe not yet lovers. A tall, goofy-looking guy she identified as Brad Beales, the linguist.

She put the photo carefully back where it was, feeling her mood sink. So much destruction and death. Such a waste.

Toreanno checked her watch and quickly made a phone call to headquarters, asking for an update. She was told that everybody was at the Greektown Casino, that Church and Stillwater might have gotten a step ahead of the Serpent. So far, no additional deaths.

She booted up the computer, found it didn't prompt for a password, and began to sift through Simmons's documents. She found the same scenarios that Derek Stillwater had been hunting. Patiently, methodically working her way through them, she came up with Scenario 27 and read it through. *Good job, Stillwater,* she thought, reading. *Nice work, Jill. Several hundred gamblers owe you their lives.*

She printed it out and decided she needed to just take the computer with her. This was serious evidence that was going to be useful in court if they ever caught the Serpent.

Before she shut down, she printed out Simmons's contact list, then cross-referenced it with the authors' names on Scenario 27. The CBCTR's Working Group appeared to have ten names, though quickly scanning through a few of the other scenarios indicated that the Working Group changed periodically. Some of the names were graduate students in various departments. Others were faculty members from different departments. Every scenario she checked had both Harrington's and Simmons's names on them, probably because they were the director and assistant director of the CBCTR.

Frowning, she took out her notebook, clicked on Scenario 1, and checked the names. She started a list of all the Working Group members. There always seemed to be ten. She saw that Agent Frank McMillan was cited as a consultant for the FBI. In addition, there were names for contacts with the Detroit Police Department, the Detroit Fire Department, the Michigan State Police, the Michigan Department of Public Health, and various emergency medical services and security firms. But those weren't actually part of the Working Group. They were people who consulted with the Working Group, who presumably answered questions and provided information on how their organization would behave under different situations.

She felt a sense of loss at Frank's death. They had been more than friends … maybe. Could have been, anyway. The saddest words on the planet: "could have been."

*We'll get him, Frank. Count on it. I promise.*

Brushing away a tear, Toreanno started a list of all the people involved in the Working Group, cross-checking them with each scenario. These people were going to help nail the Serpent. She was sure of it. They would be able to help throw a noose around William Harrington. It was only a matter of time.

# 64

*4:16 p.m.*

As DEREK MOVED PAST Calloway, the FBI agent kicked the crutch out from under him. With a curse, Derek stumbled to the ground.

Calloway leaned over him. "Derek, stick it up your ass. I'm not letting you in there without a suit. And I doubt you could beat me in a fight without the crutches, so don't even think about trying all lamed up."

Derek glared at him, then abruptly burst out laughing. "Dammit, Andy. Help me up, then."

Calloway shook his head. "Promise me, no screwing around. By the book in there. If this guy's a booby-trap kind of guy, he might be happier trying to knock off the agents and firefighters who go in after the so-called false alarm instead of the gamblers. You know the kind."

"I promise."

"By the book, Derek."

"I said I promise."

Calloway helped Derek to his feet, returned his crutch, and led him over to the tent that had been set up off to one side of the entrance. There was an FBI agent and two Detroit cops guarding it, demanding ID.

"My suit's back around the corner," said Derek.

"Sure," Calloway said with a grin. "How about I just run on over there and get it and leave you here to twiddle your thumbs. And you promise to stay put?"

Derek grinned back at him. "Not buying that, huh?"

"We've got spares, as you know. Come on, Derek. Don't be such a cowboy. You helped write these regs. Try following them from time to time."

"Rules are meant to be broken," Derek said, following Calloway into the tent. "That's why I'm so involved in writing them."

"I bet."

Calloway helped him into a suit and checked that all the seams were sealed. He handed Derek back the crutch. "Z is in charge in there. I replace Fanconi when he comes out."

"Make sure nobody gets in here without authorization," Derek said. "You know what happened to McMillan."

Calloway nodded. "I know. Take care."

Slowly, even more awkwardly than usual, Derek hobbled in the space suit through the doors of the casino. It was large and open, more ornate than he expected, with a kind of quasi-Mediterranean theme going. Greek, he supposed, or at least, the kind of Greek you create in a casino for people who have never been to Greece.

As he moved through the casino, looking for other space-suited figures, he noted the peculiarity of it all. The bright neon of the electronic games, cups of coins and tokens still sitting on the screens. They beeped and burped and whirred, waiting to be fed more money. Someone in a white suit moved toward him. When he got close, Derek saw it was Mitch Fanconi, the agent who Calloway would replace. Fanconi approached him. Through his faceplate, Derek saw a sweaty, dark-skinned face and dark eyes. Fanconi said, "That you, Derek?"

"It's me."

"Missed you at Scott Hall. Could've used the extra body."

"Off chasing leads."

"Lucky you. I hear you're behind the call here?"

"Yes. Anything?"

Fanconi shook his head. "I don't know whether to be thankful or not. Was this a solid lead?"

"Very."

"Good. Gray probably won't think so. He's got it in for you. Any special reason?"

"Now, yes. Before Scott Hall, no. Doesn't like outsiders, I guess."

Fanconi laughed. "You're not an outsider to us, and you know it. You can cover my back anytime. You need help with Gray or those upcoming hearings, you just call me."

"Thanks. Where is everybody?"

"Zoelig suited up the casino's head of security. He's taking Z through all the hiding places for security—you know, the eye-in-the-sky shit."

"Big Brother's watching," Derek said.

"Got that right. Talk to you on the flip side." Fanconi patted him on the shoulder and moved on.

Derek trudged forward, running into Zoelig and the security guy in what he assumed was the poker room, based on the poker tables and the cards and chips scattered across the green felt. The security guy looked one step from a nervous breakdown. Derek wasn't surprised. The space suits were claustrophobic as hell. Newbies always had problems before they adjusted. Sometimes people couldn't adjust. And sometimes people who worked in hot zones developed claustrophobia and had to quit.

Derek had never had problems with claustrophobia. Fear of death. Fear of his suit springing a leak. Fear of cutting his suit. Fear of opening his suit at the wrong time. Fear of screwing up in a hundred different ways, yes. But fear of being inside the suit, never.

Zoelig shifted awkwardly. "Derek?"

"Yeah. That's me. Any luck?"

"No. Hear you called this in."

"Guilty."

"What's your lead?"

"I want to know that too," said the security chief. He was a doughy-looking guy, bald, his round face pale and slick with sweat through his suit's faceplate. "But I want to get the fuck out of this suit first."

"Straight out and to the left," Zoelig said. "They'll wash you down first before you can get out of the suit. That's important."

"Yeah, sure." The security director shuffled away.

Zoelig turned to him. "Tell me."

The two men stood side by side, faceplates touching. Derek shouted to be heard over the fan and explained.

Zoelig nodded. "Good call. Very good call, Derek. Gray's going to freak if we don't find anything, though."

"Not really, he won't," Derek said. "He can blame it all on me. He's been setting me up that way all day."

Zoelig shrugged. "You noticed that, did you?"

"I'm the perfect sacrificial lamb, Z. If everything goes to hell, it's not the SAC's fault, it's that damn troubleshooter from DHS. *He* screwed things up."

"Yeah. You been covering your ass, then?"

Derek laughed.

Zoelig snorted. "Figures. When will you learn?"

"Never, probably. Let's go see if we can find something that might go boom or hiss around here."

"Haven't checked the restaurant yet."

"Let's go, then."

# 65

*4:17 p.m.*

MATT GRAY WATCHED STILLWATER walk away before turning to Jill. She didn't like the look on his face at all.

"So," Gray said, voice low. "This is your idea of following orders?"

Jill leveled her gaze at him. "Meaning what, Matt?"

Gray glanced around to make sure nobody was close enough to hear them. "Your *job*," he hissed, "was to contain him. I made that perfectly clear to you. We didn't want him running around loose, causing trouble."

"From my perspective," she said, "he's been following the leads that you didn't think were important enough to put manpower on. And he's been doing a very good, though unorthodox job. And these were real leads."

"Bullshit, Jill! *Nothing* happened here!"

"That doesn't change the fact that we found written documentation with a terrorism expert's name on it outlining exactly what we've seen here today. Or, for that matter, that this person Stillwater and I have been chasing practically signs his name at the crime scenes and booby-traps the places we might hunt for him."

"And when he assaulted me? Your job was to bring him in for that assault. Do you have problems with following orders, Agent Church?"

From Jill to Agent Church. She narrowed her eyes. "No, I don't."

"Then why haven't you been following them?"

"Matt, you're way off base on this—"

"Agent Church," Gray said, taking a step closer to her. "Did I or did I not give you a direct order to keep him in the dark and keep him out of the way?"

*Exact words*, she thought. "Yes, that was what you said."

"And did you?"

"I evaluated Agent Stillwater's suggestions, decided they had merit, and pursued them, while keeping Agent Stillwater with me so I could, quote, 'keep him out of the way,' unquote. I did my job, Matt. This guy's an expert on biological and chemical warfare and terrorism. He was in Tokyo after the Aum Shinrikyo attacks. Believe it or not, he does know what he's doing."

"Did I or did I not give you a direct order to arrest him for assault after his attack on me?"

She didn't respond.

"I can't hear you." Gray's expression was ugly.

"Yes," she said through clenched teeth.

"Yes, what, Agent Church?"

"Yes. You ordered me to get Agent Stillwater, bring him back in handcuffs, and arrest him for assaulting a federal agent. You implied, and perhaps ordered me directly, to deliver him to a holding cell at the Federal Building until today's events were completed."

"And did you?"

She raised her chin. For a fleeting moment, she wondered what she, a single parent, would do if she lost her job. An equally unsettling thought flitted through her mind: *Am I doing this because it's right, or am I doing it for whatever I might feel for Derek Stillwater?* She promptly quashed both thoughts. "I did not. I did not deem it necessary. As a matter of fact, Matt, I decided that arresting Derek Stillwater would be counterproductive in our efforts to stop the Serpent from killing more people."

"Instead," he said, "you returned with him here, uncuffed, supplied him with crutches, and allowed him to wander into a potential crime scene unescorted."

Again, she didn't respond.

*"Am I correct, Agent Church?"*

She nodded. "Yes. Those are the facts without interpretation or context."

A sneer crossed Gray's face. "And," he said, "I would like to know if you had a warrant when you entered the home of Rebecca Harrington?"

She tensed. "No, I did not. But—"

"But?"

"I was acting on a tip."

"Who supplied this tip?"

She hesitated. "Agent Derek Stillwater."

"To your knowledge, did Agent Stillwater have a warrant when he entered Rebecca Harrington's house?"

"No. To the best of my knowledge, he did not."

Gray stared at her.

In a soft, menacing voice, Gray said, "Did Stillwater have a warrant to enter William Harrington's office at the University Health Center?"

"No."

"How about for William Harrington's house?"

Jill shook her head.

Gray nodded. He waved over Roger Kandling, who was talking to Mary Linzey. He approached. "Yes, sir?"

"Agent Kandling," Gray said, "I have relieved Agent Church of active duty. She is on indefinite suspension without pay pending a review. You have witnessed this."

Kandling nodded. "Yes, sir."

Gray turned back to Jill. "Agent Church, you are to return to the Federal Building, type up your statements, and leave them with Janice to give to me. I will schedule you for a hearing and inform you of the conditions of your suspension."

"Are you crazy? You—"

"Agent Kandling," Gray said, "please escort Agent Church from the vicinity. If she resists, cuff her and place her under arrest. Do you understand?"

Kandling's expression was unreadable. "Yes, sir."

Jill looked at the two men, then spun on her heel and walked away.

# 66

*4:27 p.m.*

MARY LINZEY WATCHED THE entire exchange between the woman FBI agent, Matt Gray, and Roger Kandling. She had also seen the altercation between Matt Gray and the DHS agent, which was why she'd been questioning Kandling. Kandling hadn't been willing to be taped, but he had been very willing to give her information as an "informed source." When the female agent moved away, Kandling conferred momentarily with Gray before walking away.

She hurried after him. "Agent Kandling?"

He turned to her, a small, tight smile on his face. "Yes, Ms. Linzey?"

"Who was that agent, the woman back there?"

Kandling studied her. "Special Agent Jillian Church."

"She and SAC Gray seemed to be arguing."

He waited, not responding.

"Were they?" she asked.

"Agent Church has been suspended indefinitely."

"Why?"

"Insubordination," Kandling said. He paused. "Colluding with a possible suspect. Improper procedures."

"Colluding with a possible suspect?" Linzey had her tape recorder clutched in her hand. "And who is the possible suspect?"

Kandling frowned, shifting his weight from foot to foot. "Turn off the recorder, please."

Linzey clicked it off. "What?"

"Agent Church has been working closely with Agent Derek Stillwater. But there have been definite procedural breaches—even laws broken—by both of them today. It is for these that Agent Church has been suspended."

Mary Linzey clicked her tape recorder back on, wishing this were on camera. "Is Derek Stillwater a suspect?"

Kandling said, "Agent Derek Stillwater, with the Department of Homeland Security, has been conducting an investigation independently of the Bureau. Some of Agent Stillwater's actions are questionable at the very least, and may even be illegal. It is under investigation, as is Agent Stillwater, for events today and from the events of last month in Washington, D.C."

"Is Agent Church also being investigated?"

Kandling said, "Special Agent Jillian Church has been working closely with DHS Agent Derek Stillwater today, and both of them are believed to have conducted themselves in a manner not approved by the Federal Bureau of Investigation, the Justice Department, or the Department of Homeland Security. They are both being investigated for their unprofessional conduct today."

He turned to walk away, but Linzey said, "One more question."

Kandling nodded.

"Isn't it true that Agent Stillwater and Agent Church are the people who called the alarm here at the Greektown Casino?"

"Yes. They did."

"Is it a false alarm?"

"It appears to be a false alarm," Kandling said. "And Agents Stillwater and Church will be investigated for this as well. Their behavior seems self-aggrandizing at the very least. It is possible they are trying to glamorize themselves at this time of crisis."

She thrust the tape recorder toward him again. "So in the future, if they do something similar?"

Kandling hesitated. "Agents Church and Stillwater are no longer with the investigation into the Serpent and the sarin gas killings in any official capacity. Any statements either agent should make to the media or any other members of law enforcement should be verified with the proper authorities and treated with *the highest level of skepticism*." With a curt nod, Kandling turned and slipped into the crowd.

# 67

*4:42 p.m.*

DEREK EXITED THE CASINO, sluiced off under the HMRU's make-shift shower, and slipped back into his street clothes, thinking that he needed a real shower, food, and some rest. He was sticky with sweat and felt sure he reeked.

The crowd had thinned while he wasted time inside, and dusk was falling, turning the gray day even gloomier. He hadn't found anything, and the size of the place was causing problems in their search. And because it was a casino, there were a lot of areas only accessible by employees that required keyed and coded entrance. It was taking forever to search because they needed casino security's help, and those people weren't trained for working in the suits.

Derek had decided he was wasting his time and left it up to the Detroit Fire Department's hazmat team and the HMRU to figure out what was going on in there.

He looked around for Jill and didn't see her. He had no desire to talk to Matt Gray again. Or ever, for that matter. He decided to find Jill's car and check his e-mail and get a hold of General Johnston.

When he finally hobbled around the corner to where Jill had left her car, he found her pacing back and forth on the sidewalk, everything about her expression and body language indicating anger.

"What's wrong?" he asked.

"I got sacked."

"What?"

"Matt benched me. I'm suspended without pay." She continued pacing, expression fierce. "Dammit, Stillwater. This could have been avoided."

"Let's go talk to him," Derek said. "This isn't a good time to thin his people."

Jill turned on him. "Oh, bullshit! *You're* half the problem. I never should have gone along with this. Look, Stillwater, I could deal with the so-called insubordination issues. Matt threw that in because I was supposed to contain you, then after you punched him out I was supposed to arrest you. It's all bullshit, and he knows it. He can't get me on the containment issue, because it's a crock. You were doing your job, and even the attorney general would agree there's no cause for locking you out, at least not when you first got here. That's an internal issue that's out of our hands. As for arresting you for beating on Matt, he's crazy if he thinks that sending one of three witnesses who saw you punch him to arrest you makes procedural sense. But he's got me cold on the illegal search and seizure."

Derek sighed. "Look, I'm sorry. I just do what I think needs to be done."

"Give it a rest, Stillwater."

He leaned on the crutch and closed his eyes for a moment. "Derek," he said.

"Don't get all sentimental on me."

"Gee, just when I was starting to feel all warm and fuzzy about our relationship. What's next, Church?"

"I don't know."

"Are you going home?"

"I'm supposed to go back to the office, type up my reports, and report back tomorrow for details."

Derek stepped closer. "I need your help."

"That's why I'm in this situation, Stillwater! Didn't you hear me? I'm out. Benched. Sacked. Sidelined. Persona non grata. I'm a civilian now."

"Good. Now you can help me without answering to Gray. I can really use your help. I don't know the area, and I can't really drive with my leg all screwed up like this."

She stared at him. "You're unbelievable, you know that? You push me into the deep end, then toss me a cement block! What, you want me to lose my job for good? I'm a single parent! I can't afford to lose this job."

Derek said nothing for a moment. Quietly, "If it comes to that, I'll put in a word with General Johnston."

"The answer is no!" she snapped.

"Okay," Derek said with a shrug. "I'll get my gear. I'll get a cab or something."

He limped over to the trunk of her car. They both turned as someone shouted, "There's a body in the parking garage!" The crowd seemed to move like an animal, taking on its own life, shifting toward the new catastrophe. The media were like the animal's teeth, leading the way, charging for the parking garage.

Derek said, "You mind hanging around for a while until I check this out? Then I'll get my gear."

"I'm coming with you." She clenched her jaw in a determined expression.

Derek studied her. "You sure?"

She hesitated. "Yes. I'm sure."

They looked into each other's eyes.

"Okay," Derek said. "Good."

# 68

*4:55 p.m.*

IT WAS ON THE top floor of the parking garage a block from the Greektown Casino. The vehicle was a green and tan Subaru Outback. It was parked behind a pillar, in shadow.

Derek and Jill pushed their way through the onlookers, flashing their identification, ignoring the shouts of the media until they were standing next to Matt Gray and Walter Zoelig. Zoelig, still in his biological hazardous-materials suit, wet from being washed off, looked at Derek. "Puts a different spin on things, doesn't it?"

Derek peered into the vehicle. Behind the wheel of the Outback was a man he recognized as William Harrington. His face was pulled back in a rictus of horror, clearly dead. In the rear of the Outback were what appeared to be several gray metal canisters, almost the size of scuba tanks. Derek studied them through the window. "Those look like the canisters you mix soda in," he said.

"What the hell are you talking about?" Gray said. "I don't want you anywhere around here, Stillwater. This is an FBI operation.

251

You're not FBI. Get lost. Go. I'm telling everybody concerned to keep you away."

Gray turned on Jill. "And you've been suspended. Get out of here."

In a mild, friendly voice, Derek said, "Kiss my ass, Gray."

Gray's face turned plum. "You—"

Zoelig interrupted. "In restaurants, in vending machines for pop, the syrup comes in one canister and gets mixed with the carbonated water in the other. Haven't you ever had your Coke taste bad because the mix was off?"

"I'm dealing with a problem here, Zoelig!"

"Yeah," Zoelig said. "I see that. Try focusing on the real problem. A car filled with sarin gas. Derek's an irritation, not a problem."

"You're saying—"

"Looks like something sprung a leak in the car," Derek said.

Gray glared at him. "What?"

Derek ignored him, moving back to study William Harrington. Definitely dead.

Zoelig said, "There's a dolly cart in there too. The canisters are probably filled with sarin. He probably had plans to waltz into the restaurant, replace the containers—hell, even just put them in the storage area—and leave. Maybe there's a timer on them. Only when he got here, maybe there was a bump or a regulator busted, but whatever happened, this guy, the Serpent, died from it. We'll check it out—Andy's getting our stuff." He gestured toward the body in the car. "He's our boy, isn't he, Derek?"

Derek nodded.

Gray spun on him. "Out! You, out of here." He turned to Jill. "And you've had your orders. Try following them for a change."

Zoelig said, "Derek stays."

Gray whirled on him. "What are you ... you don't have the authority to countermand my orders!"

Zoelig smiled lopsidedly. "Actually, I do. The only person here who knows more about this shit than me is him. And I'm in charge of hazardous-materials removal and examination. If Derek wants to stay and supervise, that's up to him."

Derek shook his head. "You're fine. I'll be in touch." With a nod to Gray, he shuffled away. Jill, eyebrows arched, followed him in silence.

# 69

*5:00 p.m.*

AFTER STILLWATER AND CHURCH left, Matt Gray checked his watch.
The local news cycle started at five. If he made a statement now, it
would make it on both the five o'clock and six o'clock broadcasts.
He clicked on his radio and called the office, reading off the license
plate of the Subaru and asking for a DMV verification. Feeling en-
ergized, Gray said to Zoelig, "How soon can you get at the body?"

Zoelig sighed. "In a few minutes. Why?"

"I want to verify this guy's ID."

"Derek gave us a visual identification."

Gray sneered. "If Stillwater told me the sky was blue, I'd want
verification."

"In a few minutes, Matt. I take it you're planning a press conference?"

"Yes." Gray turned, looking for Roger Kandling, wanting him
to organize the conference in the next few minutes.

"Matt," Zoelig said, voice soft.

Gray turned. Zoelig waved him closer. Gray approached, impatient. In a low voice, so bystanders couldn't hear, Zoelig said, "Do you think a press conference is premature?"

"You're a technician, Zoelig. Stick to your area of expertise."

Zoelig glowered at him. "Gray, don't make me drop-kick you off the top of this parking structure. I'm not a technician. Are you planning on announcing that this guy is the Serpent? That the Serpent died by his own hand by accident?"

"Wait and see, Zoelig," Gray said. "Wait and see." He moved away, then turned back to Zoelig. "Oh, and Zoelig? Don't threaten me again, or you'll find yourself working anti-terror in South Dakota."

Zoelig didn't blink. "Give it your best shot, Gray."

Gray, finding his threat to be hollow, turned and strode away. He found Kandling and told him to organize a press conference in front of the casino in ten minutes. Kandling said, "Who's running it?"

"Me."

Kandling looked relieved. "Sure. Ten minutes."

And ten minutes later, Matt Gray stood in front of the doors to the Greektown Casino, the media spread out in front of him, cameras and microphones ready.

"I am Matthew Gray, special agent in charge of the Detroit Field Office of the Federal Bureau of Investigation. Here is the official statement." He cleared his throat and scanned the crowd, looking right into the cameras, lingering for a moment at the CNN, Fox, and ABC cameras, making sure he looked authoritative. "The individual calling himself the Serpent, who committed two acts of chemical terrorism in Detroit today, has died by his own hand, apparently by accident. The Serpent has been positively identified as Dr. William Harrington, the director of the Wayne State University

Center for Biological and Chemical Terrorism Research, professor of biochemistry, and adjunct professor, Department of Public Health. Harrington's body was found in his vehicle on the top level of the Greektown Casino parking garage with several canisters of sarin gas in the rear cargo area. Apparently at least one of the canisters leaked, killing Harrington before he could mount his attack on the Greektown Casino."

A reporter interrupted. "What was his motive?"

Gray said, "We'll probably never know his real motive, but it's quite possibly linked to his divorce. His ex-wife, Rebecca Harrington, an employee of the Barbara Ann Karmanos Cancer Institute, was found murdered in her Ferndale home earlier today. Rebecca Harrington's lover, and the cause of their divorce, was the assistant director of the Center for Biological and Chemical Terrorism Research, Dr. John Simmons, who died this morning during the attack at the Boulevard Café."

"You're saying this was all caused by some sort of sick love triangle?" a reporter called out.

Gray nodded. "Those elements are definitely there. Clearly, Harrington must have been suffering from some level of mental illness—"

"You mean he was crazy?"

Gray felt like he was losing control of the press conference. "'Crazy' is a legal term," he said, "not a psychological one. But yes, don't you think a mass murderer could be defined as crazy?"

Another reporter shouted, "What of your previous statements about Derek Stillwater?"

Gray paused. "Although we no longer feel that Dr. Stillwater was involved with the attack, we believe that his conduct today was unprofessional and quite possibly illegal. He is currently under investigation by the Justice Department pending a congressional hearing concerning his conduct last month for the events at U.S. Immunological Research, in Baltimore. I intend to conduct a personal investigation into his actions today as well. It is my recommendation to the attorney general and to the Department of Homeland Security that Dr. Stillwater be asked to resign."

The reporters clamored for more, shouting to be heard. Gray smiled and pointed to Steve Shay. "Yes?"

"What of reports ..."

And so it went.

# 70

*5:10 p.m.*

JILL CLICKED OFF THE car radio. She and Derek had been listening to the press conference in the car as they drove north. "*No comment,* Matt," she said to the radio. "You could have said, 'No comment.'" She tapped Derek's arm. "Doesn't that piss you off?"

Derek shrugged. He had been unusually quiet and thoughtful after they left the parking garage.

"Come on, Stillwater—"

"Derek."

"Fine. Derek. Doesn't that piss you off? I mean, really? He's trashing your reputation. Smearing you all over the media. It's uncalled for. It's unprofessional."

Derek shrugged again.

"Earth to Stillwater. Hello?"

"I'm really hungry," he said. "And I could use some caffeine. Is there a decent restaurant around here?"

"How about the Motor City Grill?"

"Whatever."

She found a parking spot behind the Fisher Building, and they entered the Motor City Grill, passed the fish tanks, and were seated by a window looking across Second Street toward the New Center One Building.

"So," Jill said, as they looked at the menus. "The Serpent killed himself."

"Mmm," Derek said.

Jill put her menu down. "Stillwater?"

The waitress appeared and took their drink orders. They both wanted coffee.

"How's their Caesar salad here?" he asked Jill.

"It's fine. What do you think about the Serpent killing himself?"

"Interesting."

Exasperated, Jill pulled the menu down so she could look at Derek. "You haven't kept your opinions to yourself all day. Now you're keeping your mouth shut. Come on, Still— Derek. What do you think?"

He leaned forward and planted his elbows on the table. "What do *you* think?"

"I think Matt's statement was premature."

"Me too."

"Why?"

"You first."

"Okay," Jill said. "They should have run everything at the garage before they made that statement. They still need to thoroughly search the casino. They need to make some sort of physical evidentiary link between Harrington, his house, his office, the car, the

Boulevard Café, Scott Hall, Rebecca Harrington's house…" She trailed off.

"And?"

Jill frowned. "And intuition."

Derek launched a cockeyed grin. "And your intuition says what?"

"It's too easy."

Derek nodded. The waitress reappeared with their coffee and took their orders. Derek stuck with a tried-and-true chicken sandwich and a salad. Jill ordered the Caesar salad he'd put in her mind. When the waitress left, Jill said, "What about you?"

"I think it's very convenient. And very careless."

"So you think…"

"I think we've been manipulated every single step of the way today, and this strikes me as being too good to be true."

Jill sighed. "So now what?"

"Well, you're unofficial. And you could get into a lot of trouble, Jill. I don't really want to jeopardize your livelihood more than I already have."

"Oh, so *now* you're concerned about my career."

Derek shrugged.

Jill considered. She leaned toward Derek. "Here's the deal, Derek. I'll help you. I'll go out on a limb and help you dig and see if we can satisfy ourselves as to what's really going on and what happened in the parking garage. But first, you have to come clean on a couple things for me."

Derek toyed with his fork. He nodded.

"Irina Khournikova," Jill said.

Derek leaned back in their booth. "You don't have a high enough security clearance for that."

"And I suppose you'll have to kill me if you tell me."

Derek toyed with his fork some more, not meeting her gaze. Finally he said, "You know better."

Jill blinked. "Fine. When we're done eating, I'll drop you off somewhere."

Derek shrugged. "Let me think. I can probably tell you some of it."

Jill cocked her head. "Is this for real, Derek? Or are you feeding me a line of bullshit?"

"Not everything that happened last month has gone public. You know that. That hearing that Matt Gray keeps bringing up, the congressional one, that's a closed-door hearing. The reason we've dropped out of the media is because there are a lot of confidential, top-secret aspects to the case. Think about it and you know it's true."

She did and she said so.

Derek nodded, as if to himself. "The real Khournikova is an agent with the Russian FSB, the *Federal'naya Sluzhba Bezopasnosti*, or the Federal Security Service. She's a Russian anti-terrorism expert."

It took Jill a second to process that. After a long silence, broken only by the tinkle of silverware and the music playing overhead, she said, "They say you killed her by suffocating her to death."

"They are very wrong," he said. "Irina Khournikova, last I heard, was back in Moscow. She may be in Mexico, though, because she's dedicated herself to hunting down the Fallen."

"The terrorist behind last month's attack at U.S. Immuno."

Derek nodded.

"But what about the woman you ..."

"She was impersonating Irina Khournikova. She was the Fallen's lover. I killed her, yes. It was accidental." Something blurred his face for a moment, a complexity of emotions. "What do you call an interrogation that accidentally results in death, Jill?" Before she could respond, he said, "They call it an assassination. She knew the location of her group's headquarters, she knew where they had taken the biological agent they stole, and she knew what they were going to do with it and when. I didn't have time to take her to headquarters and dick around waiting for the paperwork to go through. I needed to know what she knew, and I needed to know it right there. But she accidentally died before I could get that information from her."

Jill saw the pain on his face as he recounted that story. She said, "I'm sorry. And Matt mentioned something about a helicopter pilot."

She watched as Derek put a studied, neutral expression on his face. Slowly, he said, "I was working with a Coast Guard helicopter crew. I commandeered them, actually. They were shot down by the Fallen. The only survivor was the pilot, but she's in pretty bad shape. Broken back, broken pelvis, legs, burns. She's alive, but her recovery's been tough. She's not walking yet. Maybe never will."

"That doesn't seem like it's your fault."

He shrugged. "A lot of people think it is, though. Like your boss."

Jill sat back. "Okay, Derek. I guess that's enough for now."

Derek frowned. "These cases—like today—they get hairy. And I usually work alone. Sometimes, like with Cindy, and the fake Irina, people around me get hurt." He looked her in the eye. "And killed. It can be dangerous working with me, Jill. And you're not official anymore. So think about that before you agree to pursue this with me. Think about it hard. You've got a son to take care of."

She nodded. Again she thought, *Are you doing this because it's right, or because you think you have feelings about Derek?* She didn't have an answer. "I have. I have thought about it. What's next?"

Derek smiled. "After we eat, I want to check out William Harrington's body. You know where the morgue is?"

# 71

*5:20 p.m.*

MICHAEL CHURCH AND RAY Moretti crashed out in Ray's bedroom, door closed, playing Star Wars Battlefront on Ray's PlayStation 3. Michael was getting creamed. Generally he and Ray ran neck-and-neck with video games, though Ray had a slight advantage because he played more than his friend did. But today Michael's concentration was a mess. He couldn't keep his mind off the dead body he'd seen, what he'd learned about his dad, and everything else that was going on, including the feeling that something had happened between him and Ray's sister, Ann. Some connection, or something. He *really* couldn't keep his mind off *her*.

Ray crowed as his stormtrooper took out an enemy outpost with a grenade. "Take that, rebel scum!"

Michael rolled his eyes. Ray was wired. Wired even more than usual. He wondered if Ray had popped something—ecstasy or, more likely, speed. He didn't know if Ray was into stuff stronger than pot, though it wouldn't surprise him. He sensed he and Ray were coming up on some sort of crossroads. He felt like maybe there were choices he had to make. Choices like: be like Ray and get high and spend all your time chasing girls and playing video games, or think about your life and get serious about doing things, getting things done, like Ann and her plans for college and medical school. It was coming, though he really only sensed it. He couldn't identify it or verbalize it. Just a sense that more was being demanded of him and it was up to him to make those choices.

Maybe it was the concert tonight that had Ray so manic. Michael felt uneasy about that. His mom had definitely not given him permission. He knew that what he should do is just pass, say, "No, man, Mom said no, I'm going to go home." Go home, work out, do his homework, watch some TV.

"When're your parents getting home?" Michael asked.

Ray shrugged. "We'll be gone before they get here. You know, Mom won't be home till six, six-thirty, and Dad, who knows. He works all the time."

If there was any bitterness in that, Michael couldn't hear it, though he wasn't really listening for it, either.

"They're cool about us going to the concert, huh?"

"They don't give a shit," Ray said, shifting the game to another planet.

"I don't know if I should go." He threw it out there tentatively, trying to convince himself, seeing what Ray's reaction would be.

Ray froze, then jerked toward him. "Hey! What the fuck are you talking about?"

"My mom, you know, she, like, you know, she didn't want me to go, and all this shit today..."

"No fuckin' way! Pussy! Don't back out on me here. This is going to be fuckin' great! J Slim! And shit, I got those IDs I was telling you about."

*"What?"*

"I showed you, didn't I?"

Michael shook his head.

"Oh, man," Ray said. "That's right. I got them this afternoon. You remember the picture I took, right?"

Michael shook his head again. Ray was always fooling around with his digital camera, though he used it mostly to snap shots of girls' asses and tits.

Ray jumped up and scrounged through his backpack, coming up with two Michigan driver's licenses. He tossed one to Michael. It looked like an official driver's license. And there was his photograph. But his birth date had been changed, making him twenty-one years old.

He didn't know what to say.

"Isn't that the bomb, dude? We can get drinks, no problem. Hell, we can go anywhere. There's got to be a topless place around somewhere. Or maybe later we can head over to Windsor, you know…"

If anything, Michael felt even more uneasy than before. Going to the concert would get his mom all worked up, no doubt about it. He didn't expect her home tonight, though he was mildly surprised he hadn't heard from her yet. Usually she was real good about calling him if she was going to be late. And that made him worry for her a little bit. Just a tiny bit of fear, because he knew that this Serpent guy was a scary dude. Anybody who could murder somebody by taping their mouth and nose shut was evil.

If his mom didn't come home and he went to the concert and she found out, she'd be pissed. But if she found out they had used fake IDs, well…

"I don't know, Ray."

"Hey, I paid good money for these. Just stick it in your wallet and shut up."

"I—"

Michael's phone chirped. He just about jumped out of his skin. He yanked it off his belt, noted that the call was from his mom, and held the phone to his ear.

"Michael, it's Mom."

"You okay?" It was the first thing that came to his lips. Not, "Yeah," or "Hey," or "Hi." But, "You okay?"

"Yes, I'm fine. I'm sorry, Michael, but I'm still working this case. I don't know when I'll be home tonight. There's hamburger in the freezer, or, you know, spaghetti. You can fix—"

"I'm eating with Ray."

"Oh. Okay."

"Mom, what's going on? I mean, with the Serpent? Do you know who he is? Was there another attack?"

"There was something planned at the Greektown Casino, but the … Michael, I really can't talk about this now."

"Mom!"

"Michael, I'm on a cell phone!"

"But you told me—"

"Michael, you can't talk about this. All right? Dr. Stillwater and I are still working on this. I want you to be … look, Michael. If you watch the TV news or the radio, you're going to hear some things about—"

"What things?" Michael sat bolt upright, alarm radiating throughout his body.

"Just some things. Things about me and about Dr. Stillwater and some things about the Serpent. Don't believe them. Okay? They're not true. But we're still working this case. Just don't tell anybody we're still working this case."

"I don't—"

"You'll be all right? I'll call you later. I've got to go now, Michael. I love you."

"Mom—"

She clicked off. Michael stared at the phone, unbelieving. He lurched forward and popped off the video game and turned the TV to channel 7 to catch the news. That dopey guy, Steve Shay, was doing a report at the Greektown Casino. "… and the special agent in charge, Matthew Gray, says an FBI agent, Jillian Church, has been suspended pending an investigation into allegations of inappropriate conduct—"

The picture jumped to Gray's statement. Michael scowled. He hated Gray. His mom had some sort of thing going with him at one time or another—something, he didn't know exactly what. Not like they were dating or anything, but something. He didn't know if they'd screwed or what, and he didn't think of his mom like that, found it hard to believe. He knew there had been some time when she had been kind of gushy about the guy: "Matt says this" and "Matt did that," like she was hot for the guy, like he was the king turd of shit mountain. Then something happened and she got real tense at work and at home and she never talked about Matt anymore. And now the guy was dissing her on TV, and saying the same thing about Stillwater.

"Fuck, dude," Ray said. "That sucks."

"Shut up."

"Oh, defending your mommy?"

"Shut the fuck up. Asshole."

"Hey, chill. You know your mom's cool."

Michael gritted his teeth. Yeah, she was, but she wasn't telling him what was going on. He felt so confused. His thoughts were like a school of fish that twisted and turned just out of reach. Like trying to catch smoke with your hands.

"Hey," Ray said. "You want to go test out these IDs? We'll go to Hoops before the concert. They should be open. We can have a couple beers with dinner. What ya think?"

Michael felt a wave of anger wash over him. Why wouldn't she treat him like an adult? Why was she always locking him out? Dammit! He nodded his head. "Yeah. Fine. Let's do that. Let's go."

# 72

*5:40 p.m.*

THE MEDICAL EXAMINER'S OFFICE wasn't far from Wayne State University, at 1300 East Warren Avenue. A receptionist met Derek and Jill at the front desk and called an ME's investigator to come talk to them. The investigator was a short, balding black man in his fifties wearing gray slacks, a blue knit shirt, and a worn blue sport coat. His name was Jerry Ford. "No relation," he growled. He studied their IDs and said, "There's already an FBI agent in there."

Jill swallowed. "Who's that?"

"Woman. Toreanno."

She brightened. "That's fine."

"Follow me, then."

They threaded their way down to the autopsy room. There was an isolation room separated from the main autopsy area, and Ford took them to an observation center with a wall of glass looking down over it. Simona Toreanno leaned against one wall, scanning her notebook. She raised an eyebrow. "Jill. I heard you're—"

Jill raised a quieting hand. Toreanno glanced at Ford and nodded, taking in Derek Stillwater. "Who's this?" she asked.

Derek introduced himself.

"Hmm." Toreanno looked at Ford. "What can you tell us, sir?"

Ford shrugged. "Guy's dead. They're just figuring out how to get the body into this room. This is the decomp room. You know, for badly decomposed bodies. Its air system is isolated from the rest of the facility. We figure it's the best way to go with this sarin exposure."

"Good idea," Derek said. He doubted it was completely necessary, and the city didn't have facilities to isolate the 100-plus victims of the Serpent's previous attacks. Still, the Serpent liked booby traps ... "How long will it be before they get it here?" he asked.

"Any time ... oh, there we go." He turned to look through the glass. "The tall Indian guy, that's the chief pathologist, Dr. Vijay Rajanikant. Most people call him Dr. Raj. There's the intercom button." He tapped it and said, "Dr. Raj, this is Jerry. We've got a couple of FBI agents up here."

Dr. Raj glanced up at them. He was completely gowned, gloved, and masked. "Fine, fine."

Derek stepped forward and tapped the intercom button. "Dr. Rajanikant, this is Dr. Derek Stillwater. I'm with the Department of Homeland Security. I've had some experience dealing with sarin deaths."

"Very good, very good." Dr. Raj had a high-pitched, accented voice.

"But," Derek continued, "our number one priority here is to try to determine time of death. Have you taken the temp yet?"

"No, we have been too concerned with isolation. Not yet, not yet."

"I understand. Once you get things in place, would you please check liver temperature?"

"Certainly, certainly. Do you wish to tell me what this is all about?"

"After you determine time of death, I'll be glad to tell you what I'm thinking."

"Fine. Fine."

Simona Toreanno said, "Let me guess, you don't think he's the Serpent."

Jill and Derek passed each other a significant look. Jerry Ford shrugged. "You need me any longer?" he asked, despite his obvious curiosity.

"I don't think so, thank you," Toreanno said.

Ford lingered on Derek for a moment. "Been hearing about you all day on the news."

"Don't believe everything you see on TV," Derek said.

Ford nodded. "Don't, that's fo' sure. You really think that guy didn't do it?" He pointed to the decomp room.

"I'm keeping my mind open," Derek said. "But we'd better be sure or some more people might die."

"Good for you," Ford said. "Keep in touch."

"Okay, okay," Dr. Raj said. "I'm going to take a liver temperature now." In the decomp room, Dr. Raj slowly unzipped the body bag to reveal William Harrington. With the assistance of another gowned pathologist, he peeled him out of the bag and rolled him over. "I will first take the rectal temperature," he said, and using a scalpel he sliced the clothing off Harrington's body, leaving him naked and exposed on the steel table. The second pathologist carefully placed the clothing in a special hazardous-materials container.

Jill, Derek, and Toreanno watched in silence, expressionless. Raj inserted a rectal thermometer into the corpse. "Dr. Stillwater," he said, "you do understand, of course, the imprecise nature of determining time of death. You do understand?"

"Yes, Doctor. Please do your best."

"Of course, of course. My understanding is that he is believed to have died in the last hour or two."

"Sometime after 2:40 p.m.," offered Toreanno.

"I see, I see," said Dr. Raj. He removed the rectal thermometer and jotted a notation down on a notepad. Then he took the scalpel, cut a small incision on Harrington's back, and inserted a probe into the body. While he waited, he manipulated Harrington's wrist and arm.

"What do you think, Doctor?" Derek asked into the intercom.

"I think I will wait a few moments, please, please, before making my determination. Most interesting, most interesting."

Derek frowned and stepped back from the window, arms crossed over his chest. Toreanno said, "Why are you two here?"

Jill said, "We think there are some questions that need to be answered before we call this a closed case."

"Matt's smearing both of you all over the media."

"We noticed."

"You've been relieved of duty."

"Yes," Jill said, locking eyes with Toreanno.

Toreanno returned the gaze. She smiled. "Fuck the bastard. You're on my team now. I've got all the names of the people involved with the CBCTR's Working Group." She waved at the autopsy room. "I hope to God he's the Serpent, but I could never live with myself if this turned out to be some kind of trick."

Derek turned to her. "I'd like to see that list."

She handed it to him.

A moment later, Dr. Raj, after checking some numbers, clicked on the intercom. "Dr. Stillwater? Are you there, Dr. Stillwater?"

"Yes. Right here."

"You do realize, of course, that this is not precise. Not precise at all. I can only give you a range."

"I understand."

"Yes, well, you see, yes, I believe our body here has been dead for considerably longer than the three or four hours you suggest."

"How long, Doctor?"

"I would have to say from eight to ten hours, at least. Possibly even longer. Eight to ten hours."

# 73

*5:55 p.m.*

THE THREE OF THEM walked out of the medical examiner's office. Night was coming in full force, the darkness dropping quickly. The temperature had plunged, and a chill lurked in the air. Derek's eyes fairly glittered as he concentrated on what he had just learned. His leg was even stiffer now than before, and part of his mind was on the painkillers in his Go Packs. But otherwise, he was elated that his gut feelings had been vindicated, even if it meant the Serpent was still out there planning something. And probably planning it for eight o'clock, slightly over two hours away.

Agent Toreanno said, "We have to take this to Matt."

Jill stopped walking, hands up at her waist and held out in a halt gesture. "Whoa! Think that one through."

Simona Toreanno spun around. "Jill! You can't just go off and leave something like this."

"Who said anything about leaving it?" Jill turned to Derek. "Well?"

He shrugged. "I'm not going through Gray. You can. You probably should."

Jill shook her head. "No. If I … I can't bring this to him. Think about it, Simona. He won't listen to me. He'll only listen to you. In fact, if you want him to pay any attention to you, it'll *have* to be you. You can't even mention we were here. Let Matt think we went home."

Simona's dark eyes were penetrating. "You were supposed to go back to the office and file a report, though, right? Won't he be waiting for you?"

Jill shrugged. "That's minor. Tomorrow would … hell, Simona. What difference would it make now? I'm already in trouble. But if I came into his office with irrefutable evidence of an attack, he might ignore it just because it came through me. But if I—or even worse, Stillwater and I—come in there telling him he made an ass of himself at the press conference by telling everybody the Serpent was dead, that he's going to have to tell the press he was wrong and, while he's at it, shoot that particular bit of news up the chain of command, what do you think he's going to do?"

Simona nodded. "I guess … I guess it has to be me."

"Don't mention us," Derek said. "But we're going to pursue those names." He held up the list of Working Group members.

Simona sighed. "Okay. I'll see if I can get people going on it too."

"Good luck," Derek said, limping toward Jill's car.

"Stillwater!" Simona called.

He stopped and turned.

Agent Toreanno said, "You've had two strikes today with booby traps. Don't get caught in a third. Nobody's that lucky."

# 74

*6:11 p.m.*

DR. TAPLIN-SMITHSON LOOKED A lot different out of her tweed pantsuit. She was still tall and big-boned, and her frosted hair still arced to her shoulders, but she now wore jeans and a T-shirt. All vestiges of makeup were gone, and her eyes were red and puffy. She clutched a Kleenex in her left hand.

"I was so surprised to hear from you," she said. "I'm having ... well, come in. Please."

Taplin-Smithson lived in the city of Detroit, which was only partly why they had chosen to talk to her first. She lived in the Pallister Commons, not far from the first attack on the Boulevard Café. Pallister Commons was a historical neighborhood just north of the Fisher Building—large, three-story homes with wide, broad porches, privacy fences, and detached garages that were once carriage houses. There were no streets, exactly, which was confusing. Access to the garages were via alleys that ran every other street or so.

Jill and Derek had been forced to park down the street and walk in, Derek grousing the entire way as he limped along on his crutches.

The front door opened into a high-ceilinged living area with heavy, darkly stained woodwork. Large windows looked out on the front and side yards. The furniture was expensive Mission style. Paintings of what looked like Big Sur hung on the walls. A heavyset white-haired man sat in a comfortable chair, a laptop computer in his lap. He set it on the floor and walked over to meet them, hand out. Derek shook.

"This is my husband, Alan Smithson. Alan's a physician at Ford Hospital, right across the street."

"Nice to meet you," Jill said.

Taplin-Smithson took in Derek's crutches. "What happened to you? Did you get hurt in that explosion?"

"Actually, no," Derek said. "Old injury got re-hurt by a Birmingham cop today."

"Quite a day." She sighed and dabbed at her eyes. Her husband put his arm around her. He said, "It's been terrible. Thank God it's over."

Derek and Jill didn't comment.

Both doctors simultaneously said, "It is, isn't it?"

"May we sit down?" Jill said. "I'm afraid we need your help."

"Let's go to the kitchen table."

Derek and Jill followed them through the living room, past the modern kitchen, and into a formal dining room. A large multi-paned window looked over the fenced-in backyard. A calico cat glanced up from a bowl of food and arched its shoulders before nonchalantly exiting the room.

They sat down at the table. "We need you to look at a list of people," Jill said, and handed it to Taplin-Smithson.

The professor stood up and returned a moment later with a pair of reading glasses. She sat down and studied the list. "This is from the center?" she said.

"The CBCTR Working Group," Derek said. "Your name's on it."

She wrinkled her nose. "Yes, I helped from time to time. Not too often. Not a big need for a biostatistician for those scenarios." She looked over her glasses at him. "I saw the press conference. The FBI says Bill Harrington was the Serpent. That he killed himself accidentally."

"What do you think of that?" Jill asked.

Taplin-Smithson frowned at the piece of paper in her hands. She shot her husband a sideways glance. He shrugged.

"Bill wasn't my favorite person," she said, "but I never would have thought he was a mass murderer."

"Would you take a look at that list and tell us if anybody there might be a candidate? Or if anybody sticks out."

She studied Derek for a moment. "I'm supposed to look at a list of my colleagues and tell you whether I think any of them are capable of murdering over a hundred people?"

"Please," Jill said. "Just look at the list."

Taplin Smithson shot her husband another look and re-read the list. She frowned. "Well, that's sort of interesting."

"What's that?"

"Well, there are a number of graduate students on this list. In fact, Bill and Brad were always getting grad students to help with those scenarios, especially in the public health programs."

"What's so interesting?" Derek said.

She frowned again, took off her glasses, and cocked her head at Derek. "Well, this student here. Kevin Matsumoto."

"What about him?"

"Well …" She hesitated.

"Go ahead, honey," her husband urged.

"Well," Taplin-Smithson said, "he was an odd one. Brilliant, but strange. He was in the biochemistry department. In fact, he worked in Bill's lab, was one of his most promising students. But Kevin … he had some problems."

Derek leaned forward. "I noticed his name too. What kind of problems?"

She took in a deep breath. "Well, emotional problems."

"What kind?" Jill asked.

"Well, he was—"

"Was he the religious nut?" her husband asked.

Taplin-Smithson swallowed and nodded. "Well, you know, in a university situation, you get all sorts of students. Especially in a big-city university like Wayne State. Very multicultural. We get students from all sorts of religions—Christian and Jewish and Seventh-day Adventists and Muslims, even had a Quaker once. Buddhists, everything. And a fair number of seemingly normal people with nutty religious or political beliefs."

Jill said, "And Kevin Matsumoto?"

"Well, he dropped out of school. Brad was pretty upset about it, because Kevin was such a gifted biochemist. Like I said, a little bit nutty, but…" She sighed. "We're talking graduate students in the hard sciences. Sometimes these are the geekiest of the geeks, if you know what I mean. Social skills aren't always all that polished.

It's a cliché to say that, but a lot of times it's true. Kevin was like that."

"Was he Japanese?" Derek asked.

"Oh yes. In appearance? Sure. I was under the impression his mother was American. I don't think he was born in the U.S., but aside from his last name and his Asian features, he seemed to be completely American."

"And the religion?"

"Well, a few months before he dropped out of school, he started talking a lot about some religious group called Aleph. How he was a part of Aleph ... wasn't that it, honey?"

Dr. Smithson nodded. "I was thinking Alpha, but you may be right. Aleph sounds right."

Jill noticed that Derek had gone rigid, his hands clenching the armrests of his chair.

"Anyway," Taplin-Smithson said, "he got really erratic and got going on about the end of the world and how only Aleph could pave the way or save the world or something like that—"

Derek lurched to his feet and started hobbling for the door.

Jill startled, said, "Well, thank you very much," and hurried after Derek.

Jill caught up to him halfway across Taplin-Smithson's lawn. She caught his arm. "All right, Derek. Out with it. What is Aleph?"

Derek turned to her. "After the 1995 sarin gas attack in Tokyo, Aum Shinrikyo changed their name and went underground. Their new name is Aleph."

# 75

*6:15 p.m.*

MATT GRAY WAS ON the phone in his office when Simona Toreanno was ushered in. He held up a hand and pointed to a chair. Then he spun sideways to her, displaying his profile. "Yes. Yes," he said into the phone. "I understand. No, I think we got lucky on this one. No."

He listened for some time, nodding his head. Then, "Yes, sir, I understand. No, they are no longer involved. I personally saw to it that Agent Church was suspended pending a hearing. After Harrington's body was found at the casino, Stillwater disappeared. No, sir, they're still here. It's taking some time to get the three scenes and the car fit for analysis and reuse. The HMRU will be here for at least another twenty-four hours."

Simona Toreanno sat patiently, listening. Matt Gray was clearly convinced the entire situation was over, the Serpent dead. It was a convenient ending. You wrote up your reports and moved on. No prosecution attempts, no bail hearings, no unending follow-up investigation, nothing.

But if everything she, Jill, and Stillwater thought was correct, the Serpent had played them for fools, using his knowledge of their procedures and expectations to manipulate the Bureau, the cops, and the entire public health sector.

She studied Matt for a moment before letting her gaze wander around the office. A photograph of the president. An American flag. A photograph of ground zero in New York City.

Then an abrupt shift from the trappings of the office to the trappings of political success. Matt shaking hands with the president. Shaking hands with the attorney general. Shaking hands with the director of the Bureau. Shaking hands with the mayor of Detroit.

Other photographs from earlier in his career, one standing with a gun at Waco. Not a big plus on his career calendar, she thought, but who knew? Maybe Matt was proud of that debacle.

And there on his desk were photographs of his wife and kids. Pretty wife. Three kids.

The man was a pig, she thought. Jill wasn't the only one to have fallen briefly for his charms. He was good-looking, attentive, and successful. When he first took over the Detroit office, his wife and children stayed behind in Miami, and Matt let everybody think they were separated, the divorce imminent. He swept through the female ranks of the local office like the plague.

Jill was caught in a career snafu around the time Matt's wife and family moved to town and heard rumors about their affair. Matt tried to lay it all off on Jill, spreading rumors that she was a slut, that she'd slept with all of the men in the building, let alone the rest of the Bureau. Jill fought back with the weapon at hand—the truth. It got ugly before Matt solved it with apologies and forced a questionable promotion on Jill that resulted in her becoming mostly administrative rather than operative.

Some agents would have appreciated the administrative duties. But Simona knew that to Jill it had been a demotion. So did Matt. He could claim she was being groomed for command, that she needed administrative experience, but what she was being groomed for was a low-level paper-pushing position. Filing reports and compiling statistics, not solving crimes or chasing bad guys. Everybody knew it. Moral of the story: Don't have an affair with your married boss.

"Yes," Gray said. "Thank you, sir. I'll keep you updated." Gray hung up the phone and swung back toward Simona. "That was Director McCully. He's quite pleased with how this ended."

"I'm not sure that isn't a little premature," Simona said. "I was just over at the medical examiner's office."

Gray steepled his fingers. "Why?"

"Somebody needed to be."

"You were supposed to be tracking down the members of the Working Group."

"I did. Then I called the office. I—"

"Fine," Gray said with a wave of his hand. "So what? It is William Harrington, right?"

"Yes. That seems to be confirmed. But the—"

"Sarin gas?"

"Yes, I think so. Look, Matt, we received a call from the Serpent around 2:40."

"Well, actually, that reporter for NPR, Ball, he received the call. But yes, I think that was the right time."

"And we found him around what? Five-thirty or so?"

"Earlier than that, actually. Pretty close to five."

"Okay," Simona said. She took a photocopy of a partial report that she had insisted Dr. Rajanikant provide, and placed it in front of Matt.

"What's this?" He picked it up.

"Read it."

He scanned the sheet and pushed it aside. "How sure is he of this?"

"He seemed pretty sure. As sure as he's likely to be."

"As you know, time of death isn't precise."

"No, but there's a difference between eight to ten hours and two and a half hours, Matt."

Gray shrugged. "There's great variability, as you know. And perhaps he couldn't take into account the temperature and conditions in the car and the parking garage. It was pretty cold in there. And for all we know, the air conditioning was on in that car."

Simona stared at him. "That's nonsense, and you know it."

"I don't know it, Agent Toreanno," Gray snapped. "I don't know it at all. The third attack did not happen. Understand me? *It did not happen.* And furthermore, our prime suspect for the attacks was discovered dead from sarin gas at the scene of where the third attack was to occur. Which part of one plus one adds up to three for you?"

"The time of death of the body."

"There's no evidence besides that, and it's notoriously unreliable. For all we know, sarin affects the body temperature in peculiar ways."

"You don't think Dr. Rajanikant would have known that? Or Dr. Stillwater?"

She knew she'd blown it even as she said it. Matt narrowed his eyes. "Excuse me? What did you say?"

"I'm sorry. That was a slip. Nothing."

"No," Gray said, getting to his feet. "You mentioned Dr. Stillwater. What does he have to do with this?"

"Nothing, sir."

Gray came around his desk. There was something about his posture and the aggressive nature of his movements that suggested he was stalking her. "I'm going to ask you a direct question, Agent Toreanno. It's verifiable. One phone call to the ME's office and I'll know. Think about that when you answer."

She stared at him, feeling trapped.

Gray said, "Was Derek Stillwater at the ME's office?"

She hesitated before answering. "Yes."

Gray glared at her. "In what capacity?"

"Sir?"

"Why was he there?"

"I think it was his job. He wanted to confirm the time of death."

"Why?"

Jill sat up straighter. "I imagine because he thought Harrington's death was rather convenient."

"Yes, lucky for us he killed himself before he killed a couple hundred more people. Did Stillwater influence Doctor ... the ME's decision?"

"No."

Gray moved closer, looming over her. "Are you sure? Did Derek Stillwater in any way affect the ME's decision?"

"No." Firmly.

Gray turned and walked back behind his desk. He stared out at the city below him, the lights of Detroit and the traffic a moving mosaic of illumination against the early evening darkness. Voice low, Gray said, "Was Jill Church there as well?"

When she didn't answer, Gray turned.

"I expect an answer. Was Jill Church at the medical examiner's office with Derek Stillwater?"

Simona swallowed. "Matt, you have to take this seriously. This guy—"

"Stillwater?"

"What?"

"This guy, Derek Stillwater?"

"No! This guy, the Serpent. He's been playing games with us all day long. He's basing these attacks on these written scenarios—"

"Yes, I've had a chance to read the one it was all based on. Very interesting. And it ended with the attack on the casino at four o'clock, which we know didn't happen."

"But he would know we would have found that out by now. Why else would he have booby-trapped Harrington's office and his house? How—"

Matt rapped his fist on his desk. "Agent Toreanno, enough. You've given your report. Thank you. Go back to your office and write it up. And I want a written report on exactly what happened at the medical examiner's office, including the presence of Jill Church. With an accurate timeline."

Toreanno slowly stood up. "You've got to take this seriously. You've got to realize he might be planning an attack somewhere for eight o'clock tonight. We can't stand down now."

Gray turned to his computer and began tapping keys. "You're dismissed."

Feeling rising hysteria in her voice, Toreanno said, "Matt, you're being a fool."

He turned to her. "What was that?"

"Stop being a jackass! You're assuming the best. You need to assume the worst! What will happen to your precious career if the Serpent's still alive and he kills again and you shut the op down?"

Gray's voice was flat. "Dismissed. And consider yourself warned, Agent Toreanno. Another outburst like that one and you will be looking for work with Jill Church."

She started to respond, considered better, and spun on her heel, leaving his office. She clenched and unclenched her fists, frightened, truly frightened that she had two choices and neither was good. She could go to her office, file her reports, and go home and pray that William Harrington had really been the Serpent and it was all over. Or she could ignore orders, commit insubordination, and, no matter what the outcome, quite possibly lose her job, her career, and her pension.

It was no choice, really. She had to coordinate with Jill and Stillwater.

Simona headed for the elevator and was almost there when Roger Kandling appeared. "Simona!"

She turned, impatient. "What?"

"I need to talk to you for a moment. Come on."

Puzzled, she followed Kandling. She and Roger were at the same level in the Bureau, competitors in a way. Kandling was pretty much Matt Gray's protégé, being groomed for the SAC job, should Matt move on. He was a good agent: political, ambitious, smart. In her opinion, he was too by-the-book, lacking creative initiative, but in the Bureau that could be the way to get ahead too.

He led her through the office and to an interrogation room.

"What's in here?" she asked.

"I need to talk to you in private. It's important."

With a shrug, she stepped into the interrogation room, basically just an office with a table and chairs, no windows, no decorations. She stepped in. The door shut behind her. She reached for the knob, but it was locked. "Hey! Let me out!"

After a moment, Roger Kandling's voice came over the intercom. "This is by direct orders of Matt, Simona. I'm sorry. He feels it's for your own good. He knew you were going to go off on your own, and he doesn't want you to get in trouble. Just relax and—"

Simona didn't pay attention to the rest. She couldn't believe this was happening. But maybe she could. Matt Gray wasn't a dummy. He'd likely know she would pursue what she felt was the correct avenue.

Instead of screaming and shouting, she took out her cell phone and dialed Jill Church's number.

# 76

*6:25 p.m.*

KEVIN MATSUMOTO, ACCORDING TO the DMV, lived in a small house in Ferndale. Jill pulled a photograph of Matsumoto from his driver's license file and downloaded it to her laptop. Like most driver's license photos, it was somewhat useless. Matsumoto's headshot indicated a dark-haired Asian male with a goatee, an angular face, and a sullen expression. She didn't think the expression was significant, because she had yet to see a really perky expression on anybody's face in a driver's license headshot.

The vital information indicated he stood six feet tall, weighed 175 pounds, and had brown eyes.

Derek studied the photograph while she drove to Ferndale. "I wonder what he's doing now," he said.

"Plotting to kill somebody."

"That's not what I meant. I mean, he quit school. Did he re-up at one of the other universities around here, did he get a job, or what?"

"He was a graduate student in biochemistry. If he had his bachelor's in chemistry or biochemistry, he may well be working somewhere."

"With access to all the ingredients to make sarin."

"Is it hard to make?"

Derek shook his head. "Not for a grad student in biochemistry. Not for a halfway decent undergrad in chemistry or biochemistry."

Jill's phone sang. She answered it, listened, and said, "Okay. We're on top of things. I'm sorry, Simona. Why don't you just sit tight…" She listened. "Yes, you might do that. All right."

She put her phone away.

"What was that all about?" Derek asked.

"Matt Gray's locked Simona in an interrogation room. I told her to sit tight and not make waves, basically. She said she's still got her cell phone, but the charge is low. She's going to make some calls, let other agents know what's going on, maybe go over Matt's head."

Derek sighed. "Is Gray always this nutty?"

Jill laughed, a short, disgusted bark. "He's been more paranoid than usual lately. One thing you have to keep in mind about Matt. We've all got our areas of expertise. When they wanted an SAC in Detroit, they had to take a couple things into consideration. The Bureau's pushed all the communist hunting and organized-crime work to the back burners and put the majority of our resources into fighting terrorism. That's fine, I guess. But in Detroit, there are a couple different issues to be concerned about in fighting terrorism. One is immigration and border security. The Ambassador Bridge to Windsor is the busiest commercial border crossing in the United States. And Michigan has a huge international border with Canada. Secondly, Detroit and Dearborn have the largest Shiite

291

Muslim populations outside of the Middle East. So when they wanted a new SAC, they were really looking for somebody who either had experience dealing with immigration and border security, or somebody with experience with an Arab population. Matt worked port security in Miami for years before he came here."

"So he's not really an expert on domestic terrorism."

"He's not operational in that sense, no."

"That doesn't exactly explain the raving paranoia."

"No. That's more..." She hesitated. "Matt's got a few personal problems. One is he's married with three kids. Matt sleeps around."

Derek turned at the bitterness in her voice, but he chose not to ask the obvious question. "And that makes him paranoid?"

"This is sort of unsubstantiated," Jill said, turning off Woodward onto 8 Mile Road. They moved from light commercial to what looked to Derek like light industry, a few factories manufacturing things like septic tanks and machine shops making tools and parts in support of the auto companies.

"Go ahead."

"Well, Matt's wife is the daughter of Senator Walker."

Derek thought. "Republican from Georgia?"

"Right. And chair of the Senate Ways and Means Committee."

"So his father-in-law's got a lot of clout."

"Very much. And Matt's wife has been suspicious of his philandering for some time. Rumor is, the marriage is on the rocks and if she goes to *Daddy* with the truth, Matt's career is likely to be toast."

"So he thinks everybody's out to get him?"

"He has good reason not to trust most of the female agents in his office."

Again, Derek didn't comment. After a moment's silence, he said, "And *that's* why he's a raving paranoid?"

"It's a factor. We think *Daddy's* been watching how things have been going in this office very carefully. Just hints and rumors we've been getting from other agents. You know, 'Hey, I hear Senator Walker's concerned about how things are operating up there.' That sort of thing."

"Just because you're paranoid...," Derek said.

"Right. Maybe they *are* out to get you."

They pulled up in front of a small bungalow in what looked to be a working-class neighborhood. It was on the edge of a light manufacturing strip, a row of boxy houses, probably two bedrooms, small yards, single story, carports rather than garages. Kevin Matsumoto's house was dark. There was a small concrete stoop in front. It looked like it was sided with wood or asbestos siding, the drapes drawn, a few untended shrubs along the front of the house. There was no car.

They studied the house for a moment. Derek voiced their thoughts. "I don't know how to go in there safely."

"I was afraid of that."

"Any suggestions?" he asked.

Jill shook her head, her jaw firm, eyes hard. "Sometimes..."

He looked at her, a question in his eyes.

"Sometimes you just have to knock on the door," she said.

Derek scratched his jaw. "I've got another option, actually."

"What's that?"

"Try a window."

# 77

*6:31 p.m.*

DEREK AND JILL WALKED around the house, their flashlights beaming around the foundation and at the windowsills. Derek took every opportunity to peek in the windows, but on most of them drapes were drawn. What he saw otherwise was unremarkable.

"Can you tell if the windows are wired?" Jill asked.

"No."

Jill thought he had gotten surly and quiet since getting out of the car. Maybe it was what Simona had said about nobody being lucky three times.

"There's always the door," she said.

Derek shook his head. "Let's try a window." He stepped over to a rear window and studied it for a moment. With a sudden motion, he smashed out part of the glass using the butt of his gun. In the neighborhood's silence, it seemed loud. They waited. Nothing changed. Off in the distance, a dog barked. Farther off they heard traffic.

Derek reached in through the broken glass, unlocked the window, gripped the frame, and opened it, sliding it upward. Carefully he removed any chunks of glass. "All right," he said. "I'm going in."

"No," she said, a hand on his arm. "I'll go first."

"I'll take the risk, Jill."

"Shut up. I'm smaller and I don't have a bum leg. Now cup your hands."

Derek frowned, then obediently stooped and laced his fingers together. He boosted her up to the window so she could squirm through. After a moment of rustling, she reappeared. "There's a back door. I'll open it for you."

"Be careful!"

"Of course."

He waited. It seemed interminable, though it was probably only a minute or two. The rear door opened silently, and Jill waved him over. Once he was inside, she said, "Flashlights?"

"Just turn on some lights," Derek said. "Flashlights will attract more attention." Jill turned on a light, and they found themselves in a tiny kitchen. The appliances looked like they had been around since the fifties or sixties. The decor had the feel of the seventies, with yellow and green ceramic fixtures and tile. Dirty dishes teetered in the kitchen sink. Against one wall was a small Formica table with aluminum tube legs. A copy of the *Detroit Free Press* lay strewn across the table, as well as a cereal bowl of brown milk, a juice glass with dried orange juice on the bottom, and a grimy spoon. On the table was an opened box of Cocoa Puffs.

They moved from the kitchen into the living room. It was small and cramped, the furniture worn and old-fashioned, as if Kevin Matsumoto had either inherited his parents' leftovers or picked everything up at a garage sale. The only thing new was the TV, a flat plasma screen attached to one wall. More newspapers were piled in messy stacks. The carpeting looked old and ratty, speckled with debris as if it had never been vacuumed. Next to an old armchair were piled chemistry textbooks and a scatter of other books and technical journals. Derek leaned over and picked up one of the books, showing it to Jill. It was *The Anarchist Cookbook*.

"Figures. I wish that thing had never been published," she said.

Derek scanned the room, focusing on several photographs on the wall. He stepped closer. "Shit."

Jill joined him. "He looks familiar." She pointed to a photograph of a round-faced Asian man with a Fu Manchu mustache, scruffy black beard, and mane of pitch-black hair worn long.

"Shit," Derek repeated. "That's Shoko Asahara."

"Who?"

"The head of Aum Shinrikyo. After the gas attack, he was arrested, tried, and found guilty. They sentenced him to death by hanging, but so far it hasn't happened. Oh, damn. I forgot…"

Jill turned. "What?"

"Shoko Asahara was the name he took when he started the Aum. His given name was Chizuo Matsumoto."

"You don't…"

"I think Asahara had five or six kids by his wife. After Asahara and his wife were convicted, the kids ended up living with remaining members of the Aum, who started calling themselves the Aleph. Asahara had a lot of followers in a lot of countries."

"So Kevin could be his son."

"Or think he is."

Jill swallowed. "Let's keep looking."

There were two more rooms. One was clearly a bedroom. Dirty clothes erupted from a laundry basket. It smelled rank, of sweat, dust, mold, and dried semen.

Derek stuck his head into the sole bathroom. He sniffed. "The chemistry lab," he said. "Can you smell it?"

"I smell something."

It was a small, cramped room, the tub looking like it had never been scrubbed, a moldy pink shower curtain pushed to one side, damp towels on the floor like twisted snakes. Derek eyed a closet. With slow, deliberate movements, he stepped into the bathroom and turned the closet's knob. It opened without any resistance. There were four shelves. The top two held soap and razors and deodorant and all the other paraphernalia of a single man's bathroom. The bottom two shelves held rows of chemicals and Pyrex laboratory vessels—beakers and Erlenmeyer flasks of varying sizes. Derek studied the labels on the chemicals. "DMMP," he said.

"What?" Jill asked.

"One of the four ingredients needed to make sarin."

"It only takes four?"

"Yeah, ain't chemistry wonderful? He's our boy."

He backed slowly out of the bathroom and looked across the hallway toward the second bedroom. The door was closed.

"I really don't like the fact that door is closed," Derek said.

Jill nodded, her heart hammering in her chest. "Suggestions?"

He sighed. "No. This is the guy. We need to find out what he's got planned next." He held up the atropine injector he had brought with him. "The person who stays in the hallway gets this. I suggest I be the first one in."

They looked into each other's eyes. She said, "He likes bombs too."

"A real Renaissance man, our Kevin. Here. Take it."

She took it. Derek studied the door. It was uninformative. "Step back," he said.

After she moved down the short hallway, he reached out, hand shaking, and gripped the knob. Slowly, he turned, sensitive to any resistance. There wasn't any.

Once it was turned all the way, Derek opened the door the same way. Also nothing unexpected. Once the door was open halfway, he stopped. He wiped sweat off his forehead and craned his neck. He panned his light around the room, shook his head, and reached in and turned on the overhead light.

This room had been the Serpent's work room and office. There was a long workbench filled with tools and wires and mechanical and electronic objects. At another table there was a computer system. Blackout blinds were pulled over the two windows.

"Let me check the floor," Jill said.

Derek nodded.

Jill joined him, got down on her knees, and began to gently feel the carpet. She peered around the door and said, "Uh-oh."

"What?"

"The door's wired. Good thing you didn't open it any more. It looks like it's set to go off if the ..." She fell silent.

"What?"

"Look!" Jill jumped to her feet and pointed. On the wall behind the door was a digital readout. The wires from the door ran to the readout. Bright red letters counted down: 10, 9, 8 ...

There was a touchpad beneath it.

"Get the hell out of here," Derek said.

"Derek—"

He grabbed her and shoved her out into the hallway, glanced around the room, and leaped over to the computer desk.

7...

6...

He snatched a pad of paper off the desk and rushed for the door, getting tangled up with his crutch.

5...

4...

Jill caught his shirt and dragged him out of the room, nearly carrying him.

In his head, Derek counted: *3...*

Jill flung open the front door.

*2...*

They tumbled outside onto the concrete stoop.

*1...*, Derek thought.

They raced across the lawn.

*0...*

Nothing happened. They turned to look at the house. "Maybe it was just an alarm," Jill said.

The house erupted, glass and wood exploding outward. The compression wave slammed them off their feet. By the time they came to their senses, the small house was engulfed in flames.

# 78

*6:40 p.m.*

JILL ROLLED OVER AND pressed her hands to her ears, which hurt. Every sound seemed muffled—the flames devouring the house, the distant cry of sirens, the murmur of voices from neighbors appearing to see what had happened. Even Derek's voice.

He said, "You okay?"

Jill looked over and saw he was sitting up, staring at the house.

"Can't hear very well," she said.

He nodded and pointed to his own ears. "Me neither. Hope it passes soon."

She pulled herself to a sitting position and cautiously climbed to her feet. For a second she swayed, but then her equilibrium kicked in and she steadied. She reached down and helped Derek stand up.

"Where's your crutch?" she said.

He gestured to the crutch lying in the grass fifteen feet away.

Jill nodded and jogged over and retrieved it for him.

Derek frowned, scanning the ground. "I dropped it. Where is it?"

"What?"

"The notepad I took off his desk."

"Was there something on it?"

"I don't know. I didn't have much time. But I thought I ought to grab something."

"Let's hope it was worth it."

One of the neighbors trotted over. He was a big, burly guy with a shaved head and a gray goatee. Even though the head and goatee made him look tough, Jill thought he was a puppy dog. Something about the attitude suggested he was a nice guy. He wore faded jeans and a gray sweatshirt and looked like he might spend some time in the gym. "Hey, you two all right?" His voice was a little high-pitched for such a big guy.

"I think so," Jill said.

"What the hell happened?"

"House blew up," Derek said. "Duh!" He limped away, scanning the ground for the notebook.

Jill frowned. She turned to the neighbor. "You know the guy who owns this?"

"Owns? No. It's a rental. Kid lives there, young guy, anyway. Japanese, I think. Odd kid. I've talked to him once or twice. Not too friendly." He gazed uneasily at the house. "He in there?"

"No," Jill said. "Any idea where he might be?"

The neighbor shrugged. "Don't know. He works strange hours, comes and goes."

"Any idea where he works?"

"Palace."

Jill said, "Of Auburn Hills?"

"Yeah. Offered my daughter tickets to a concert a month or so ago, said he got them because he worked there." He licked his lips. "She turned him down. He's a creep."

Jill said, "Any idea what he does at the Palace?"

He shook his head. "Hey, here's the fire truck."

Jill turned to see Derek struggling to catch the notebook, which was being blown around the yard by the wind. Under different circumstances it would have made her laugh. She ran over and picked it up. She jogged back to Derek with the paper. In a low voice, she said, "I really don't want to spend the next couple hours explaining this."

"I'm a bad influence on you, Agent Church," he said, taking the notebook from her. "I'm with you, though. Let's go."

The firefighters almost blocked them in, hooking up to a hydrant about fifty yards down the street, the street quickly clogging up with rescue vehicles and police cars. Flashing red, blue, and white lights cut the darkness. Jill helped Derek into the car, walked over to the neighbor who had been so helpful, and handed him a card, saying, "Give this to a cop. Tell him to tell the firefighters that nobody's inside."

He studied the card. "FBI?"

"Yes."

"What's this about?"

"Thanks!" she said, not answering, and ran back to the car.

"Hey!" he shouted. "You're not staying?"

She fired up the ignition and slowly threaded their way out of the neighborhood. Derek, in the passenger seat, turned on the map light and studied the notepad.

"Well?" she said.

"It's … blank." His voice was so laden with disappointment that Jill thought he might break into tears.

"We'll think of—"

"Wait. It looks like he may have written over it. Um, I'm about to trash evidence here."

"We just fled a crime scene, Derek. What difference does it make?"

He found a pencil and lightly rubbed it across the top page. "I have a feeling a document examiner somewhere is having a heart attack right now," Derek said.

"Anything?"

Derek angled the page this way and that, squinting. "Numbers and letters. Like he's calculating something."

"That's all?"

Derek frowned. "'0.5 mg × 21,454 = 10,727 mg. Total.' And then it says: '25% dispersion???'"

"What's that mean?"

Derek was silent. "It also says: '1,700 mg/70 kg × 21,454 = 36,471,800 mg. Total.'"

"You've lost me."

"Seventy kilograms," Derek said. "That's like the average person's weight. A hundred and fifty pounds or so. Oh shit."

"What?"

"And point-five milligrams is about the lethal dose of sarin gas. Or in other words, 1,700 milligrams per 170-kilogram or 150-pound person."

"That's all it takes to kill somebody? Half a milligram?"

"Fun stuff. And both times he multiplies it by 21,454. He's trying to figure out the dosage of sarin needed to kill 21,454 people!

Jesus! And he talks about a 25 percent dispersal rate. He's got more calculations, adding a quarter more to these numbers. That's got to be some sort of guess. If you're aerosolizing a space, how much of it lands on the floor or whatever. But twenty-one thousand people?" Derek angled the sheet closer to the light, then held it up so the light shone through the back of the piece of paper. "It says: 'airborne exposure limit: $0.0001$ mg/m$^3$.' Yes, he's definitely calculating how to kill over twenty-one thousand peop—"

"Tonight at eight o'clock?" Jill asked.

"That would make sense."

Jill let out a little cry, half gasp, half controlled scream. *"Oh dear God!"*

# 79

*6:55 p.m.*

KEVIN MATSUMOTO, OTHERWISE CALLING himself the Serpent, moved through the crowds at the Palace of Auburn Hills. It was a huge, circular arena, industrial in flavor, with white concrete walls and exposed girders and duct work. Once through the entrance and ticket areas, a broad tiled walkway encircled the actual arena. Vendors and strollers hung out here, hawking jewelry, memorabilia, and food.

The J Slim concert didn't officially start until eight o'clock, though a few thousand people were already here, milling around, checking out the arcade, and buying T-shirts, CDs, travel mugs, and posters. Others were here starting their party early, eating dinner at one of the restaurants or snacking on pizza, pretzels, and popcorn, just as likely paying five bucks for a beer or a gin and tonic.

Kevin grinned, watching some idiots standing in line for a J Slim T-shirt. Forty bucks for a T-shirt with this asshole flipping the bird! They looked like they deserved it. Torn jeans, motorcycle boots, J

Slim tank tops, their hair spiked with gel, skull-and-crossbones earrings, tats on their arms, probably temporary. Somebody bumped him and he smiled pleasantly, though the person who bumped him recoiled at his expression. "Hey, get a life," she snarled, beer in her hand. She wore low-rise jeans, her puffy exposed stomach showing off a pierced belly button, her shirt pink and tight, nipples protruding.

*You're dead*, he thought, and smiled harder, wondering what people saw in his face when they looked at him. Wondering why when he thought he was covering up, being normal and friendly, people seemed to sense just how much rage he felt. How much hatred.

They would speak his name in fear. Kevin Matsumoto, rightful head of Aum Shinrikyo reborn. His half-sister, Rika Matsumoto, ran Aleph now. She would not recognize his rightful place at the head of Aum. She was younger than he was. He had been born before Aum, before Chizuo Matsumoto was reborn as Shoko Asahara. Kevin was the first-born, the son of Shoko Asahara. Him. Not her. After tonight, the world would be forced to realize that only the true son of Aum could have been responsible for the day's destruction.

Using the Palace ID he had reprogrammed from one he stole before he quit, he moved toward the backstage areas, making sure he didn't get into the areas where J Slim and his band were hanging out with local disc jockeys and the people who had won free backstage passes. No, he didn't need that. Besides, security was tight there.

Instead, he moved to the technical equipment area, checking the smoke machines. They were actually using two different types of machines: smoke machines and foggers. The foggers were behind and below the scenes, set up on both sides of the stage. They were large barrels filled with water. At the top of the barrels were baskets that contained dry ice. You lowered the baskets into the water, and it produced a carbon dioxide fog. A heating element made the chemical reaction churn along even harder. Large hoses ran from the sides of the foggers and out to the main floor of the Palace. This was very effective and cranked out a lot of fog.

The main-floor guests were going to be in for a shock as J Slim took the stage to the machine gun rat-a-tat-tat of his drummer, the throbbing buzz of the synthesizer, and the laser lights.

And everybody else was going to be in for a surprise as well.

Kevin, in his job at the Palace as part of the technical crew, had arranged for smoke machines to be set along many of the upper beams that crisscrossed the infrastructure of the Palace. These were commercial smoke machines manufactured by the Roscoe Corporation. What Kevin liked most about these was the remote control. With the push of a button, the machines would kick in, producing smoke out of a chemical reaction of water and glycol. There were dozens of the machines installed around the arena, strapped to the front of luxury suites and bolted to overhead beams.

As J Slim made his big entrance, the lights would dim and the band would fill the cavernous building with an electric thrum and a heart-thumping drum line. The concert was sold out, slightly over twenty thousand people, and they would probably keep chattering or more likely cheer and scream. Oh yes, they would scream. The music would crescendo, rising to a howling wall of noise that was almost deafening. Colored spots would flash. Lasers would shoot everywhere, their effect increased by the carbon dioxide fog and artificial smoke that swirled through the air and across the main floor.

Kevin had loaded all the fog and smoke machines with canisters of sarin gas. With the punch of the remote control button, sarin gas would flow onto the main floor and drift down from the rafters and suite overhangs. Kevin doubted that he would kill all twenty-one thousand concertgoers. He expected, as they began to realize what was happening, that people would stampede for the exits. He predicted a lot of people would die in the chaos, either from the gas or being trampled to death.

Some would escape. People at the higher levels might even get lucky. Sarin was heavier than air and accumulated at lower levels.

Kevin predicted that tonight's final attack would make the death toll at the World Trade towers look like a picnic. Thousands were going to die. Thousands.

The thought made him smile.

# 80

*7:05 p.m.*

JILL SLAMMED ON HER brakes and swerved to the curb. Derek damn near catapulted through the windshield. Hands flung out in front of him, he bounced hard against the shoulder harness, cursing. Jill fumbled for her cell phone, panic etched across her face. Derek watched, unclear as to exactly why the number had caused such a strong reaction.

Jill, phone pressed to her left ear, muttered, "Come on, Michael. Answer, dammit!" Her face twisted in frustration. "Michael, it's your mother. If you're just out and about, call me immediately. Whatever you do, don't go to the Palace tonight. Understand? We think there's going to be...there's going to be an attack there tonight! Don't go!"

She violently jabbed off the button, said, "Voice mail," then punched another number.

Derek pulled out his tablet computer and booted it up. While he was waiting for it to kick on, Jill said, "Dammit, Michael! It's Mom.

If you get this, call me immediately. Whatever you do, don't go to the Palace. We think the Serpent's going to attack there again. Understand? *Don't go there.* And if you *are* there, leave immediately!"

Derek's tablet PC popped on. He picked up a satellite signal and went online. He Googled "Palace of Auburn Hills." A concert schedule indicated a sold-out show at eight o'clock at the Palace of Auburn Hills that night. J Slim.

Meanwhile, Jill was clicking through her phone's address book, scowling. Finally she tried directory assistance and was connected to the Morettis' number. "Hello! This is … Ann? This is Michael's mother, Jill Church. Is Michael there?"

Derek glanced away from his computer screen to the taut, frightened expression on Jill's face. He had a pretty good idea what she was being told and felt an unpleasant tingling feeling in his stomach.

Jill said, "Does Ray have his cell phone … yes. Thank you. Are your parents …" She listened some more.

Derek reached over and gripped her free hand. She at first shot him an annoyed look, then softened to one of gratitude, squeezed back, and let go.

"Okay. Now, Ann, you need to listen to me very carefully. If Michael or Ray call you, tell them to come home immediately. They *have* to leave the Palace. Do you … I … no. Thank you."

She clicked off, her face white. "Michael and his friend Ray went to the Palace for the J Slim concert." She smacked her palm against the steering wheel. "I told him he couldn't go! I told him no! Dammit! Why—" She glanced over at the screen of his computer. He was on the official Palace website again. "Is there a number there?" She held up her phone, scanning the computer screen.

Derek turned it so Jill couldn't see. "Hang on. Take a minute." His voice was calm, soothing.

"Dammit, Stillwater! My son is there!"

"I know that. Take a minute. Think. What's going to happen if they start an emergency evacuation of this place? If all of a sudden they come on the loudspeaker and say there's been a bomb threat or the event's been canceled, everybody should head for the nearest exit immediately? What is the Serpent—let's call the prick Matsumoto—what's he going to do?"

Jill's eyes grew wide. "Dear God! He'll—"

"He'll set it off immediately, that's what he'll do. Right. He'll know the game's up and he'll take out as many as he can. But we know what he looks like and we know where he is." He checked his watch. "And we've got slightly less than an hour to get there. How far—"

Jill slammed the car into drive and floored it. "It's going to be tight."

# 81

*7:15 p.m.*

Simona Toreanno sat slumped in the interview room at FBI headquarters, staring at her cell phone, which was now officially without charge. She was isolated and didn't know what to think any longer. Her anger had burned itself out, and what she now felt seemed a lot like despair.

The door opened. Matt Gray stood there, head cocked, looking at her. He said, "I've received a couple interesting telephone calls in the last half hour, Simona. One was from the director." He shook his head. "Going over my head like that—"

"You are so full of shit, Matt! You had your stooge lock me up, for God's sake!"

"And then I received a phone call from my father-in-law." Clearly he was angrier about the call from Senator Walker than the call from the FBI director.

"And you'll listen to him?"

Matt's eyes glittered. "Here's the latest news, Simona. Jill Church and Derek Stillwater were last seen fleeing a crime scene in Ferndale. A house explosion. The house was being rented by a man named Kevin Matsumoto. Matsumoto is missing. Matsumoto, as it so happens, is on your list of people who created scenarios for that Wayne State think tank. I made a few calls and managed to get some background information on Matsumoto. You see, Simona, I *am* doing my job here. I am conducting my due diligence. But I've got a couple of rogue agents undermining my chain of command. You do understand that, right?"

"What did you find out about Matsumoto?"

He met her angry gaze. "What I found out is pretty damned scary. Honors student in chemistry from Waseda University, Tokyo. He was in the doctoral program in biochemistry at Wayne State University, but he dropped out. He is reported to be a genius. I ran him through INS. It gets interesting. His mother's name was Julie Hawkins. She's in our files as well as INS's. Julie Hawkins spent time in Japan as a college student in the eighties, then dropped out and disappeared. Then in the late eighties, she shows up as a member of Aum Shinrikyo. Her parents freaked out—justifiably, in my opinion—and hired a deprogrammer who dealt with cults. This guy and his team go to Japan and kidnap her and her son and return them to the U.S. Julie Hawkins doesn't handle it and has a nervous breakdown, and her parents institutionalize her. She committed suicide in 2000. The kid was raised by his grandparents, but from a few calls I made, it wasn't a happy situation. The kid's had a history of mental problems, but considering his parents, maybe he came by it naturally. Anyway, he went to college in Japan on scholarship. At least, we think so. It's possible it was funded by a group called Aleph, which is Aum Shinrikyo's new name."

Simona swallowed hard, trying to digest all that information. "What's he doing now? What did he do after he quit Wayne?"

Gray shrugged. "I've got people on it. Now here's the plan, Simona. You have one chance to hold on to your career. No matter what happens after tonight, I will request that you be transferred elsewhere. Whether you are merely reprimanded and transferred or fired from the Bureau is entirely up to you. Do you understand?"

He was offering her some sort of a deal, and she was willing to take it if it got him off his ass. "What do you want me to do?"

"You, me, and Kandling are going to go after Matsumoto. We have forty-five minutes before a possible attack. If there's going to be one. If we ..."

She was on her feet. "Deal. Give me your phone."

Gray looked startled. "Why?"

"I'll call Jill."

"She's not—"

"Oh, grow up, Matt. You want to save your own ass? Then find out what she and Stillwater know. It's the smartest thing you could do, no matter what you're trying to accomplish. Don't you realize they're on the right track and we're not?"

Anger flashed across his face. He shrugged. "Perhaps you're right. Here." He handed her his phone, waiting.

Simona tapped in Jill's number and waited. "Jill? Simona. Matt's willing to listen. What's ⎯" She went still. The muscles in her throat tightened, and she closed her eyes. "Okay. I ... I don't know what we'll do, but we'll ... yes. I understand. I'll be in touch."

She clicked off the phone and handed it back to Gray. "Is the HMRU still around?"

Gray nodded. "They've gone back to Scott Hall to work on cleanup and decon."

Simona was already on the move. "This is going to be tricky. Come on, Matt. Let's get everybody moving."

"Where?"

"The Palace of Auburn Hills."

# 82

MICHAEL CHURCH AND RAY Moretti stood in line to get J Slim T-shirts. Both clutched tall plastic cups of beer in their hands. Ray was getting wasted in a hurry. Michael only sipped his own beer, wasn't sure if he liked it. They'd stopped at Hoops and tried out their fake IDs. No problem, though the bartender eyed Ray a little suspiciously. He'd had two beers then, Ray had had three, and Ray was getting a little loud and dumb. The loud wasn't exactly new. The dumb wasn't either, for that matter, but Michael hadn't realized just how dumb Ray could get.

"Look at her," Ray pointed. "Check out her ass. What you think? An eight?"

He was loud enough that everybody around him looked over. A couple of guys looked where he was pointing and hooted. "A seven, man. But check out those tits!"

"Low standards," another said. "Big, but fat. Not a bad ass, though."

Michael felt uneasy. It wasn't just the girls. It was something else. The way some of the people looked at them disapprovingly. And something else besides that. Probably that he was so far off the reservation right now.

Ray elbowed him, spilling beer. "What ya think, Mike? How about her?"

Michael looked over at the girl Ray was pointing at. She saw the gesture and gave them the finger. Then she pointed at Ray and held up her hand in a zero gesture. Michael had to smile at the same time his face flushed with embarrassment. She was pretty hot, and he liked that she wasn't embarrassed—instead, she got ticked and dished it right back.

"Chill, dude," he said.

"Is this fuckin' great or what?" Ray crowed.

The guy in front of them glanced back. He was an older guy, maybe in his thirties, with deep-set blue eyes and a round face. He slouched in his denim jacket, a gray painter's cap shading his face. He took in Ray and said, "Might want to pace yourself, bud. It's gonna be a long night."

"Mind your own fuckin' business," Ray snarled.

"Chill," Michael hissed. He flashed the guy an apologetic look. "Sorry."

The guy just shrugged.

Ray went back to his pussy hunt. Michael wished he'd stop. He had a little bit of a headache from the beer. And he really didn't want to get piss-drunk. If he did, they'd never get home in one piece, assuming he could find his friggin' car out there after he'd had too much to drink.

He ignored Ray for a minute and took out his cell phone. He'd turned it off. But he needed to see if his mom had called. He'd need someplace quiet to talk to her and convince her he was actually over at Ray's. He figured she was all tied up with the Serpent and wouldn't be home anytime soon, and that was okay. She hadn't actually given him a final "no" about the concert tonight, though he knew she actually would have if she hadn't taken off to the city so fast.

"Calling your *mommy*?" Ray asked, knocking back a big swallow of his beer.

Michael flashed Ray the bird and waited for the phone to come on. Almost immediately it chimed, indicating he had a message. Damn.

"Hey, get me an XL in that one there," Michael said, pointing to a black T-shirt with the big, distorted white face of J Slim on the front and a list of concert venues on the back.

"You don't want that one?" Ray pointed to the classic J Slim with two raised middle fingers.

Michael patted his chest. "Got that one. Here." He thrust money into Ray's hand. "I've gotta go check this. Hold my beer."

"Fuckin' A, man. It'll be gone if you don't hurry your ass."

Michael walked quickly away from the concessions, looking for a door outside. It was damned loud here. He double-checked that he had his ticket and his hand stamped, and stepped through the doors onto the west entrance sidewalk. It was cool outside, a breeze blowing out of the northwest. The air smelled rank. The Palace was just south and east of a landfill, and when the wind blew right, it smelled like garbage.

He had a good strong signal here, and he punched in to retrieve his call. His jaw dropped as he heard his mom's message about leaving the Palace, about the Serpent planning an attack. Heart hammering in his chest, he punched the auto dial for his mom's cell. A wild moment of panic gripped him. He wanted to run. He wanted to drop the phone and sprint for his car and get the hell out of there

He bit his lip and cooled off. Okay. Now what? What was he going to do?

# 83

JILL AND DEREK RACED north on I-75, ripping along the expressway in the left lane at eighty-five miles an hour, at least as much as possible. Traffic was moving pretty well, but as they sped past Crooks Road, traffic seemed to get thicker and more erratic. They found themselves alternating between sudden slow-downs to twenty-five miles per hour that freakishly cleared after a mile and jumping back to seventy, seventy-five, eighty miles per hour.

Jill's phone rang. She flipped it out and punched it on. "Jill Church."

"Mom? It's Michael!"

"Oh, thank God. Are you at the Palace? If you are—"

"Mom, what's going on? He's here?"

"Yes, we think he's going to do something big at eight o'clock. Now Michael, you and Ray have to leave. Immediately. We're on our way."

"But what about all the people here? They're not evacuating or anything. What about all these people? It's a sold-out show."

"Michael, listen, if—"

"Haven't you called this in? What's going on?"

"Michael—"

"Tell him," Derek said. "Now's the time."

Jill wanted to punch him. "Michael, just listen to me." She didn't like the edge of hysteria that had crept into her voice. "Just listen to me, please. You and Ray, you have to leave."

"Who is this guy?"

Jill clutched the phone. Suddenly the cars in front of her slammed to a halt, brake lights flashing one after another ahead of them. "Shit!" She dropped the phone and stomped on her brakes. The car bucked and her tires squealed on the pavement, but they stopped in time.

"Where's the phone?"

"You drive," Derek said. "You're going to get us killed. I'll talk to him."

Derek picked the phone off the floor and said, "Michael, it's Derek Stillwater."

"Dr. Stillwater! Is this for real?"

"Yes. It's for real. Do what your mother says. Go get your friend and get out of there."

"But what about—"

"Michael? Or is it Mike?"

"Either way. Look, Dr. Stillwater—"

"Derek."

"Fine. Derek. Look, I can't just abandon all these people."

Derek looked at the clock on the dashboard. They had less than thirty minutes. Traffic had congealed and was barely moving. Jill's hands were white-knuckled on the steering wheel at ten and two o'clock, her jaw set in a fierce expression of concentration.

"Mike," Derek said, "listen to me very closely and don't interrupt for a second. Your mother and I are on the way. We're … just a second. Where are we?"

"Between Adams Road and the Square Lake interchange," Jill said through clenched teeth. "About ten miles away."

Derek stared at her. That far? With a swallow, he turned his attention back to Michael. "Okay, Mike. Here's the situation. Your mom and I are on I-75 between Adams Road and the Square Lake interchange. We're on our way. We know what this guy looks like and—"

"There's no way you can make it here in time," Michael said. "Once you get past Square Lake and M-59, it's Palace traffic. There's really only one exit, and it'll be backed up for a couple miles. If you make it before eight it'll be a miracle."

Derek said to Jill, "He says we'll never make it. Is that true?"

The look on Jill's face said it all. "It'll be close," she said. "Hopefully Matt's doing something."

Derek closed his eyes for a moment. "Okay, Mike. You're right. We might not be able to make it in time. So you and your friend need to get the hell out of there."

"I can set a fire alarm off or call security. Get people out. I can't just leave everybody to die."

"No! No! Look, this guy, Kevin Matsumoto, the Serpent, if they start evacuating, he'll set it off early. We've—"

"Kevin Matsumoto? Do you have a picture?"

"Michael, are you listening to me?"

"You listen to me," Michael said. "Do you have his picture?"

Derek glanced over at Jill. She was listening. She cocked her head, pulled her car onto the left shoulder, and started racing down the side of the road. Derek swallowed. This was bad. They weren't able to drive fast on the shoulder, and a deep ditch divided the north and southbound lanes. One bad patch of pavement or a swerving vehicle, and they wouldn't get to the Palace at all.

"Yes," Derek said. "I have his picture on my computer. It's off his driver's license."

"You can e-mail it to me."

"What are you talking about?" Derek stared at the clock. 7:33 p.m. They were just coming up on the Square Lake interchange, and it looked like there was an accident on the left-hand side, multiple cars. He saw it the same time Jill did, who suddenly cursed and hit the brakes. For a moment, the wheels on the left side slipped off the shoulder onto the soft road bank. The car fishtailed.

Derek swore and dropped the phone to hang on. Jill regained control of the car and signaled to merge back into the stream of traffic, which the driver wasn't especially willing to let her do.

"Just butt in," Derek said. "Where's the fucking phone?"

With a sudden spurt of gas, Jill moved back into traffic to the squeal of brakes and honk of horns. Derek scrabbled around the seat until he found the phone. "Michael? You still there?"

"Yes. E-mail me the picture of this guy. I can look for him."

Derek swallowed. "How am I going to do that?"

"I've got e-mail on my phone. You can e-mail it to my address and I can bring it up on my phone. I can look for him."

Derek closed his eyes. *Dear God.* "It's a bad idea," he said. "You and Ray should—"

"You either send it to me or I'll have him paged."

"Don't do that! God damn it, Michael!"

Jill snatched the phone out of his hand. "Michael, you get out of—"

"Mom, it's the only way. You can e-mail this guy's picture to me and I can look for him. It's a long shot anyway."

"You will do no such thing, Michael! You get Ray and get out of there. Leave this up to us."

"You're stuck in traffic and you won't even evacuate!"

"Michael—"

"Mom." Michael's voice was low and surprisingly steady. "Mom," he said, "what would Dad have wanted me to do?"

Jill clenched the phone. "Michael, listen to me—"

"No, you listen to me. If I haven't seen this guy by five minutes to eight, I'll get out of the building. I promise. It's our only hope."

Jill scowled. She looked at Derek. He was watching her. He said, "It's too much for me to ask."

She swallowed hard. Took in a deep ragged breath. "Michael … Michael, be careful. Promise me, five minutes to eight and you and Ray are out of there."

"I promise."

"Be careful. I'm giving the phone back to … to Derek. Michael … Michael, I love you."

"I love you too, Mom."

She handed the phone back to Derek and clenched the steering wheel as if it were a life preserver.

"Mike? I need your e-mail address. Okay. Got it. Hang on."

Jill slowly pushed the car through traffic, finally making their way onto the right shoulder. She floored it.

Using his tablet PC, he forwarded the photograph of Kevin Matsumoto to Michael's e-mail address. "Confirm when you've got it. And Michael?"

"What?"

"Two things. He used to work at the Palace. He might be wearing a uniform of some kind. And two, if you identify this guy, don't engage with him. You understand what I mean?"

"Don't confront him."

"Right. Don't confront him. Don't talk to him. Don't do anything but keep an eye on him and let us know what's going on. Hear me?"

"Yes, sir."

"Seven fifty-five, you and your friend are out of there."

"Yes, sir."

"Good. Call me right back to confirm you got the photograph."

He ended the call and held the phone stiffly in his hand. They were coming up on the interchange, and traffic was starting to move a little easier now that the accident was behind them. Jill edged back into traffic and floored it.

# 84

*7:35 p.m.*

Michael Church paced outside the Palace for a minute or two, restless, nervous, brain buzzing, giving Stillwater time to mail the photograph and for it to move from server to server to server. Finally he launched his phone's browser and connected to his e-mail and downloaded the photograph Stillwater had sent him. He studied the face on the tiny screen, suddenly worried that he wouldn't be able to recognize the guy if he saw him, and realizing that he had only twenty minutes to find him. A surge of adrenaline swept through him—fight or flight. He clenched his fists, tasting something metallic and bitter. Fight.

He hurried back in, returning to the concession line to hook up with Ray. Ray wasn't there. Michael scanned the crowd, looking for Ray hanging out somewhere. He didn't see him anywhere. Had he bought the T-shirts and headed back to their seats?

Glancing at his watch, Michael again scanned the crowd, this time looking for Kevin Matsumoto. *This is impossible*, he thought with a sinking heart. *There are just too many people here.* He took another look at the photo and started walking. Ray was on his own. He hoped he would run into him, tell him what was going on. First, though, he wanted to make a quick circuit of the arena walkway before even considering moving into the main area.

Sweating lightly, Michael strode along, scanning faces. He found as he moved on that he was able to quickly skip the women, the African Americans, the kids who were too young, the few older people.

His mind made a quick shift to looking for males in their twenties with dark hair and goatees, latching onto the shape of Kevin Matsumoto's head, his ears, his nose. And constantly, in his head, time ticked by. He had to give himself enough time to find Ray and get them the hell out of here if things went bad.

Time. He had never felt like this before, this sense of urgency and purpose.

Where was the Serpent?

# 85

*7:36 p.m.*

THE SERPENT MOVED ONE last time through the corridor that encircled the Palace. He was enjoying the crowds, reveling in the thought that he controlled their destiny. He was their God, determining their life and their death.

His senses were finely attuned to everything. He heard the loudspeakers playing a recording of J Slim in the background as a warm-up to the real thing. Felt the wafts of air, cold from the exterior doors, warmer from the heating system, the heat of thousands of bodies. He smelled their sweat and smelled the beer and the pizza and the popcorn. Heard the voices, talking, laughing, loud, boisterous, so energetic.

*One last time*, he thought. *Then I'll get in place.*
*The Serpent will get ready to strike.*

# 86

RAY MORETTI WANDERED OUT of the men's room, a bag with the two T-shirts clutched under one arm. When Michael went off to call his *mommy*, Ray knocked back the rest of his own beer, then began on Michael's. He was pretty much trashed, he knew, and didn't really give a shit. Ray didn't much give a shit about anything. Nobody paid Ray much attention. Not his mom or dad with their high-toned careers, not his bitch of a "perfect" sister with her straight As and her plans for college and all that shit.

Ray could tell Michael was turning out to be just like her, worrying all the time, talking about studying, about the karate class he taught, talking about college, wondering what he wanted to do with his life.

*Asshole!*

Ray didn't worry about any of that. Life was short. He watched his parents work all the time, lecturing him on how hard they worked to pay for their big mortgage on their big house, how it was a good thing they worked hard to make good money so Ann could go to medical school, how he needed to find his direction.

Fuck! He looked at their lives and didn't think that was such a great thing. Eleven-hour workdays, long commutes, worrying, worrying, worrying.

They needed to party. Not some three-martini cocktail party, either. Not some Club Med vacation spent talking about work, calling in at the office or checking your e-mail three times a day.

He didn't want to grow up to be tight-asses like his parents.

All Ray thought about was partying and getting some pussy, and that was just fine by him.

When he stepped out of the bathroom and there was still no Michael, he said, "Fuck it," ignoring the glance of a guy passing him, and headed for their seats. Michael would find him after he got done talking to his *mommy*.

# 87

*7:38 p.m.*

JILL AND DEREK SCREAMED along northbound I-75, Jill swerving in and out of traffic. The right two lanes were bumper to bumper, traffic jamming up at the Palace exit at Lapeer Road. Jill stayed in the left two lanes, racing past the cars on her right. Off to their left, Derek glimpsed a white dome. "Is that it?"

"No. That's the Pontiac Silverdome."

Derek set aside his tablet PC, dragged one of his Go Packs into his lap, and began to rummage through it. He drew out an extra clip of ammunition for his gun, the first-aid kit, and the atropine injector. Dropping them into various pockets, he pulled out a small book, opened it, and held up a photograph to the interior light.

Jill, concentrating on her driving, glanced over. "What's that?"

He held it so she could see. "My ex-wife."

"Pretty."

Derek nodded. "She's a doctor in Texas now. Our marriage couldn't survive our careers." His hand crept to the chain around his neck, the one with the Saint Sebastian's medal, the juju beads, and the four-leaf clover. Was he superstitious? No, not really. But he believed in luck, good and bad. He had been very lucky today. He hoped his good luck would hold.

"Hang on," Jill said. She pressed the gas and jerked right, fist slamming down on the horn. With a roar she ripped across traffic, cut off a pickup truck, and blasted onto the looping ramp to Lapeer Road and the Palace of Auburn Hills. Tires screeched and horns wailed as she raced along.

Ahead of them was a cutaway entrance to the south Palace parking lot. It was blocked by an Oakland County Sheriff's patrol car, lights flashing. Jill spun onto the cutaway and pulled up to the sheriff's deputy, who stood next to his car. She rolled down her window and held out her identification. "We've got an emergency situation. We need to get in. Right now."

The deputy was a young guy with dark, curly hair and a thick mustache. "Yes, ma'am. Go right ahead."

He moved a pylon aside and Jill sped past. Derek took one last look at the photograph and slipped it back into the book, laying it carefully back into the Go Pack.

Jill rocketed past the parking attendants, skidding to a halt in front of the closest entrance. She killed the engine and jumped out of the car. Derek clambered out, messing with his crutch. Jill punched her son's cell number into her own phone.

"Michael. We're at the south entrance. Where are you?"

A sheriff's deputy approached. "You can't park there," she said. "Sir, you can't park there."

Derek turned and flashed his own identification. He waved at Jill. "This is Agent Church, with the FBI. Have they contacted you yet?"

"Who?"

"The FBI."

"No, sir. What's this all about?" Her blue eyes were inquisitive, her pale skin flushed from the cool temperature. She was a tall, broad-shouldered woman with strong-looking hands.

Derek shook his head. Figured. You couldn't count on Gray for anything. He quickly outlined the situation for the deputy. He held up the tablet PC and showed her the image of Kevin Matsumoto. "We've got to find him before eight o'clock. And we've got to do it without him knowing it. We can't spook him."

The cop frowned. "Maybe we can coordinate with security."

"Good."

He turned to Jill, who was listening closely to whatever Michael was saying to her. To Derek she said, "Go on. I'm going to link up with Michael."

Derek paused. "He'll be all right."

Jill's face looked wan and tired. She nodded. "Let's go, Derek. Keep your line open."

"Got it." He turned and followed the deputy into the building. Jill returned to her car and drove off, heading to the opposite side of the Palace.

# 88

*7:39 p.m.*

THE FBI's HMRU HELICOPTER, a Bell-UH-1 Iroquois, or "Huey," lifted off from the Detroit Medical Center helicopter pad with Zoelig and the HMRU team, Matt Gray, Roger Kandling, and Simona Toreanno on board. Once above the buildings, it headed due north.

Matt Gray sat up front, next to the pilot. "How long?"

The pilot checked his readouts and said, "It's about forty miles, so probably fifteen or twenty minutes."

Matt swallowed, looking at his watch. He turned to Simona. "It's your ball game. Get Palace security on the horn and give them an update."

Simona nodded and began to work the phone. What she thought was: *Matt's isolating himself from screw-ups. If this goes to hell, I'll be the one responsible.*

Beneath them, the city of Detroit slipped by. They raced northward along the river of light that was I-75.

# 89

*7:43 p.m.*

MICHAEL CHURCH DIDN'T WANT to admit it, but he was relieved when his mother called. He was getting increasingly freaked out by this. There were so many people! And that was just on the walkway around the Palace. There were people milling around outside and the arena itself was slowly starting to fill up, and there were luxury suites that he didn't have access to.

She'd asked where he was and he'd told her he was by the north entrance. She'd told him to stay put, that she was on her way. She'd asked where Ray was, and he'd told her about missing him. She hadn't responded to that, and—

It took a minute for his brain to consciously lock on to what he was seeing. He blinked. That guy...

A guy who looked just like Kevin Matsumoto was moving toward him. Michael thought he was staring and didn't want to attract the guy's attention, so he turned, glanced at his cell phone to verify the picture, and put the phone to his ear, pretending to listen to someone on the other end.

The guy walked by him, not three feet away. He wore black pants and a red shirt that said Palace Staff on the left breast, and he carried what looked like a tool kit of some sort in a bag he had slung over one shoulder. He was tall, with narrow shoulders, long arms, and a brisk, aggressive stride.

For a moment, Matsumoto's gaze flicked over Michael. Then he moved on.

Michael felt a chill. There was something about the guy's expression—so cold—that gave him the creeps.

And yes, it was Kevin Matsumoto.

When Matsumoto was past him, Michael turned to follow, punching in his mom's number.

# 90

*7:46 p.m.*

THE PALACE SECURITY OFFICE was tucked away in a corner behind the box office, and Derek was sweating heavily by the time he and Deputy Angela Pushman got there. The chief of security was an elegant-looking man with silver hair and glasses. Despite his appearance, he wore jeans, a white dress shirt, and a navy sport coat. He stood up and took them in, his voice soft and gentle. "Hello. I'm Bruce Lippman. Is there a problem?"

Deputy Pushman said, "This is Derek Stillwater, with the Department of Homeland Security. There's—"

Derek checked his watch and said, "We have reason to believe there's going to be a sarin gas attack here at eight o'clock."

Although Lippman didn't act noticeably perturbed, he did straighten his back and focus on Derek. "Credentials," he snapped. He tapped his Timex and looked back at Derek. "This is rather short notice, Agent—is it agent?"

"Agent Stillwater or Dr. Stillwater. We're afraid a mass evacuation will just set him off, and we haven't known very long. Have you received a phone call from the FBI? They're supposed to call."

"No, we have not."

*Dammit*, Derek thought.

"Please, sit down, Doctor. You … do you need a wheelchair or something?"

*I need a vacation*, Derek thought. "No, I'm fine for now." He thought Lippman must have a bit of the rebel in him, wearing jeans when all the rest of the staff wore dark slacks. Trying to be a regular guy, maybe.

Derek gave him his ID. "I'm working with an FBI agent. Her son … we don't have time for a long explanation. Do you have security cameras?"

"Of course."

"Let's take a look." He handed the tablet PC to Lippman and said, "This is the guy we're looking for."

Lippman glanced at it and scowled. "That's Kevin Matsumoto."

"Yes. He works here, correct?"

Lippman shook his head. "*Worked* here. He quit a few days ago. We weren't sorry to see him go. Kevin had a tendency to involve himself in things he wasn't supposed to. And he made people nervous. A strange kid. Always talking about the end of the world. We got complaints that—"

"I don't care right now, dammit," Derek said. "What was his job?"

"Part of the technical crew. Lights, sound system, electronics. The whole deal here. We not only have concerts and basketball games, but rodeos and tennis matches and hockey games, and Matsumoto was handy around equipment like the ice machine, the Zamboni, and the smoke machines."

Derek said, "Smoke machines?" He twitched, his instincts kicking in and kicking in hard.

"Well, yes. For, you know, fog. We have foggers and smoke machines, for special effects."

"Where?"

"Some are on the main floor. Some are set around the upper beams and below the overhangs of the luxury suites."

Derek rubbed his forehead and checked his watch again. He said, "Show me the fog machines. Can you take me down there right now?"

"You think—"

Derek nodded. "I sure as hell do, Mr. Lippman. I sure as hell do."

# 91

*7:51 p.m.*

JILL ANSWERED HER PHONE. It was Michael. She heard a babble of noise in the background—people talking, recorded music, the shuffle and clatter of people walking. Michael's voice was an excited whisper. "I've got him."

"Where?"

"He's walking, we're just past the north entrance."

"Okay," Jill said. "Okay, Michael. Good. Keep an eye on him, but stay back. Don't let him know you're back there, okay? Whatever you do, don't engage with him."

"Yeah, yeah ... uh, he's out of sight, he just headed into some sort of—"

Suddenly the connection dropped out.

"Michael? *Michael!?*" Jill stared at the phone. The readout said: CALL ENDED.

She punched redial but got an OUT OF SERVICE message and was transferred to Michael's voice mail.

Jill screeched to a halt next to a long white limousine and sprinted for the entrance.

# 92

*7:52 p.m.*

WHEN KEVIN MATSUMOTO DISAPPEARED around a corner marked Palace Employees Only, Michael Church picked up his pace. It was a door with a card reader as a lock, and it was just swinging closed. Michael lunged forward, catching the knob just before the door clicked shut. As he did, the hand holding his cell phone slammed against the concrete-block wall with the sound of breaking plastic.

He sucked in air, blood rushing in his ears. He glanced at his phone. The little screen was shattered. Michael thumbed the power button. Nothing. *Oh shit!* He tapped the button again, shook the phone. Nothing.

He glanced around, shook his head, put the phone in his pocket, and slipped through the door, allowing it to close behind him. He was in a long, narrow corridor. At the end of the corridor were two doors. One said Engineering. The other said Deck.

Michael jogged down the hallway, his footsteps a muffled, thudding echo on the tiled floor, and studied the doors. With a shrug, he opened the door marked Engineering. He stepped through and realized he was in the power plant for the facility, some sort of trunk line for all the heating and cooling ducts, the furnaces and air-conditioning units. It looked to be a large room jammed with equipment. It was hot and noisy, the roar of the machinery deafening. It was also empty.

He stepped back out and gripped the knob to the door marked Deck. *What the hell*, he thought, and stepped through.

A stairwell marched upward. Trying to still his beating heart, Michael listened carefully. High above him he heard footsteps. It had to be Kevin Matsumoto.

What was he supposed to do? His phone was busted, nobody knew where he was. He looked at his watch and saw it was 7:53. Only seven minutes left.

Michael rushed up the stairs.

# 93

BRUCE LIPPMAN BROUGHT DEREK Stillwater out of a hallway into an open area behind the stage. It was a mass of electrical connections, wires and cords strewn across the floor like a snake pit. Three men huddled over a checklist. They looked up when Lippman and Derek entered.

Lippman said, "Steve, this is—"

"Show me the fog machines," Derek demanded.

Steve, a wiry guy with shaggy brown hair mixed with gray, eyed Lippman, who nodded.

"One's over there." He pointed to a barrel. "The other one's over here."

Derek hobbled over and studied it. "Anybody opened it lately?"

"It's loaded with dry ice, ready to go when we get the signal."

"Who's setting off the smoke machines?"

Steve frowned. "What's this all about?"

"Who, dammit?"

"Go ahead, Steve," Lippman assured the man. "We don't have time to explain."

"I've got the remote. I'll set them off at the right time. I'll be in the lighting booth. What's going on?"

"Let me see the remote control," Derek asked.

Steve unclipped what looked like a garage door opener from his belt. "It's got a decent range."

"And Kevin Matsumoto set these up for you?"

Steve's face twisted. "That jerk. Quit without giving notice, just got up and walked out. Left me short-handed."

"Did he set them up?" Derek repeated. His hands shook, and it was all he could do to keep from grabbing this guy and throttling the information out of him.

Steve shrugged "Yeah, sure. Changed the frequencies so they all run off a single remote."

"Have you tested it today?"

"What? No. Why? They're all set to go."

Derek pried open the device, removed the batteries and pocketed the remote control.

"Hey!" Steve reached for it, but Derek brushed his hand aside.

"What's the range on this thing?" Derek said. "Can you set it off from outside?"

"No. We tried once, just for fun. Too much interference. Anywhere inside the arena. Anywhere inside the arena, but it's not reliable out in the halls. Line of sight works better. What's going on?"

Derek turned back to the barrel. "When did the dry ice go in?"

"About five minutes ago. Bruce, what's going on?"

Lippman raised a hand. "Just cooperate, Steve."

"Who put it in?" Derek asked.

"Me and Frank." Steve jerked a thumb at one of the other guys.

Derek nodded and opened the top of the barrel. There was a mesh tray filled with dry ice. It could be lowered into the water. He reached in and lifted out the dry ice tray, setting it on the floor. A huge block of dry ice smoldered and vented carbon dioxide. Reaching into his pocket, Derek pulled out his flashlight and directed it into the water.

Steve looked past him. "What the hell's that?"

The bottom of the barrel appeared to be filled with red metal canisters. Coils of tubing ran from a central regulator into the outflow hose. A red light glowed on what looked like a radio receiver. Derek recognized it immediately as being similar to the radio receiver that had been used at the Boulevard Café.

Derek took a deep breath. He didn't have time. If the Serpent had booby-trapped these devices ...

"Move back," he snapped, and plunged his fists into the water.

# 94

*7:55 p.m.*

MICHAEL CHURCH ARRIVED AT the top of the stairs feeling only slightly winded. Only moments before, he had heard a door close above him, so he felt confident Kevin Matsumoto had gone to the top and not taken any of the other doors he had encountered.

The final door was blank metal with no sign indicating what lay beyond. Steeling himself, Michael pushed through it.

He found himself standing in a gallery at the very top of the Palace. There were entrances to a number of the fourth-level luxury suites. Panic gripped his heart with icy fingers. Had he lost the Serpent?

Off to his right, he glimpsed Matsumoto stepping through another door, this one marked Authorized Personnel Only. Michael leapt toward it, sprinting the distance and lunging against the door just before it shut completely. There was a card reader on this door as well.

He pushed through. Another flight of steps, industrial metal, bare walls.

He rushed upward, reckless. Time was ticking away too fast.

Out another door, and he found himself standing on a metal gridwork at one end of the Palace. The entire arena was below him. He was at the very top of the building, among the girders and catwalks. Pennants dangled nearly at eye level proclaiming the Detroit Pistons' championship seasons and the retired numbers of Pistons stars. A huge, four-sided TV screen dangling from the center of the roof, PalaceVision, loomed large, still dark. The Palace arena spread at his feet, a huge, scooped bowl filled with people, probably a couple hundred feet across, and easily a hundred feet down.

Off to his right, Kevin Matsumoto moved determinedly toward a catwalk that angled all the way across the space. Matsumoto focused straight ahead, not looking back at Michael. Michael slipped along the wall, trying to keep to the shadows, not wanting Matsumoto to see him.

Matsumoto stepped out onto the catwalk, walking toward the middle of the space.

Michael increased his speed, trying to close the distance. Sweat dripped down his forehead and stung his eyes. He blinked, wiping his face with his sleeve. He didn't want to go out on that catwalk. It looked like it was about five or six feet wide, a steel grid, with a railing on one side, a drop of about a hundred feet off the other. Michael felt like a clamp was being tightened around his guts.

This was for real. This wasn't some fantasy, some TV show or movie, some heroic video game. This was real.

Matsumoto was moving toward the center of the space, turning toward the railing. Michael saw that he held something in each of his hands. He thought one looked like a remote control. He wasn't sure what the other was.

Taking a deep breath, Michael stepped onto the catwalk, ignoring the dizzying depth beneath him, and headed toward the Serpent.

The Serpent turned then to see him. Something peculiar flashed across the guy's face. Surprise? Relief? Shock? Anger?

Michael didn't know. He felt his concentration both narrow and broaden, similar to what he experienced when sparring in karate—focusing on the opponent but staying attuned to the environment and other possible threats.

A smile burst across Kevin Matsumoto's face, and he held up the remote control. "Don't even think about it," he called out.

Michael didn't hesitate or pause for even a second. He broke into a flat-out sprint along the catwalk toward the Serpent.

# 95

*7:56 p.m.*

JILL WAS FRANTIC. WHERE was Michael? What had happened?

She spun in the entryway, looking for her son. Looking for Matsumoto.

No one. The crowds thinned as they streamed into the arena.

She held her phone in trembling fingers, debating what to do. She punched in Derek's number. It rang and rang, then was abruptly picked up.

"Hello?"

She didn't recognize the voice. For a moment, she wondered if she had dialed the wrong number. "Hello? Who's this?" Had something happened to Derek? Who was this?

# 96

*7:56 p.m.*

DEREK RIPPED THE Tygon tubing out of the fogger outflow hose, gripped the entire assembly of gas cylinders, braced himself, and lifted it out of the tank. Turning, he set it down on the floor, studied the device, turned off the regulator valve, and examined the radio receiver. It looked straightforward. He took his gun and slammed the butt down on the radio. With a crack, the light went out.

He picked up his crutch and moved across the stage to the other barrel. Lippman said, "Is it … neutralized?"

"I hope so. Put a guard on it. Nobody gets near it, touches it, moves it until the Bureau's HMRU people get here."

He stood in front of the second barrel, lifted off the top, and set aside the dry ice tray. He looked at Lippman. "So far so good. Keep your fingers crossed." He hoped the reason these didn't seem to be booby-trapped was that the cylinders took up too much room in the tanks and any additional explosives would have displaced too much water. Or maybe the water had provided too much of a technical problem. Or maybe Matsumoto didn't booby-trap his gas bombs, just the houses of his victims.

Derek reached in and repeated the procedure. His phone rang while he was up to his elbows in the water.

"Answer it," he said, still focusing on the task of immobilizing the sarin canisters in the fog machines.

Lippman took the Iridium phone off Derek's belt and answered. "Hello?"

He listened for a moment. Lippman said, "It's Agent Church. She's lost contact with her son."

"Tell her to get to the highest point in the Palace. That's where this guy will be."

Lippman looked surprised. "Up in the suites? Or the catwalk?"

"My money's on the catwalk."

Lippman put the phone to his ear. "He says he believes the Serpent will be at the highest point in the facility. That would be the catwalk. Where are you?"

He listened. "There's an elevator near there. Take it to the top level and go right. There's a door to the utility levels. It requires a card reader. I'll get somebody up there."

Derek set the canisters down and smashed the receiver. He took the phone from Lippman and said, "I'll meet you there." He turned to Lippman. "Where?"

"Let's go." Lippman spun on his heel and led Derek toward an elevator. Lippman was on his own phone, calling his security people, telling them where they needed to go.

Lippman looked at Derek. "The FBI is on its way. Are we going to be in time?"

Derek shook his head and took out his gun again, checking that it was loaded and ready. "I'm afraid this is in the hands of a sixteen-year-old kid."

# 97

*7:56 p.m.*

AS MICHAEL SPRINTED THE distance toward Kevin Matsumoto, his brain clicked into what he sometimes thought of as "combat calculus," a not-quite-conscious assessment of his opponent. He noted the remote control in Matsumoto's left hand. That was the primary objective.

He noted there was something in Matsumoto's right hand. He didn't know what it was. It was small. He didn't think it was a gun.

He noted that Matsumoto had raised the left hand and shown him the remote control. It suggested Matsumoto was left-handed.

He noted Matsumoto's size, his build, the way he moved.

He noted the look on Matsumoto's face when he started his charge, a look of surprise.

In the few seconds before they collided a hundred feet above certain death, Michael Church's mind calculated a thousand different factors.

Kevin Matsumoto spun toward him, bringing the right hand forward, keeping the left hand raised.

Michael, moving fast, came in low, slamming his left arm down on Matsumoto's right, spinning into a right elbow thrust to Matsumoto's solar plexus, immediately snapping his right arm out and clamping onto Matsumoto's left wrist and twisting.

With a surprised cry, Matsumoto dropped the remote control. It clipped the railing, bounced on the catwalk's grid, and skittered away.

With a shout, Matsumoto punched Michael in the face and dived after the remote control.

Michael jerked his head to the side, the punch grazing his cheekbone. Michael used the momentum to shift and bring his left hand into Matsumoto's ribs, following with a flurry of short blows to the killer's chest and ribs.

But Matsumoto wasn't interested in the fight. He was interested in the remote control. With a guttural cry, Matsumoto shoved Michael away.

Michael fell backward under the impact, smacked up against the railing, lost his balance, and fell to the catwalk.

Matsumoto tried to leap over him. Michael grabbed his legs and brought him crashing down.

Matsumoto kicked out, catching Michael in the jaw with his booted foot. Michael jerked his head, stunned.

Matsumoto lunged away, scrabbling toward the remote control.

Michael reached out, caught a pant leg, and yanked hard.

Matsumoto's legs fell out from beneath him, and he crashed down on the walkway with a grunt, the remote control still out of reach.

Beyond them, Derek Stillwater appeared on the walkway, followed by Bruce Lippman. Derek moved fast despite the crutch.

Matsumoto kicked out again and caught Michael in the shoulder with a hard slash that knocked Michael toward the unprotected edge of the catwalk.

For a heart-stopping moment, Michael balanced on the edge, legs sliding out into open air. With a cry, he gripped the catwalk and swung himself back over, rolling to his feet. He leapt after Matsumoto, who headed for the remote control.

Suddenly Matsumoto turned to face him, raised the right hand, and sprayed something into Michael's face.

Michael gasped. His vision darkened. He shook his head and tried to breathe, but his lungs seemed locked up. It felt like he had lost control of his body. He caught just a glimpse of glee on Kevin Matsumoto's face before he crumpled to the catwalk.

# 98

*7:57 p.m.*

CURSING HIS BAD LEG, Derek hurried across the catwalk as fast as he could. On the far end of it, with a vast gulf between them, he spied Jill emerging at the other side of the arena.

The two men—Kevin Matsumoto and Michael Church—were battling. Matsumoto shoved Michael. Michael bounced off the railing, lost his balance, and fell to the catwalk. For a moment of horror, it looked like Michael would roll right off. His legs swung out into space.

"No!" Derek screamed, pushing himself to move faster.

Michael caught his fingers in the catwalk's mesh and levered himself back onto the grid, rolling in a smooth, graceful motion onto his feet. With leopard-like fluidity, he leapt after Matsumoto, who rushed toward the remote control.

Derek was closing in when Matsumoto turned his back on him, facing Michael. He raised his right hand and sprayed mist directly into Michael's face.

Derek saw Michael freeze, his hands raising in a defensive motion in front of him, gasping loudly, clutching at his chest.

Derek was almost to the remote control. He bent to pick it up, and Matsumoto whirled toward him and rushed forward, shoulder down.

Derek, off-balance, swung his crutch in a hard arc, catching Matsumoto in the leg and knocking him off balance.

Matsumoto stumbled over the remote control. It skittered away, behind Derek.

Matsumoto swung his arm wildly. *"Get out of my way!"*

Derek swung the crutch, again catching Matsumoto in the knee. With a howl, Matsumoto dropped to the metal walkway, clutching his leg. From his crouched position, Matsumoto glared up at him. As if spring-loaded, Matsumoto launched himself.

Derek braced himself.

But it was a feint.

Matsumoto's right hand came up.

Derek felt a spray of liquid on his face and tried to hold his breath. He hoped the atomizer was almost empty from being used on Michael. He exhaled sharply, then rubbed his face with his sleeve, anything to minimize his exposure. Too late. His vision dimmed. His lungs seized up.

He tried to reach Matsumoto, tried to get one last grip on the Serpent before he passed out ... before he died ...

But ...

Derek slumped to the metal catwalk, struggling to breathe.

# 99

*7:58 p.m.*

JILL CHURCH RUSHED DOWN the catwalk. She had never felt fear like this. "Michael!" she screamed, her voice ragged with emotion. "Michael!"

He collapsed to the catwalk, and Kevin Matsumoto grinned.

She saw the grin, saw the glee—the joy!—in his face as he sprayed sarin gas into her son's face.

As she ran, she reached for her gun. Her son! He had killed her son!

Derek Stillwater raced across the catwalk from the other end, reaching for the remote control. Kevin Matsumoto exploded into motion, throwing himself at Derek like a football tackle.

Derek struck out with his crutch, knocking Matsumoto off balance.

The gun was in her hands. She closed the distance.

Michael writhed on the platform, hands clutching at his throat.

She saw Stillwater swing the crutch again. She heard Matsumoto scream, saw him drop to his knees.

And then Matsumoto leapt to his feet and sprayed sarin gas in Derek's face.

Jill saw Derek stagger, try to reach for Matsumoto, hands outstretched...

Jill stood over her son, gun out, standing in a perfect Weaver stance, feet shoulder-width apart, oriented at a forty-five-degree angle to her target. Her right arm extended, elbow locked. Her left arm was tucked close to the body, hand supporting the right hand. "Kevin!" she shouted.

Matsumoto turned to glare at her. He reached for the remote control.

Jill fired.

And fired.

And fired.

Kevin Matsumoto jerked at each shot, dark red blossoming on his chest. His body twitched like a marionette. He reached one last time for the remote control.

Jill fired again.

The bullet took him in the heart and he toppled sideways, off the catwalk. He spiraled awkwardly to land with a visceral thunk on the concrete stairs a hundred feet below.

She knelt next to Michael. "Michael! It's Mom! Michael, hang on!"

Derek Stillwater gasped out, *"Jill."*

She looked at him. In his outstretched hand, he held the atropine injector. She jumped to him, snatched it out of his hand. There was only enough for one dose.

"Derek—"

"Do it," he whispered.

She turned back, broke open the injector, and slammed it home into her son's thigh, injecting the antidote into his bloodstream.

With a last, desperate prayer, she turned to Derek and plunged the injector into his leg, hoping there was still some atropine in the cylinder, that it would at least slow down the effects of the poison. He groaned, but did not move. She turned back to her son.

"It'll be all right, Michael," she said, holding his hand. "Hold on. It'll be all right. You did great. Absolutely great! Hang on! Hang on!"

# 100

*9:03 p.m.*

JILL SAT WITH MICHAEL in the emergency room at Beaumont Hospital in Royal Oak. It was the only Level I trauma center in Oakland County. There had been some discussion on where to take Michael and Derek, but the FBI agent who ran the HMRU, Zoelig, had loaded them into the Huey and raced off toward Royal Oak.

As she'd climbed into the helicopter with her son, Jill had seen Matt Gray turning to the media available and taking credit for the successful operation. It figured, she thought. Gray was like a cat. He always landed on his feet. She had watched the paramedics and the HMRU doctors working on Derek and her son, noticing the taut, worried expressions on their faces as they took Derek's vital signs and injected him with drugs. It had been a horrible, sinking feeling for her. Only a partial success. And now Derek ... she didn't want to think about it. He had meant ... something to her. She didn't know what, exactly. Some personal *frisson*, a little bit of attraction, or potential for something more. Maybe it was just the stress of the crisis, strangers drawn together. She hoped—prayed—Derek would make it.

Now, in the hospital, she turned her attention back to her son. Michael lay on an examining table, an IV in his arm, an oxygen mask over his face. He looked up at her. He said, "I'm sorry."

She shook her head and stroked his hair. She leaned close to him. "I can't tell you how proud I am of you right now, Michael. Do you realize you saved thousands of lives? You're a hero. You were so brave …" Her voice broke and she wiped at her eye. "Michael, your father would be so proud of you. You're an awful lot like him."

Michael smiled and closed his eyes.

Someone at the door cleared his throat. Jill turned to see a tall, broad-shouldered man in a dark suit standing in the doorway. It took her a moment to recognize him.

"General …"

General James Johnston, secretary of the Department of Homeland Security, raised his hand and said, "May I come in?"

"Of course."

Johnston was a grizzled man in his early sixties with a military bearing. It was there in the straightness of his spine and the set of his square jaw. It was there in the clear, arrowlike way he aimed his gaze at people. He held out his hand and introduced himself.

"I understand you were instrumental in preventing this final attack. Thank you very much. Good work."

"Thank you, sir." She shook his hand. "I was … it was really Derek who did it, sir."

Johnston shook his head. "He couldn't have done it without you. I understand you have some problems facing you with Agent

Gray. I'll help you with that as much as I can. And if you tire of the Bureau, I promise you there will be a future with us at DHS."

"Thank you, sir. Thank you very much."

Johnston turned to Michael. "And this is the young man who took on the Serpent single-handedly. I'm very impressed, young man. Very impressed. We're all thankful. Good work, son."

Michael shook his hand. He moved the oxygen mask aside and said, "Sir, is Dr. Stillwater all right?"

Johnston looked him directly in the eye. "I'm sorry, son. Dr. Stillwater didn't make it. We tried, but we weren't able to get him treated quickly enough."

Michael blinked. "I—"

Johnston patted his shoulder. "He was a good man. And a good friend. I'm very sorry."

He stepped back, nodded, and said, "If you need anything, Agent Church, just let me know. I'll have my staff contact you shortly." He looked at her closely. "And don't feel guilty about the choice you made. It wasn't really a choice after all, was it?"

She shook her head, words catching in her throat.

"All right, then. Good work to both of you."

Johnston turned and walked out of the examining room, closing the door behind him.

Jill sat back down and looked at Michael. She felt hollow. How could Derek Stillwater be dead? It was heartbreaking. She liked him. For a moment there...for a moment there, she had hoped there might be something more. There had been something about Stillwater that reminded her of her late husband. The impatience, the oddball charm, the overall competence. Was what she felt grief for Derek, or for him?

Michael took a deep breath of oxygen, then pushed the mask aside. His eyes were filled with tears, but he blinked them back. She could see the effort he was making to be strong, to be a man. But he already was, she realized. And a fine one at that. He said, "I wanted to talk to him about …"

She took Michael's hand. "I'll tell you about your father. It's about time I did. Anything you want to know."

# EPILOGUE

*9:23 p.m.*

DEREK STILLWATER OPENED HIS eyes. He felt like shit. His entire body ached and throbbed. His vision was poor. He found it difficult to focus. Sarin affected the eyes, called miosis, making the pupils constrict. Everything seemed a little dark, despite the lights shining brightly in what apparently was a hospital room.

He turned to see General James Johnston sitting next to his bed. Johnston looked up from a report he was reading. "Hello, Derek."

"So I died and went to hell."

Johnston grunted. It might have been a laugh. "You're alive, my friend. A little worse for wear, but Zoelig was able to get atropine and a few other things into you and get you here."

"Where's here?"

"William Beaumont Hospital."

Derek closed his eyes. He had no memory of getting here. He vaguely remembered gunshots and Jill appearing. He remembered offering her the atropine injector. Then he had no memory after that.

"The Aum are back," he said.

Johnston nodded. "So it appears."

"Kevin Matsumoto may be the son of Shoko Asahara. We need to get in touch with the Japanese—"

"I already have." Johnston held up the report. "My counterpart in Japan faxed me this immediately. Here, look at this." He handed Derek a photograph. It was of Kevin Matsumoto and a Japanese woman in what looked like a bar.

Derek struggled to focus his eyes. It read, *Rika Matsumoto and Kevin Matsumoto (American). Zengenjimachi, Miyakojima-ku, Osaka.* It was dated six months earlier.

"That's Rika? The head of Aleph?"

"Yes," Johnston said. "The revered daughter of Shoko Asahara. They've also sent me a transcript of part of their conversation, although they didn't get all of it. You know the Japanese National Police have the core of Aum Shinrikyo that aren't in prison under round-the-clock surveillance."

"For the last ten years. I thought it was going to end soon."

Johnston shrugged. "I doubt it'll ever end. Here, want to read?"

"My eyesight's not so hot. What's it say?"

Johnston glanced at the report. "She insists that her father was always faithful to her mother and she doesn't believe that Kevin is her half-brother. He says a DNA test can prove that he is. She insists that he's welcome to join Aleph, but he is not a child of Shoko Asahara and has no right to be the leader, that's her birthright. Then Kevin gets angry, tells her he's going to prove that he's the rightful leader of Aum, gets up, and stomps out of the bar."

"Nice of them to share that with us after the fact."

Johnston nodded. "Hindsight is 20/20. And so much for inter-governmental cooperation."

"It never occurs to them that a biochemistry graduate student who think he's the rightful heir to Aum Shinrikyo might have some nastiness planned?"

"Sakamoto Tsutsumi, my associate in Japan, assures me they would have gotten it to me or the FBI eventually."

Derek closed his eyes and groaned. *Such bullshit.* Suddenly he turned to Johnston. "Did Michael make it?"

"He's better than you. He'll be fine."

"Gutsy kid. Takes after his dad."

"Yes, I understand you knew his father."

Derek nodded. "A good man. And Jill's a good woman too. She's got some guts, once she starts thinking for herself. I look forward to seeing them."

Johnston stood up and looked down at Derek. "That may have to wait a while. You're officially dead."

Derek groaned. "Oh boy. This is hell after all. What are you doing here? How long have you been here?"

Johnston shook his head. "I got in around eight-thirty. I left as fast as I could after receiving a disturbing telephone call from an FBI agent named Simona Toreanno. But it's a long story and not what I have to say to you right now. I received some top-level intelligence today, Derek. About Coffee."

Derek struggled to sit up. "*What?!*"

Johnston pushed him gently back down. "Rest. Take it easy. They think he's somewhere in the United States. I thought it might be good, especially since this opportunity came up, for Coffee to think you're dead."

Derek rested against the pillow, thinking, Kevin Matsumoto and Aum Shinrikyo momentarily forgotten. Richard Coffee. He called himself the Fallen, or the Fallen Angel. The leader of a cultlike group of terrorists determined to obtain a weapon of mass destruction and wreak havoc on the world. A man he had once called a friend.

The Fallen Angel was back in the country.

Derek thought about what General Johnston had done. He smiled. "It's like the Irish toast, isn't it?"

Johnston looked puzzled. "What's that?"

"A famous Irish toast." Derek smiled again, thinking. Planning. "May you find yourself in heaven before the devil knows you're dead."

## ACKNOWLEDGMENTS

I would like to thank the "lunch club" at Henry Ford Hospital's cytogenetics lab. Those lunches were some of the best things about working there. Thanks to Judy Bailey, Jessica Sanchez, Nicole Ballard, Bedford Embrey, Jill Crouchman, John Hou, Trish Ritchie, Martha Chu, and the various people who rotated in and out of our group.

Thanks to Sameera Pirzada for her assistance in translating Jimmy Buffett into Urdu.

Thanks to my agent, the amazing Irene Kraas, not only for selling this manuscript, but for making me go back to the dig site and work a little bit harder.

For my exceptional team at Midnight Ink: Barbara Moore, Kevin Brown, Wade Ostrowski, and Brian Farrey.

Thanks to the people who taught me everything I know about Sanchin-Ryu karate: Vicky Clay, Mike Clay, and Dana Bickerstaff.

For Leanne, Sean, and Ian, who make it all possible and all worthwhile.

And special thanks to the various functionaries and website-content folks at the Department of Homeland Security, the Federal Bureau of Investigation, the Detroit Police Department, Wayne State University, the Greektown Casino, and the city of Detroit who either answered questions or provided information.

Read on for an excerpt from the next
Derek Stillwater Novel by Mark Terry

# Angels Falling

COMING SOON FROM MIDNIGHT INK

---

LIEUTENANT CHARLIE WALKER TRACKED the van rolling down the road toward Checkpoint Delta through his M24 sniper rifle's scope. He had the crosshairs centered on the driver's head, finger caressing the trigger. *Pow!* he thought. *Pow. Pow.* Calm. Like target shooting. Not real flesh and blood. Not a person. Not a human being. Just a target. He rehearsed the kill in his mind. Two shots through the driver's head. Shift so he could watch the passenger jump out. *Pow.* Pick him off. Anybody in the rear? Shift to the right, catch them as they scrambled out of the back.

Wearing a ghillie suit, a Nomex flight suit camouflaged with leaves and brush, he hid on a hillside overlooking Cheyenne Hills, a sprawling five-star resort outside Colorado Springs at the foot of the Rocky Mountains. A member of the Colorado National Guard's 19th Special Forces Group, Charlie was invisible among the shrubs and underbrush that covered the slopes.

Darkness covered the hillside, the sun still blocked by the surrounding mountains. The thin Colorado air was cold for mid-June. At sunrise, the temperature would jump dramatically. It would be damn near impossible to lay out in a ghillie suit in scorching, 80-degree sun. He wasn't looking forward to it. It would be a long, hot day. Already he was coated with a slick of sweat. His stomach grumbled. He had a peanut butter energy bar in his pocket and a canteen of lukewarm water. But he knew a cold six-pack of Coors was waiting for him when he was done.

He also had to pee. When this van passed through, he would crawl over to a stand of aspen and relieve himself. He had considered the aspens for his sniper nest, but it had a partially obstructed view of Checkpoint Delta. In the hot daytime sun, he might consider it, at least part of the time. The open sunlight would be brutal.

Charlie peered through AN-PVS 7B night-vision goggles, everything glowing green. Charlie slowly swiveled his rifle, tracking the vehicle, a red panel van. The National Guard was manning checkpoints at strategic sites along all entrances to Cheyenne Hills in preparation for the G8 Summit. The summit would officially begin at ten a.m. with the arrival of twenty heads of state and their entourages. Checkpoint Delta was just west of Cheyenne Hills West, one of the fancy castle-like resort buildings on the west side of Double Mirror Lake.

The red panel van slowed to a stop by the checkpoint. Charlie focused the crosshairs of his rifle sights on the driver's-side door and waited. How many times tonight? Twenty? Thirty? A hundred? Over and over during the night he repeated the routine, and nothing exciting happened. He didn't think it would. This G8 thing was a big, big deal. The Secret Service ultimately ran security, overseeing Brigadier General Frank Cole's command of the National Guard troops. From what Charlie could see, Cheyenne Hills was zipped up tighter than a plastic baggie.

Charlie had only two minutes to live.

## ABOUT THE AUTHOR

Mark Terry is a full-time freelance writer, editor, and novelist. He also has a degree in microbiology and experience with infectious disease research and genetics. He lives in Michigan. Visit his website at www.markterry books.com.